Out of *Play*

Nyrae Dawn and Jolene Perry

Entangled Publishing, LLC
2614 South Timberline Road
Suite 109
Fort Collins, CO 80525
Visit our website at www.entangledpublishing.com.

Edited by Heather Howland
Cover design by Heather Howland

Print ISBN   978-1-62266-010-0
Ebook ISBN   978-1-62266-011-7

Manufactured in the United States of America

First Edition August 2013

The author acknowledges the copyrighted or trademarked status and trademark owners of the following wordmarks mentioned in this work of fiction: Grammy; Advil; UAF; UAA; Corvette; Ford Ranchero; Ice Road Truckers; Twenty Questions; Jell-O; Diet Coke; Mack truck; CSI; Seinfeld; iPhone; Victoria's Secret; McDonald's.

This book is dedicated to my mom. Thanks for teaching me to believe in myself. It's because of you that I never gave up, and saw my dreams come true.

—Nyrae

To Melissa, Heather, Beth, Monica, Andrea, Jamie, Julie, Betty (both of them), Vivian, Emma and all the other tough Alaskan chicks I've been privileged to know—this is for you.

—Jolene

Chapter One

Bishop

Bishop! Bishop! Bishop!

The chants from the crowd won't stop rattling around in my head.

Bishop! Bishop! Bishop!

I stumble from the car to the front door, catching my foot on the step and slamming into the side of the house. The world around me blurs. It always does after a show.

Look, it's Bishop Riley from Burn!

Left, right, and left again, I look over my shoulder like the paparazzi are still behind me, their voices mixing with fans that haunt me. What kind of rock star can't handle crowds? It's pathetic. *I'm* pathetic the way I let the anxiety practically swallow me whole.

Just get inside. I need to get inside, and then it will all go away.

I wave my personal guard back into the car before grasping

the handle, desperate for quiet. But as soon as I push the door open, it's like I'm back on stage again, everyone wanting a piece of me. People are everywhere, closing in. No one's supposed to be here. She promised. Maryanne fucking *promised* there wouldn't be a party tonight.

I shove my way through the people crowded in her living room. The crowd's screams during my drum solo overtake me, wipe away the high I get when my sticks slam down on the drums. No one's staring, but it feels like they're climbing inside my skin, gnawing from the inside out.

I need Maryanne. She said she had a surprise for me, and it sure as hell better not be this party.

Someone hits me on the left, scoots around me on the right. Each touch amplifies the screaming in my head, the vice twisting around my throat. I flex my hands, wishing I had my drumsticks.

"Bishop!"

I cover my ears, but then I realize it's Maryanne calling my name.

She bounces over to me, a big-ass smile on her face. "Come with me!" She's yelling, but I can still hardly hear her.

My feet tangle again as I go up the stairs and follow Maryanne down the hallway. With each step, the vice around my throat gets tighter, flashes of the show tonight playing in my head.

10,000 people.

Burn! Bishop! Burn!

It mingles with the phone call from my asshole dad. He

wants more money, he always does. It's the only way to get him to leave us alone. I squeeze my eyes shut, everything becoming too much.

We slip into one of the rooms…and it's quiet. Blissfully fucking quiet, the noise of the party muted by the walls. I turn on Maryanne, hating the way my hands shake. "You better have something good."

She holds up a pill bottle and grins.

My mouth goes dry. "What is it?"

"Come and see." Laughing, she backs away. As soon as I step toward her, she tosses the bottle at me. When I get the lid off, I toss the pills in my mouth and grab the beer Maryanne hands me to wash them down. Pills and beer gone in three seconds flat. Gone the way we used to be before I had the money to pay Dad off, when he would find us in whatever new town we moved to so we could escape him. Only the pills make me feel a whole lot better than leaving did.

Maryanne trails her fingers down my stomach. "How many did you take before you got here?"

"A couple. I only had a few with me, though."

"Here." Maryanne hands me her beer, and I down that as well.

It doesn't take long for the edge to start drifting away, for the vice, the voices, the hands grabbing for me to fade.

My cell rings.

Shit.

I pull out my phone, knowing I'll get hell if I don't answer. People are always checking up on me.

"Where'd you disappear to?" Blake, my band's lead singer, asks. "I thought you were coming over."

The room is spinning. How the hell does a room spin? I fall onto the bed to see if that makes it stop. Nope. My body tingles all over. It's such an incredible feeling. So much better than the hands ripping at my skin during a show or the chanting trapped in my head.

"B.R.?"

Oh, right. I'm on the phone. "Paparazzi wouldn't stop following me," I say. "I had to ditch them." *True.* The word sounds funny, so I keep playing it over. *True, true, true, true.*

"You could have ditched them and still come over. I thought we all decided the band would hang together after the show tonight."

We did? Little bits and pieces try to form in my brain, but struggling to figure them out takes too much concentration. Blake's trying to kill my buzz. I'll be damned if I let that happen. The spinning starts to slow down, and I'm pissed about it. The dizzy was way better than dealing with him. "It's not that big a deal."

My upper teeth brush against something on my bottom lip, and it startles me. But then I realize it's my lip ring, and laughter starts pouring out of me. I don't want to stop. I don't remember the last time I laughed this hard—the last time I let loose with people who weren't in my head.

Burn! Burn! Burn!

It's more than our band's name when they yell it like that. It makes me feel like they're burning me alive. My high starts slipping more…

I want to grab onto to it. Find something else to take to make sure it doesn't go away for the rest of the night.

"Bishop, you need to take this shit seriously. I can only cover for you so long before—"

Wait. "Cover for me? What the fuck does that meant?"

"Mean."

Mean? What is he talking about? The spinning slows to a stop. He's giving me shit for something all of us do. *They're* going out tonight. There's no difference if I do it with or without them. And at least I have an excuse. They don't feel like they're going to lose their shit on stage like I do. Not that I'd ever tell any of them that.

"Bishop," Maryanne whines. "You're ignoring me. I don't like to be ignored." She falls onto the bed next to me and runs her fingers down my chest again. My heart picks up. *This* is what I'm in the mood for. Not Blake's shit.

"Is that Maryanne?" he asks.

Bishop Riley! Burn, Burn, Burn!

My buzz is sizzling away…

"Gotta go." I hang up the phone and drop it on the bed… floor, I don't know and don't care. Maryanne's skirt is short— so short. "What'cha want, B.R.? I know you want more."

Do I? Yeah, I do. Just a few minutes ago, I was laughing. It takes the stress away so I can be happy.

I think she bats her eyelashes at me, but I can't tell. Maryanne gets up and walks over to the dresser. A bottle of vodka flies at me, which I almost don't catch. With a slow smile, she pulls out two more pill containers. The stress immediately seeps out of me, just that easily. I deserve to party once in a while. I'm tired of people telling me otherwise. I don't know anyone who doesn't let loose sometimes. Who doesn't need help relaxing after the crazy schedule we keep? The rest of the time, I just maintain. We all have to maintain.

For once, I want to do more than just maintain.

I get up and grab one of the bottles out of her hand, don't bother reading it before trying to twist off the top. It takes me three tries to open the stupid thing, but I finally get it before shaking whatever's left into my mouth.

"B.R. What about me?" Maryanne swats my arm, but I ignore it. I'm so tired of getting shit from everyone. Tired of feeling on edge all the time, like my own heart wants to eat me alive. I just want it all to go away. After fumbling a couple times, I finally manage to open the vodka before I down some, pills and all.

What feels like a second later, my legs go weak. The spins pick up again, but it feels like my head and not the room. Maryanne starts laughing and dancing around. I try to watch her, but a sheet keeps dropping over my eyes.

The room lurches. I fall to the floor. Maryanne's laughing, and I'm fighting to talk, but nothing comes out. Something tries to crawl up my throat. That stupid sheet drops down again, but it doesn't go away this time. Why won't Maryanne take it off? She keeps laughing…laughing…

Soon, there's nothing left.

• • •

I try to open my eyes, but it's like they've been sewn shut, giving just enough to partially lift, only to fall closed again. They're puppets on a string, someone pulling the lines so they don't listen to me. The thought makes me want to laugh. When I try, the sound won't come out. My throat burns. My tongue's dry as hell, and I'm heavy, paralyzed or something.

Oh, shit. Am I dead?

My heart starts pounding a really killer drum solo. If my heart's beating, I can't be dead, right?

I try to sit up. It's a no-go, so instead I focus on my eyes, fighting like crazy to pull them open.

"He's coming around," someone whispers. Mom? I think so but can't tell. When I feel a hand against my head, I know it's her. She's done that since I was a kid, and I want nothing more than to lean into it. That has to be good. If I can remember stuff like that, I have to be okay.

Do I *want* to be okay?

"Bishop?" Mom whispers again. The pain in her voice slices me open. I hate it when she's hurting—hate it more that I'm pretty sure I fucked up big, and I'm the one who made her feel that way.

"Ma?" My voice won't come out right. There's something in my throat. I fight to open my eyes, but they sort of flutter instead. First, I only see fog, but slowly it starts to clear, and she's leaning over me, her brown hair hanging down. She smiles, but a tear slips down her face and lands on my cheek.

I'm supposed to protect her, not make her cry.

Yeah, I totally screwed up.

This time, I try to move my arm but realize it's strapped down. Tubes are all over the damn place: on me, hanging from stuff. There's a constant beep that I must have missed before.

Panic sets in, and I try to push up again. To do something, *anything*. Since my arms aren't happening, I go for my legs. Try to get up.

"Shh. It's okay, honey. Just relax."

I can't stop. I'm freaking the hell out here, and she wants me to relax?

"He's too agitated," a voice I don't recognize says. "We're going to give him something."

Give me something? Yeah, that actually sounds good.

Mom's face starts to blur. The last thing I notice is she's not even trying to smile anymore, and then I welcome the darkness that takes me over again.

• • •

"I'm not going to Alaska." When I feel my heart kick up, I fight to slow it down by squeezing the arms of the chair.

My band's manager, Don, doesn't even attempt to hide his anger the way Mom's trying to hide her sadness.

Don crosses his beefy arms and leans against his desk. "You're going."

I shove out of the chair, and it crashes to the ground behind me. "First of all, I'm an adult. You can't make me do shit. Second, it was an accident. A *onetime* accident."

I still can't believe it happened. Waking up and finding out I could have choked on my own vomit? I've never been that messed up before. It was a really bad night, and I got a little carried away, that's all.

Pills are a way to unwind. A way to stay calm when I feel like I'm cracking apart.

Mom's shaking hand moves to her mouth, and she gasps. I didn't even say anything, but it's the first time we've even partially put it out there since I woke up in the hospital a week ago. "Ma, I'm sorry. Seriously, you know I didn't mean anything. It was…" I shrug. "I don't know. Just something to do, or whatever. I was tired after the show and all that press stuff. It helps me relax. It's not like I do it all the time." When Maryanne hooks me up, I can make a whole bottle last over a month. That's nothing compared to some of the people I know. Not that I could tell my mom.

"Bishop…you could have *died.*" Mom's crying again, wiping tears with her pink-painted nails. I hate myself a little more for making her feel like this. "Do you realize how serious that is?"

Do I realize how serious that is? That's the stupidest question I've ever heard. "Yeah, Ma. I'm the one who woke up with a tube down my throat."

That only makes her cry harder. If possible, I feel even shittier. Mom doesn't deserve this crap, doesn't deserve my screw-ups since she's given up everything so I can be here. Too bad I can't seem to make myself do anything about it.

Don clears his throat. "If you understand how serious it

is, you get why you're going to Seldon. Your mom and I have been talking, and we think—"

"Don't talk about me like I'm an idiot. I don't need you two discussing shit behind my back."

When he speaks again, Don's voice is hard. "Do you know how long I've been in this business, Bishop?"

Right now, I couldn't care less.

"Over twenty years. I've seen a lot of talent come and go. I've seen people make it big and people screw it all up." He shakes his head. "I've seen people *die.*"

"I—"

"Shut up and let me finish. I believe last week was an accident, but I don't believe this was a onetime thing. You might think I'm an idiot, but I can tell when someone's high. I've been around the block with musicians both in better and worse shape than you. I also know you're on the edge. If you keep going the way you are now, you'll take a header right off it. It starts out as a way to relax, then you start losing control once in awhile like last week, and before you know it, you don't have any control at all. I've seen it."

"We just want you to take a little break, sweetie," Mom adds. "That's all. Get a clear head and see what you're doing."

Looking at her hurts too much, so I look at Don instead. It's easier to be pissed at him.

"You're lucky you have people who care about you. Not everyone has that. I've been around long enough to know that even though you're making me money now, you get worse and you're going to start costing me money. It's Alaska or rehab.

You choose. We can keep Alaska quiet, which honestly is a damn blessing. The press doesn't know what happened last week, and we might be able to keep it that way. They find out and *every*thing changes. It's not about the band's music anymore. It all turns into 'How's your drummer? Staying clean?' I won't let you screw up my band up like that, Riley."

I hate the way he pulls that last name bullshit. Don looks at me all cocky, like he knows he has me. Music awards are all over the walls of his stupid office, taunting me. *Our* Grammy from last year.

"And if I refuse?" The look on Mom's face tells me I broke her further. Don's scowl says he's beyond pissed, but what the hell? They're not the ones getting shipped away.

Bishop! Bishop! Bishop!

Focusing, I think of the pills I have back at home. After dealing with this, I deserve one

"You're a natural drummer, kid."

I shake my head, wishing my hands would stay still. He knows it pisses me off when he calls me *kid* even more than the last name thing.

"You're one of the best I've seen, and you're still a damn *teenager*. I'd hate to lose you. The guys would hate to lose you, but you're no good to us if we have to worry about you swallowing your own tongue because you're too fucked up to see straight. One night leads to two, to three. You'll keep getting closer to that cliff and I'll be damned before all our hard work goes to waste because you couldn't handle it."

Handle it? How do I handle this? The feeling that everyone at a show is inside me, taking over my insides and jumping on my heart. Pills are the only things that dull the chaos in my head.

Mom reaches over and touches my shoulder. "I only want you okay. I don't care about the band. I care about you. We need to do what's best for you."

If that were true, she wouldn't be listening to Don. "The guys won't go for this. They have my back." We're on top of the world right now. Three number-one singles in the past six months and he wants me to hide out?

He rubs his beard. "You disappeared for a day in Tokyo. You passed out and missed that interview in New York. You missed a band meeting the same day you downed a bunch of pills. They're not going to have your back on this. And they've also been instructed not to talk to you while you're gone. You're stepping away from everything while you're there."

"I—" They're not allowed to talk to me. The guys, my *bandmates*, know about this. They sold me out. I've talked to every one of them this week and no one said anything about Alaska.

Don cuts me off before I can think of something to say. He sighs, his body going a little limp like he actually cares. "We have nothing going on for the next couple months. The guys are all taking some time off. This is the perfect chance for you to figure out what you want. To back your ass away from the cliff. You have two months to get it together or you're out. That'll give us enough time to pull someone in before the tour."

Out. As in out of the band. It's like the crowd is inside my chest again. I struggle to slow my breathing. This is my *life*. *Drumming* is my life. "You're going to take music away from me?"

I look at Mom, but she lets her eyes drift closed.

"No, kid. *You're* going to take music away from you." Don's stern face doesn't change.

"I don't have a problem," I blurt out.

"Then it won't bother you to take a vacation."

I throw my arms in the air. "Fine, but I don't call Alaska in February a vacation spot. I get to pick the place."

Don actually laughs. "You lost your chance to negotiate. It's Seldon, Alaska, or nothing. Troy grew up around there, and he and Gary go back every once in a while. You can't get into much trouble there and unlike L.A., it's the kind of place you can hide out, because I swear to God, if I see your face plastered on a tabloid cover like you're Lindsay fucking Lohan, you're out. I'm not dealing with that shit anymore."

Mom shifts, her serious matching Don's. "It'll be an adventure, Bishop. We've never been to Alaska. It'll be like when you were younger—just the two of us."

Those words shock my system. I feel like I really am trying to swallow my tongue like Don said. I can't do this with Mom. Can't handle the way she looks at me. Can't handle her chewing her pink-painted nails, scared I'm going to lose it at any second. Push her graying brown hair behind her ear and know I'm probably giving her more of it.

I shake my head. "Not her. I...I can't go with her. If it's her, I walk." I look at Mom, hoping she'll get it. Hoping she sees I'm not trying to hurt her, but instead she gasps, her chin starting to tremble.

She looks over at Don, and I know he'll save her, but he surprises me by saying, "No. Gary's been through this before. He's got this."

Mom looks as surprised as I am that he's sending me with his brother.

. . .

We decided it would be better if no one knows who I am. And by we, I mean Don, but whatever. I get it. It's not like I want people to know I'm stuck in some shithole town with people who probably marry their cousins.

We dyed my bleached hair back to its original dark brown. Don wanted my lip ring gone, but there's no way I'm losing it. They're already shipping me off like some degenerate drug addict. I think I'm being pretty damn accommodating.

Frustrated, I put my feet up on the dashboard.

"How are you feeling? Any withdrawal symptoms or anything?"

What? I look at my bodyguard, Gary. "First of all, it's been over a week since the party. If I were going to withdraw, wouldn't it have already happened? Second, I'm not a pill-head! I don't take that shit every day. That's what you guys don't get."

"You don't have to take something every day for it to be a problem." There's a tenseness in Gary's voice I don't often hear from him, but I ignore it.

After what feels like a year, Gary pulls off the snow-covered road and into a snow-covered driveway in the middle of too many snow-covered trees to count. "It'll serve you guys right if I get attacked by a bear or something." As soon as I say it, I realize how stupid it sounds, but I don't care.

"Bears are asleep this time of year," is all Gary says.

Ignoring him, I look at the microscopic cabins in front of us. They're the size of the hotel rooms from when we first started. Now, we always stay in suites.

"They don't usually rent them out this time of year, so we paid for the whole thing. They don't know who you are, so now's the time to tell me if you're going to create an alias."

I drop my head to the side and look at him. He's Don's brother, but their last name is where the resemblance ends. Don's huge. Gary's small and thin. Don's all business. Gary thinks he's a comedian. Don is straight as they come. Gary is gay. There's something about Gary that makes you not want to screw with him, though. Maybe it's his big-ass, bodybuilding boyfriend.

"This isn't a game, man. It's my life."

Gary shrugs. "Your call. You need to at least lose the last name, though. You can be like Madonna. All the really cool rock stars go by one name." He winks.

I curse under my breath. We just got here, and I'm already over it. "Funny."

I move to get out of the car, but he stops me. "You can do this, Bishop. I know it's tough, but you can do it. Troy was a whole hell of a lot worse than you before he got clean. He went to rehab, and when he finished, we came here to recoup. Not the cabins, but his parents' house. Did Don tell you Troy grew up here?"

I'm still trying to sort through what he said. I never knew his boyfriend used to be an addict. And I hate that they're comparing me to that. After pulling my arm away, I get out of the car. He's right behind me. "Since we have the whole place, I want my own cabin." Really, I'm still thinking about Troy and how they think I need the same treatment as someone who went to rehab.

He walks to the trunk and opens it. "We're next door to each other and you get random check-ins. I'll also be searching your cabin often, and before we separate, I'm looking through your bag and your clothes. You go anywhere, you have to ask first. I want to see you before you go and when you come home. You also can't be gone for longer than a couple hours at a time."

"Excuse me?"

"I'm not done. We also have sit-down talks at least once a week. We're also getting you on some kind of schedule. When Troy got clean, he started working out. I'm starting you with an hour walk daily. Sometimes we'll go together, others you can go alone. It'll be good for you to have some time being at one with nature." Gary's eyebrows go up. He's obviously enjoying this.

I groan, but it's really just a cover. My heart's beating a million miles an hour. There's no time to think about the walk or any of the other shit he said. Gary's going to search my bag.

My mind flashes to the pills I have tucked in a little slit in the back. I think it's hidden, but there's a chance he'll find it. "I'm in a town the size of a shoebox. I have no car and definitely no friends. It's not like there's anywhere I'm going to go…well, except on your walks, I guess." I'm hoping this diverts him so he doesn't realize I'm freaking the hell out.

Gary laughs, and I suddenly want to punch him in the face. I used to like him better than Don. "Such a grouch. Now get over here and help me with the bags."

I take a step forward, somehow slip in the snow, and fall on my ass. Gary laughs harder.

I fucking hate Alaska.

Chapter Two

Penny

Adrenaline rushes through me as I fly behind the enemy's goal with the puck in my possession. The screaming crowd barely registers over the sound of my breathing and skates against ice. This game could get us into the semifinals, and we're so close to the end.

Ten seconds left.

I know where each player is—most of us have been on the same teams for years—and I can pick out any of the guys by the way they move on the ice.

I barely dodge the opposing center, and Mitch is weaving up the middle. He's about to veer to the left and will be in front of the goal in perfect time. He just has to get around the defense. I'm watching out the corner of my eye as I keep the puck close. Mitch and I have more assists and goals than anyone else in the state, and that's really saying something. There's a lot of talent up here.

Okay. Focus.

Time slows as it always does when I'm moving this fast. Each push of my skate, each hit of my stick against the puck registers in my brain so I don't screw up.

Five seconds left.

Just before number eight tries for a steal, I snap my stick and shoot the puck straight to Mitch who slams it toward the goal. Number eight rams me into the wall, forcing the air from my lungs, but I don't tear my eyes from the net. The goalie reaches up and makes contact with the puck on the tip of his glove. I hold my breath until it falls just to the inside of the red line.

Despite my protesting ribs, I throw my hands in the air and scream as the buzzer rings. Number eight wasn't fooling around. My side's killing me. Mitch crashes into me for a hug, and the rest of the team mauls us.

All the shit I get from outsiders for being the only girl on the team is totally worth it for this.

. . .

"Pen-ny! Pen-ny!" the guys chant as I step out of the girl's locker room. I love this—the high from the game, from the crowd, from my guys. My white-blond hair is still soaked from the shower, and my whole body aches. They were a rough team, and I wonder how many bruises I'll have tomorrow. I shift my huge hockey duffel higher on my shoulder, sending another wave of pain through my left side.

"Party's at Matt's place!" Mitch tosses an arm over my

shoulder, making me shift my bag again as we head for the door. He'd never insult me by asking to carry it. "You coming?"

"I'll be there." There's a part of me that wishes the guys were online gamers or D&D nerds or something so I didn't have to deal with the partying, but at least they're serious enough about hockey to not get into anything major. They also don't say a word when I take their keys.

"Heard back from Michigan yet?" His smile is wide, and his dark hair flops over his forehead. "Their women's team is pretty hardcore."

My chest sinks because even Mitch doesn't understand that I really want to keep playing with the guys. I don't want to go to Michigan. I don't want to go to Illinois or Washington or Wisconsin. I've given up explaining that I actually *do* want to stay in Alaska and go to UAA or UAF, so I usually give the most non-committal answers possible. To Mom, to Gramps, to everyone because apparently they all have a plan for Penny Jones that doesn't include my input. "Not yet."

"Do you have to check in at home first?" Mitch asks quietly.

"Yeah. Mom's working tonight, so I definitely need to stop by." I love Gramps, and it scares me to leave him at home for too long. So far, his confusion hasn't gotten dangerous, but I still worry. He was too tired to come to my game, and that doesn't happen often.

"When's your mom going to hire someone to stick around him?"

I can't think about that yet. It's too drastic. "Not until we have to. He's had a lot of good days lately." Even as I say the words, I know he'll go downhill no matter what we do.

Mitch gives me a squeeze because he's known me long enough to understand what I need. "Want me to do your check-in with you?"

"No." I know Mitch would, but I also know he'd probably rather not. *I'd* rather him not because he'll bring his girlfriend with him and watching them might kill my buzz from the game. I want to head straight to the party, even though I'm not a drinker. Someone has to be there to make sure the guys don't accidentally kill one another playing some daredevil game while wasted.

"I'll be keymaster until you get there, cool?" He gives me another squeeze.

"Thanks." I breathe a sigh of relief. Mitch gets my need to keep our friends safe—even when they're too shit-faced to give a crap either way.

I glance at the door where Mitch's girlfriend, Rebecca, is scowling at me. Like she always does when I stand close to Mitch. She's perfectly dressed and perfectly made-up with her tiny, curved body and perfectly smooth brown hair. The exact opposite of the kind of girl who could understand Mitch. Whatever.

He gives me a peck on the side of his head before dropping his arm and his bag and running to pick her up. This always appeases her, and generally makes me realize that I might not be as okay with him and Rebecca as I'd like to be. He's dated before, but Rebecca's different. She's been around longer, and he shows no sign of wanting to move on to someone else. It sounds crazy, but Mitch has always been a given with me. He's my best friend, and I've never had a doubt that someday there would be a Mitch and Penny.

The little pang of longing or loss or jealousy is brief, but only because I'm good at pushing it away.

"Good game, Jones." Freddie and Chomps—well, David, but we all call him Chomps—slap me on the back as I step around Mitch and Rebecca who have just become a twisted-up mess of hormones in the doorway. Chomps is defense and about as big as you'd expect a guy with a nickname like Chomps to be. He and his girlfriend aren't this obnoxious. It might have something to do with the fact that they've been dating since, like, eighth grade and are likely to get married within two months of graduation, but still.

"See ya, Lucky Penny!" Mitch manages a short wave before he's again sucked in by the vacuum that is Rebecca's lips. Or maybe it has more to do with her boobs.

"Shove it, asshole." I grin as I push open the second set of doors even though I'm not feeling it. The thought of losing Mitch makes it hard to breathe. I just need to get home and do my check-in so I can meet up with everyone, then I'll be fine again. I'm sure.

The snow's coming down hard, and there's probably already a foot of the heavy, wet stuff in the parking lot. Good thing Matt lives close to me, because if he didn't, there's no way I'd drive in this mess just to watch the guys get trashed.

Bitty, my red truck, spins sideways out of the parking lot,

and I give her a bit of extra gas just to kick up some snow and keep her sideways a bit longer. Once she gets traction again, I shove her in four-wheel drive for the trip home.

I flick on the radio to my favorite rock station and crank it up—anything to keep my high from the game for a while.

When I glance behind me, Chomps's truck is on my tail, filled with guys, also skidding sideways and spraying snow. It sucks to have to check-in at home instead of riding with them. It's bad enough I miss the locker room talk. Then again, they probably talk about girls whenever I'm not around, so maybe I should be glad I'm not there.

What matters is they take care of me on the ice, and I take care of them. A team. At least for a few more games. And then comes the part I don't want to think about because I'm not ready for anything to change.

• • •

I live in the crazy house off the corner near the river.

This is Alaskan direction speak. My Gramps and Gramma lived in a trailer, and then they built around that. And then they added on to that, and then they added on again. Gramps lives in the trailer part that's now shielded by our house, but it still looks like a trailer parked in the basement when you're inside.

At last count, we had five different kinds of siding on our three and a half story house, in five different colors of brown and blue, and a half junkyard's worth of cars off the left side for Gramps's hobby. To the right are the perfect, tidy little log cabins and manicured yard (now buried under several feet of snow) that Mom and I rent out in the summer. Two of our small cabins have lights on, and I remember we have guys up from California.

Hopefully, the renters won't stick around for long. It's annoying having to worry about guests during hockey season—especially rich ones who expect special treatment just because they've rented out the whole place during winter. It's our *off*-season. Who else is going to be here?

I put my truck in park and see Gramps line-dancing in the second story kitchen. Gramps in the kitchen usually means he's not all present, but he's happy. It's his normal. Mild dementia, and what the doctor says might turn to Alzheimer's, hit two years ago when Gramma died. In his lucid moments, he tells me it's better this way. He doesn't miss her as much as he would if he always knew what was going on. It both breaks my heart and relieves me.

In his spots of drastic confusion—anything goes. Fortunately, those don't happen often. It's another reason I wish Dad was still around because maybe if Gramps hadn't lost both his son and his wife, his mind would still work.

I kick off my winter boots in our large entry and jog up the wooden stairs to the second story where we live. Other than the hole I call my room, downstairs houses a bunch of freezers, Gramps's food storage, and a big rack for all my hockey, snow-machining, and motocross gear. Gramps is big into "preparedness" even though it's borderline paranoid. I'd blame the dementia, but he's had this little quirk for as long as

I can remember.

"Hey, Gramps."

He stops mid-dance step with a fresh pie in his hand. His long beard touches the top of Gramma's old white and red checked apron with frilled lace on the edges. He says the apron brings him luck in the kitchen. I'm not about to argue since I don't know how to cook, and most of what he makes is delicious.

"Lucky Penny! How are ya, my girl!" He grins wide, wrinkling the skin around his eyes.

"I'm good." He sets the pie on the counter with a flourish, and I wrap my arms around him for a quick hug.

"What'cha got there?" I ask as my stomach starts to grumble. I have no idea how many calories I burn in a game because I've never been a calorie-counting kind of girl, but I do know I'm always starving when we finish.

"Steak and strawberry pie." He smiles proudly.

My stomach turns—first because no one should put a piece of steak in their mouth at the same time as a strawberry, and second, it means he's not doing as well as I want him to— at least not tonight. Definitely not good enough for me to feel okay about ditching him for a party.

He picks up the faded, red hot-pads and does a few dancing steps to the god-awful country music he's listened to since I can remember. His gray ponytail hangs halfway down his back and swings a bit as he two-steps to the other side of the plywood-floored kitchen.

"You want a slice?" he asks.

"Nah. I ate after the game." I swallow the lump that formed in my throat, and tears spring to my eyes. I know Gramps says he doesn't care he's like this, but I know better. I'm wondering if it'll hit him before or after he takes a bite of the stupid pie.

I pull out my phone and text Mitch.

WON'T MAKE IT. NOT HAVING A GOOD NIGHT HERE.

Mitch answers in less than a minute like he always does.

SAY THE WORD AND A FEW OF US WILL BRING THE PARTY TO YOU.

Maybe I haven't lost Mitch to Rebecca. At least not totally. I lean against the large wooden picnic table set in the middle of the kitchen. I know the guys would come here, and Gramps might love it, but if Mom ends up home at a decent hour tonight, that's not going to work. I never seem to know what her schedule at the hospital is—mostly because she picks up whatever nursing shifts she can get. And now that I'm thinking about it…it's been probably two weeks since Mom and I spent any real time together. She must really be pushing for extra hours.

THANKS ANYWAY. C U MON AT SCHL.

SORRY PEN

I start to write back and tell him not to worry but don't bother. He'll worry no matter what, because he's a good guy that way.

REBECCA SAYS SHE'LL KEEP THE KEYS

Irritation rushes through me. I'm sure she's doing it so Mitch will be given another chance to tell me how she's trying to get along with the team, and how I might be overreacting to the stupid stuff she does, like pressing her boobs against the Plexiglass that surrounds our rink.

THX I write back only because I can't be a bitch and say nothing.

I slump lower in my seat and realize the music's stopped. Gramps is staring at the untouched pie.

"Kinda weird, isn't it?" he asks. "To put both steak and strawberries in the same place."

I want to lie. I want to tell him that everyone makes steak and strawberry pie, but I swore to him I'd tell him the truth — even when I really don't want to. "A little."

He sighs and pulls off Gramma's apron, hanging it on the hook next to the window.

"Dessert instead?" he asks, trying hard to lighten his voice.

I cock a brow. "Depends on what we're having?"

"Ice cream." He chuckles as he pulls open the freezer door. "It's too bad. I think I really nailed the crust."

I have to laugh, even though I'm blotting tears away again. Nobody as good as Gramps should ever have to deal with losing his mind.

"Don't worry, Penny. I know how to get two bowls. I think we're safe." He's trying to tease as he sets the bowls on the counter, but his hands shake as he does it. He's not so far gone that he doesn't realize when he does something weird, and it makes me hate again that this is happening to him.

He hits the power on the radio and the horrid country oldies station blares through the house. As much as I hate the twang, it means that things are about as right as they're going to be. There's definitely comfort to be gained from that.

• • •

Mom's at the table in the morning looking out over what's probably two feet of fresh snow. Her blond hair isn't as bright as mine, but she keeps it long and wrapped up in a braided bun most days. Mine hangs perfectly straight to my shoulders—long enough for a very small ponytail. I shuffle into the room, huddled in my sweatshirt.

The February sun reflects off the wood walls, making the house feel warmer, even though the frost on the edges of the windows says it's probably well below zero.

"Morning, Penny. Heard you helped win the game last night." She smiles over her cup of coffee.

"We all played well." I nod. "Haven't seen you in forever."

"Brandy said you passed to Mitch for the winning goal." Her brows go up, and the corners of her mouth twitch. Brandy is Chomps's mom.

"Yeah, I did." I replay the pass in my head. Perfection. But my whole left side is still a bit sore. Nothing a hot tub and some Advil won't fix.

"I got another letter from the sports director at Minnesota. It's big, Penny." Her smile is wide and full of pride. "They've been national champions more often than not in the past five years."

I know it's big. They're good. Really good. I steel myself, knowing she's trying to bait me into another conversation about college that I don't want to have. "Both UAF and UAA have good programs, and then I'd still be in Alaska and not so far away." And still playing with guys like I've been doing since I was eight.

Mom frowns. "UAA doesn't even always have a women's team, Penny. Don't you wanna—"

"Can we talk later?" I ask because the fact that UAA only *sometimes* has a women's team is why I want to go. Not that there's anything wrong with a girl's team—it's just not me.

I stare at the table, hoping she'll drop the subject because I really don't know how to answer in a way that'll keep her happy, and me in Alaska where I want to be. Mom, Gramps, and everyone else thinks it's important to get out—explore the world, figure out who I am or whatever. I already know who I am. Running away to college isn't going to help me learn something I already know.

Her frown holds for a moment, and then her face softens. Like she's decided she'll let it go for now. Thankfully.

"Did you go to the party last night?" she asks.

I sit at the end of the bench on our table, unsure yet if I want to be sitting or not because now I'm thinking about Gramps. If I tell the truth, she'll know he's not doing as well as I want him to.

"I take it that's a no?" She sets down her mug, a look of concern on her face.

"Gramps made an odd pie last night." I let out a sigh and

push to standing. Thinking about Gramps hurts too much. I need food.

"I wondered why no one had cut into it." Mom re-shuffles on the bench and takes another long drink. "You okay?"

I shrug because I'm definitely not okay, and I pull out some bread. Gramps has yet to mess up a loaf of bread.

"The cabin renters came in a couple days ago," she says.

"I saw." I slide my bread in the toaster. "How long are they here for?"

"Undetermined." She holds my gaze for a while.

"Okay."

Mom's never wanted people living in the cabins, so whoever it is must be giving her some serious dough for her to even consider allowing someone there open-ended.

"Don't worry. I warned them that we only do breakfasts in the summer and that they'll be alone for all their meals. So, just the regular stuff, you know. Bedding laundry, garbage, maps, answering stupid questions like why we call them snowmachines instead of snowmobiles…" She gives me a wink.

"Okay." It means more work for me, but also a bit of cash. Mom and I split the profit from the cabins, so while it sucks, it's doable. I need parts for my old Corvette anyway.

"How was your night?" I ask as I spread butter across my toast, licking the extra off my fingers.

"Oh, fine." Her eyes don't meet mine as she stands and walks for her room. "I need a shower."

"Oh-kay." I stand a bit stunned at the abrupt end of our

conversation as Mom's door closes between us. We don't have a perfect relationship or anything, but this was our first talk in a while, and it was going fine until it was…just over.

Her shower turns on, and it's stupid to just stand in the middle of the kitchen with my toast, so I sit and rest my feet on the low windowsill. Smoke billows from the chimneys of two cabins, and the snow reflects the sunlight in billions of tiny sparkles like it does when it's this cold. A guy steps out. One who looks the same age as I am. I wasn't expecting that. Maybe I should've been paying more attention the past couple of days.

When I'm about to give up on staring and hit the hot tub, he lights up a cigarette. I scan him again. Brown hair that's too evenly colored to be natural and a coat that probably cost more than my whole bag of hockey gear. I can see his frown from here, making me wonder why he's spending so much money to stay here if he looks so pissed off.

I'll definitely be doing some digging when Mom leaves for her shift.

Chapter Three

Bishop

I've been here for three days and it feels more like three years. Gary's in and out of my cabin a million times a day. He checks the whole cabin and me each time like I'm in prison or something. Once in awhile, he acts like he's just coming to visit, but I know it's an excuse to check up on me more often. To make sure I haven't either died of boredom, or went outside and drowned in all the snow. Who the hell would want to live in a place where it gets this cold? I freeze my balls off every time we take one of our walks. I'm still trying to figure out the point of those. We don't even talk…just *walk*. I'm pretty sure I could walk in L.A. if that's all I'm here for.

But no. That would be too easy. And I'm sure he's torturing me with snow-hikes because he thinks I'm in here snorting cocaine or something. Which is ridiculous. That's not something I mess with.

So I drink a little. Take a few pills here and there to help me get by. It's not like I don't have a prescription for some of them. This is a hard life. Don, of all people, should get that. He's managed enough bands to know how it is. To know how you start to feel like you're losing your mind.

I don't have a problem.

Gary managed to miss the pills in my bag, and I've only taken one in the three days I've been here. It's not like I can tell him that, though. He'll blow it out of proportion and call his brother. Don's pretty good at turning stuff around on me, and Mom goes along with everything he says.

Case in point: me sitting in this tiny cabin in the middle of nowhere. She never would have made me do this on her own, and it's definitely not what's best. I can't even relax inside if I want to smoke.

Trying not to shiver, I take a drag of my cigarette. Sitting on the porch with the door open isn't giving me any heat. And they said this was supposed to be a vacation.

After putting out my smoke, I go back inside, shrug off my coat, and start pacing the cabin. I'm starting to go stir-crazy. I'm not used to sitting around like this. My hands are shaking, so I rub them on my jeans hoping it will help. The longer I stay locked behind these log walls, I feel like they're shrinking on me. Like they're closing in...in...in, trying to crush me. Trying to squeeze the life out of me. It feels like it does when I'm in a crowd. Like I can't suck in enough air. It's ridiculous. What kind of fucking rock star can't deal with a crowd?

My head is all hot and my feet are cold. Gary said it's because of the oil stove and heat rising. I don't get why the people don't just put in a regular heater. This is Alaska, not the stone ages. I'm pretty damn sure everyone in California has a regular heater, and we hardly even use the things.

I push the hoop in my bottom lip around in the hole while I pace. This is so screwed up. The longer I stalk around the room, the faster my heart starts beating. The more I feel like I'm going to explode if I don't get out of here soon.

It's just this place. I miss my house, my drums. That's all it is. I've had drumsticks in my hands for as long as I can remember. It's crazy how I can love something and hate it at the same time. Playing is my life, the crowds suck it out of me.

Again, I try to find something to do with my hands, but they have minds of their own and keep trembling.

I lean against the kitchen counter and do that deep breathing bullshit my doc told me to do when I feel on edge. *In. Out. In. Out.* When it doesn't work, I busy my hands by pushing them both through my hair and lean over.

In. Out. In. Out.

Still nothing.

The walls move in another foot, and that's when I know I have to get out of here. Pushing off the counter, I go straight for the front door. It's open about two seconds before I remember I'm in *Alaska* and my junk is liable to freeze off if I don't stay as warm as possible.

About ten steps later, I'm in the tiny bedroom off the main room of the cabin. There's a beanie on the chair, which I slip on. I turn for the door, but something stops me. I don't know what it is. My anger, annoyance, whatever it is, I turn and head for my suitcase. After looking around to make sure Gary didn't sneak up on me, I push two fingers inside the hidden spot in my suitcase. One of the small white pills I stashed comes out easily. The ones for anxiety that I actually have a prescription for, Gary's in control of.

Right now, I need more than I'm prescribed.

It's just because I'm trapped in this snowbound hell, I tell myself as I swallow it dry, grab my jacket from the living room, and then head outside. If I take these instead of going to Gary, maybe he'll report to my parole officer, AKA, Don that I'm doing well and can go home.

There should not be this much snow anywhere. It comes all the way up to my knees. White and trees is all I see for… well, for as far as I can see. The drugs are starting to kick in. I already feel the tightness in my muscles start to lessen.

I glance over at the cabin next door just as Gary steps out. His cell glued to his ear, probably whispering sweet nothings to Troy or whatever it is they do. "What are you doing?" he calls to me.

Really? Walking is supposed to be part of my "therapy". Not that he's let me do it alone yet. Does he think I'm going to buy something from the moose on the corner? "I'm pretty sure it's called walking. Maybe you remember it. We spoke about doing it every day. Don't worry. I'm not leaving, *Dad.*"

He gives me a huge smile and a wave, like he's the happiest person in the world.

And now I suddenly want to puke. Nice.

As I trudge through the snow, the shaking eases up, and

I actually feel like I can breathe. Still, it's not as good as the smog-filled air in L.A. Yeah, I said that. It's almost like things are *too* clear up here, if that makes any sense.

Or maybe I'm going crazy. I heard people get depressed in Alaska since it's dark like ninety percent of the time.

I head for the far end of the property and toward the freaking wilderness, wishing someone had told me to buy some boots before I got here, but the last thing I want is to end up as breaking news. I can see the headline now: TEEN DRUMMER BISHOP RILEY OF THE BAND BURN MISSING IN THE ALASKAN WILDERNESS, WHILE HIS "BABYSITTER" WAS BUSY ON THE PHONE WITH HIS BOYFRIEND AND HIS MOM AND MANAGER WERE PARTYING IT UP IN THE LAND OF FREAKING NORMALCY WITHOUT HIM.

I make a quick u-turn to avoid finding one of those sleeping bears Gary was talking about. My feet are cold as hell as I pass my cabin again and start toward the main house—if you can call it a house. I've never seen anything like it with all the different floors and obvious additions. I mean, it looks kind of cool, but also makes me wonder if we're renting cabins from a bunch of nutcases.

I'm walking around the other side of the house when I see the leggy blonde standing by a kickass Corvette. Deprived as I am, I take a minute to admire them both. I've seen her come and go a few times. Not close enough to see her face, but the rest of her is gorgeous. Her hair is just past her shoulders, stick straight, and I swear it's only a few shades darker than the snow.

She's tall. Taller than I usually go for, but not too tall to appreciate. She's curvy in all the right places. Yeah, definitely something to appreciate.

And the car? The car is incredible, too. For the first time in a while, I remember the 1970 Ford Ranchero sitting in my garage back home. It's one of the first things I bought when we got signed. I've always wanted one, a piece of shit I could fix up myself. If I weren't a drummer, that's what I'd do: rebuild cars.

The plan is already set on what I want to do to mine. She'll be incredible once I ever get a chance to work on her. She's been sitting there for over a year.

Why haven't I worked on my car?

The Snow Queen pushes off the car, and I try to turn so she doesn't realize I was staring at her, but she catches my eye before I get a chance.

Two thoughts slam into me at once. First, she's unreal beautiful. Not plastic in the way the girls I know are. Big eyes, slim lips and a nice little smile. And second, I totally don't feel like talking to her. I'm out of my element here. The last thing I'm in the mood for right now is trying to befriend the locals. Plus, she might recognize me, and that'll make things a whole lot worse. I should have grabbed the hat Gary bought me instead of the beanie. Obviously *that* would make a huge difference.

If I thought it would get me home, I'd *tell* her who I am, but knowing Don, he'll find a way to blame me and I'll get sent somewhere even worse. Though I'm not sure where would be worse than being in the snowy wilderness with no real civilization.

Shoving my hands in my pocket, I move to turn away when I hear, "Hey!"

"Damn," I mumble under my breath before I start to walk her way. Maybe she can let me know who delivers all the way out here. Chinese sounds bomb.

"What's up?" I nod my head before looking toward the ground. I'm awesome at disguises.

I hear her chuckle and glance up at her to see her eyes are on my feet. Yeah, I know I'm not wearing the right shoes. She doesn't have to be cocky about it. "Something funny?"

"No, no." She tries to play it off, but I can still see the smirk lingering. "Can you help me with something real quick?" she asks, while I'm busy watching her face. Trying to look for any signs that she recognizes who I am.

"Sure." I shrug, finding the ground again with my eyes. She leads me to a huge toolbox—one of those tall, heavy ones.

"I'm Penny Jones, by the way," she says over her shoulder. The garage door is open and she's only wearing a hoodie.

"Bishop Ri—" Oh, shit. I forgot I'm not supposed to use my full name. I look at her as she licks her bright red lips. "Ripe."

Her forehead wrinkles. "Bishop Ripe?"

Yeah. So I'm an idiot. Who gives a shit? "Problem with that?"

Penny shakes her head, but I can tell she's fighting another laugh. Not that I wouldn't be laughing in her situation.

"I need to roll this over to the car, but the wheels are messed up. Sometimes they fall off, so can you stay on the other side just in case?" Her voice is kind of a mix of snark and sweet—the sweet feels like a contrast to her strong, tall build. And somehow, I have a feeling the quiet sweetness is her camouflage. Like she's a black widow or something and could bite my head off at any second. Or maybe I'm being paranoid because I'm in the land of Ice Road Truckers.

"I'll push it over for you." The car's at the end of the garage, but it's a slight decline.

"If only one person could do it, I wouldn't need your help. If you wanna push, let me hold this end steady." She doesn't sound pissed, but maybe a little annoyed. She stands in the front like I'm actually going to need her help with this thing. I can be a little annoyed, too.

"It'll be fine," I tell her before getting behind it and pushing. Seriously, how many people does it take to push a toolbox?

"Whatever you say." She stands back and smirks, like she knows a private joke I'm not a part of.

Holding my end I start to walk. The thing slides as easily as it should and I start to wonder if she really just wanted an excuse to talk to me or something.

I keep pushing and walking, when suddenly the front wheels fall off and the thing to comes to a dead stop.

Unfortunately for me, I don't have super breaks and can't stop that quickly. My head rams right into the stupid metal box in front of me. "Shit!" I grab my nose, which pulses with pain.

"Oh my God!" The Snow Queen steps toward me, but I hold my other hand up to tell her to stay put. I definitely don't need the "I told you so" from some Alaskan chick I just met. Especially someone as smug as she seems to be.

"I told you to let me help. Are you okay?" She's cocking her head to each side like she's trying to look around my hand. There isn't nearly enough concern in her voice considering I probably just broke my nose. Our publicist is going to freak if Don's stunt ruins his promo photos for our next tour.

"I'm fine." Then I feel something running down my wrist. Nice. I'm bleeding. I ran into a toolbox, broke my nose, and now it's not only bleeding but I look like I'm crying in front of the Snow Queen. I should have packed a few more pills. I had no idea there would be so much stress up here.

"Tilt your head back and come inside. I'll get you cleaned up." Still no worry. Like this is no big deal and people break their noses in her garage all the time. But then she glances back and I think there might be a little concern in her eyes.

Part of me wants to tell her I'm not going anywhere with her, but it's cold and my nose hurts so I follow her out of the garage, around the front of the house and through an unpainted metal door. When we walk inside, the only light comes from a small window lighting up racks of helmets and black duffel bags of who knows what. Snow gear hangs from a bar on the wall and almost every other surface. The floors and wall are wooden, and there are about five refrigerators down here. That's strange as hell.

Maybe it's where they keep the bodies.

Fucking Don and his need to get me up here—he'll be sorry when I end up in pieces in someone's freezer in a crazy house in Alaska.

I pause when my eye catches the back corner of this big open space. It looks like there's an old trailer stuck inside the house. A trailer. Inside the house. Definitely crazy people.

She jogs up the open wooden stairs, and once again, I follow. The stairs stop in the kitchen, which is really just half the upstairs with a huge-ass picnic table in the middle of it and windows all along the front. I can see Gary is still outside, that same grin on his face. God, they talk more than teenage girls.

My eyes are still watering, but this is the craziest house I've ever been in. I blink a few times. The other half of this floor is full of old couches, an ancient TV, and has a few dead animals on the wall. It's creepy. I need to get my ass back to California.

"Sit," she tells me, and I find myself plopping onto the bench, resting my weight against the table. I drop my head back and she gives me a towel. "Pinch it."

"I know what I'm doing." The last bloody nose I got was when I got in a fight my freshman year. I pinch my nose like she says anyway, though, and look at the wood ceiling. Maybe I should tell these people it's possible to make houses in something other than wood.

"I'll be right back," she says.

I wish I had stayed in the cabin and let the walls close in on me.

She stops close when she comes back, and something like vanilla mixed with oil and gasoline drifts around me.

"This might suck a bit at first." She chuckles before cramming something up one of my nostrils.

"What the fuck?" I yell, pushing forward.

She doesn't even flinch or apologize or anything. "I know it sounds crazy, but all the hockey players use tampons for bloody noses. They're the most in-demand item in the first aid kit."

"So you help with the team or something?" I'm trying to be nice here, but it's a struggle.

She frowns and shoves something up my other nostril, harder than the first.

Wait. "*Tampons*?"

"Feel better?" She gives me a fake smile that tells me she knows damn well I don't feel better and that I did something to piss her off.

"Yeah, incredible. You've got an awesome bedside manner. Thinking about being a doctor?"

She looks like she wants to punch me, which is kind of funny and strangely hot.

"Absolutely. Everyone likes doing stuff they're good at, right?" She gives me a small smile like she's having fun with me, not mocking me. Yeah right.

I don't know how to react to this and, honestly, I'm done playing games with her. My feet are soaking wet and cold, I'm covered in blood, my nose aches. Oh, and I have feminine products shoved up my nostrils. "Listen, thanks for…" Breaking my nose? Actually, I'm not sure I have anything to thank her for.

I stand up. It feels like the bleeding is completely stopped, I *might* admit it could be the tampons, which are coming out the second I leave this place. Now all I want is something good to eat and the lumpy cabin mattress.

Not that I've been sleeping or anything. Long days and longer nights when my eyes won't stay closed and my brain feels like it does on stage.

"I'm going to head back. Do you have the number for any delivery places?"

The smirk is back. "Delivery? Didn't anyone tell you, you're not in Kansas anymore, Toto?" Then she does it. She laughs and even though it might be kind of funny, it pisses me off. She must be able to tell because she says, "I'm sorry. I'm not laughing at you. I swear."

"Nice. Thanks for the hospitality, Snow Queen."

I still hear her giggling as I walk away and head down the stairs. I'm going back to my stupid cabin, and taking some ibuprofen because of my broken nose. Hopefully along the way, I'll forget I ever saw this chick. I'm just about to close the door when I hear. "Catch ya later, Bishop Ripe."

Did I mention I fucking hate Alaska?

• • •

"The fresh air is nice, isn't it?" Gary nudges me with his arm.

"No. Not really. It's cold. Why are we walking again?"

From the corner of my eye, I see him shake his head. "Do me a favor and take a deep breath."

I huff.

"Humor me, Bishop."

Since there's no point in pissing him off, I do as he asks.

"What do you smell?"

We're walking down a deserted Alaskan road in the winter. I'm not sure what I'm supposed to smell. "Nothing. Cold, I guess."

"There you go! That's good." He nudges me again. "Did you know you could smell cold?"

Looking at him, I roll my eyes. "Honestly, it's not something I've put a lot of thought into." But you *can* smell the snow and frost in the air. It freezes the inside of my nose. "Why does this matter again?"

Gary doesn't answer that. "Look around and tell me what you see."

It's on the tip of my tongue to tell him I see this being a stupid fucking thing to do. "Trees, a road, more trees, painted lines on said road, more trees."

"Troy used to climb these trees all summer when he was a kid. Not these in specific, but you know what I mean. His parents told me they could always find him climbing. He built his own tree house, too. I've seen it. Of course when he got older, he stopped. How many adults go around climbing trees for fun, right?"

"Right." Shrugging, I hope that's the right answer.

"When we came up here after rehab, you know what we did?" There's a sentimental tone to Gary's voice that I don't understand.

"I give up. What did you do?"

"We climbed trees. We built another tree house. Sounds crazy, I know. But he enjoyed it. It took him back to a time when things were easier. When were things simple for you, Bishop Riley?"

Instead of replying, I cross my arms. This is fucking stupid. It's not like I don't get what he's trying to do.

Suddenly, Gary's foot shoots out, playfully. I don't realize it in time, though, and I stumble with his mock attempt to trip me. "Come on. You've had enough for today. Let's go get the car, drive to town, and buy you some boots."

"Finally!" Without another prompt, I turn and we head back toward the cabins. The chanting in my head has been replaced by Gary's voice.

When were things simple for you, Bishop Riley?

Chapter Four

Penny

I sit in the kitchen with my coffee, staring out the window at the cabins. It's probably rude to always be watching, but I can't help it. These guys don't ski. They don't have snowmachines. They don't seem to know anyone up here. They walk. Like every day. Normal people don't go on walks in the winter when there are a million better things to do outside, *all* of which are faster.

If I had to guess, I'd say Bishop is pretty pissed about the whole situation because I have yet to see him without a scowl. That Gary guy's always going to his door to stand and chat for a minute, and then leaving. There's something about the situation that feels off, and I want to know what it is. I dug through all Mom's paperwork for the cabin business, but all I came up with was Gary's name on the cabin rental, his name on the VISA, and nothing else.

Bishop steps outside and lights up another cigarette,

reminding me how seriously hot he is. He really has the whole dark, brooding thing going on. I'm sure part of it is because most of the guys I know my age, I've known for a while, or I know their family, or am friends with their cousin, or something. This guy is all new, *felt* all new when I patched up his nose, and he looks…misplaced up here. But more than that. He looks misplaced *inside*. That's not something easily fixed. And maybe that's where the whole brooding thing comes from.

"How's my button nose this morning?" Gramps grins at me from across the table. His blue eyes are so bright, and his face so filled with his kid-grin, that he looks like an expectant three-year-old.

There's no way to hold in my smile at something he's said to me since I can remember. "My nose is not a button, Gramps."

He reaches across the table and lets out a loud beep as his finger makes contact. "I beg to differ."

I wrinkle my nose, but I'm glad he's having a good day today.

"Why are we looking so introspective this morning?" he asks.

"The guys. In the cabins." I jerk my chin. "Just trying to figure out their story."

Gramps gives me his pro eye of suspicion. "Trying to learn, or harassing that boy?"

I freeze for a moment and scramble for something to say that won't give up the fact that I've maybe been watching Bishop more closely than I should, and maybe enjoyed fixing his nose more than I should. "What?" I wonder how well I pulled off innocence.

"He left here bloody with a tampon in his nose. You need to stop doing that." He chuckles and stands, heading for the fridge.

"What? They work great! It's not like I *gave* him the bloody nose or anything." *Like I've been known to do.*

He shakes his head.

And yes. Okay. The tampon might not have been totally necessary, but I wasn't lying when I said it's one of the most used things in our first aid kit.

"You got an offer from Boston University to check out their rink." He reaches into the fridge. "Possible scholarship."

Another college. I'm good, but I didn't think I was good enough to get so much attention for it. They're the fourth team this month, and if I wanted to leave state, and if I wanted to play on a women's team, they'd be worth listening to. Time to change the subject. "Gramps! You're not supposed to open other people's mail! It's a federal offense," I tack on for added seriousness.

He snorts. "Distraction may work with your mother, Lucky, but it won't work with me."

"I'm sticking around." I shrug. "No point in running all over the country when I know where I want to be."

"Penny." He turns and leans against the counter. Gramps is all here and all serious. "I'm going to live or die whether you're here or not, and so's your mom."

"That's not the point, Gramps." I stick my chin out. I can't miss it. Him. Gramps can't always take care of himself, and with Dad gone, Mom can't take care of him, either. She barely sleeps. Just works, eats, and lately, is only doing the occasional stop by home.

"The point is that you have some serious talent, and it shouldn't go to waste." Gramps mimics my set jaw, which makes me immediately pull mine back in.

"I've got a good thing going here, Gramps. Both UAF and UAA have seen me play enough to take me on the men's teams, and I could probably be an assistant coach at my high school." Every one of those things is something I want to do. Why would I leave? I hate that they try to push their choices on me.

His brow wrinkles in worry. "College players are a lot bigger than the high school boys, Penny. Even Chomps. Maybe playing on a men's team isn't a good idea."

"Is that what your son would say? Dad's the one who got me playing with the guys in the first place." I shove back my hair and push out a breath. Gramps blinks a few times, hopefully reading me well enough to change the subject.

He rubs his thumb across my chin, tilting his head to the side one way and then the other way until I can't hold in my smile. "Why don't you work on your car today?"

I'm surprised he didn't ask if we were both working on my car. For Gramps, it's like therapy. It's something he has yet to have a hard time remembering how to do. "For a while. I've got practice today."

"Sunday?" His brows go up.

"Semifinals are coming up." We barely lost state last year.

I'm determined to make it all the way this year. Semifinals, and then finals, and we *have* to go all the way.

• • •

My Corvette sits here. Just like it has for years. I got it running last summer, but it never worked right. The car was my dad's project until someone left a party after washing a handful of pills down with too many drinks and hit him while he was out riding his motorcycle. I was ten.

I suck in a breath and shove the thought away. Normally, it's a good thing to be in the room with this car, but sometimes it just makes me miss Dad more. Puts an ache in my chest that I don't think will ever totally go away.

I run my hand up the side of the body toward the hood. The car is ugly now, but it'll be perfect when I finish. 1975, buffed out and ready to paint—once I get some more money and decide on a color. It's the engine that's still giving me fits.

I lean under the hood and stare at the same problems. We're basically rebuilding a rebuilt engine. Not easy. And as I stand here, the puzzle that I usually can't wait to get my hands on doesn't feel like it wants to be touched. So much for this distraction before practice. Gramps is napping anyway, and it's not the same working without him here.

Instead of cleaning, or trying to get the wheels back under my toolbox, I sit in the driver's seat, which reminds me that I have to find a steering wheel that's in better shape. The top is off the T-top. No one appreciates T-tops anymore, but I think it's perfect. Especially for up here. It's not like there's months and months of time when I could have a convertible top down.

Sliding my hands across the wheel turns the ache in my chest to hurt over missing Dad. There's too much stuff in my head today. Gramps telling me I need to get out of town. Some guy who looks like a rock star with a tampon up his nose. Mitch with a girlfriend he actually seems to like, and who doesn't seem to mind putting up with him.

I slump lower in my seat, feeling like with the end of hockey season, and the end of my senior year, things are going to change a lot more than I want them to.

• • •

"Where's your ball and chain?" I shove Mitch from behind as we warm up on the ice.

He frowns. "She'll be here later." Mitch hates me harassing him about her. She's just...such a *girlie girl*—preened and high-maintenance, with her dark hair always shiny and smooth or done up in tiny curls. My stomach flips. I have no idea how to make myself that way, or even if I'd want to.

Mostly, I hate that he hates me teasing him about this. It means, again, that whatever I feel for him is not something he feels, and that he either doesn't care that Rebecca's starting to come between us or hasn't noticed. I'm not sure which is worse. I push around him and start doing laps while I wait for the rest of the guys to get on the ice. It's like silk today. Smooth and fast. Almost fast enough to make me forget the one thing I shouldn't be thinking about today with the mess my head is in.

Mitch got wasted after we lost in the finals last year, and it was my first time drinking more than one beer. Our kiss hadn't been perfect. It was sloppy and forced because we'd been drinking, but the point is that we both wanted it. He kissed me. I kissed him. Mutual. Mitch and Penny, just like it was supposed to be.

I woke up practically in a minefield of bodies in Chomps's basement because no one was in a position to get their keys back the night before.

"I'm sorry Penny. That was out of control last night. We shouldn't have…you know." Mitch looked down with this weird grimace like he'd been waiting for me to wake up and was bracing himself to tell me.

And if I'd just kept quiet, I wouldn't have been able to be rejected another time. "I'm okay with it. I mean. I think it can work." And I even leaned forward. Toward him, but not nearly as far as he leaned away.

It's like he didn't know where to look. Where to put his hands. Where to put his body. He wanted out, and I didn't know how to make him want me as someone more than his friend.

"Sorry," he said with a low voice full of pity.

I rubbed my face to hide my tears, which were an awful mix of sadness and humiliation. "We're cool, Mitch." And my voice sounded okay, even though I was breaking.

"You here, Jones?" Matt slaps my helmet as he races past snapping me back to the present.

I have to get my head in the game or I'm going to get hurt.

Rebecca puts her lips on the glass, and then her chest. Mitch races to the edge, and I swear part of her doesn't think we all see her doing this.

Practice is no place for this kind of ridiculous flirting. Mitch rests his helmet against the glass so they can do some sort of stupid kissy face thing that's completely beneath him.

"Totally whipped, hey?" I elbow Chomps and tilt my chin toward Mitch, hoping he'll break up their ridiculous show.

Chomps cackles before speeding across the rink and doing a half-bump, half-slam into Mitch's backside.

"Sorry, man!" Chomps yells as he speeds away, Mitch right on his tail.

"*Chomps*!" Coach shouts.

"S'up Coach?" He slides to a stop next to him in the center.

"Don't 's'up' me. We're five days away from semis and you just slammed one of your own. Not okay." Every word has that hard edge of anger he gets when he's seriously pissed. Not good. His dark hair is closer than military cut, and his jaw is clenched and brow's pulled together.

Now I feel bad I started this, but there's not much I can do about it now.

"Okay!" He blows his whistle for us to gather and starts shouting orders.

Mitch bumps my arm. "What's with the sour face, Pen?"

"Does she need to watch over you wherever you go?" I whisper back. But I'm standing too close and looking at him in a way I shouldn't. Mitch and I *are* close, though, so it's always muddying the lines for me. He meant it the other night when he said he'd have come to my house. And he'd have left Rebecca behind to help. Or at least there *used* to be a point where he'd have left her behind. I'm not sure anymore, and I hate how that weighs me down.

"I like her here, and she doesn't mind sitting in a rink for hours to be with me. So yeah, it's cool. Becca's cool." His eyes are on me, but I look away. Talking about deep stuff before practice won't help my concentration any. I keep my eyes on Coach. I know the question will be all over Mitch's face—*are you sure we're okay? That kiss was a year ago.* Or even worse, he'll look sympathetic. The problem is Mitch knows me well enough that I'm easy for him to read. At least the rest of the team hasn't caught on…or I don't think they have.

It sucks when he says he likes her. Part of me wants him to be using her. Okay. *All* of me wants him to be using her. Maybe it'll be better when he goes to college next year. I stick the guard in my mouth and try to focus on Coach. After sitting in Dad's car, still barely seeing Mom, and watching Rebecca's boobs smashed against the glass, I need to skate.

• • •

It's lightly snowing, which is my favorite time to sit in the hot tub. The flakes melt before touching my skin, but the cool drops of water still feel good. The ten-person hot tub was a present from Gramps when I hurt my back a few years ago, and we can fit a mess of people in it. Too bad Rebecca doesn't see that there are like six other places *not on Mitch's lap* that she could be.

Chomps's girlfriend, Trinna, has no problem sitting *next* to him and not being so…overt.

Also, I'm fine in a sports bra and black boy shorts from my bikini. Rebecca's suit would fall off with a tug of one tiny little string. Mitch's hand traces her collarbone as their faces rest together, and they kiss again—the kind that spreads black heaviness in the pit of my stomach because he's never looked at one of his girlfriends the way he looks at her. The hot tub was not a good idea.

"Pizza's here!" Matt yells. "Damn am I glad Ditch thinks you're hot." He kicks me under the water.

I shrug. I know I'm the only one out this far that he'll deliver to, but I've never given much thought as to why. He just always has.

A sliver of light from the closest cabin catches my eye, and Gary walks toward Bishop's door. When Bishop appears in the doorway, his eyes narrow as he sees Ditch climb out with three large pizzas. Right. He would be pissed since I told him no one delivered out here. I don't feel *bad*, more like itchy, uncomfortable.

Just as Ditch gets out of the delivery-mobile, Matt leans over. "Who's the pretty boy?"

I follow his gaze to Bishop's scowl and the back of Gary's head as they talk. "Why? You want me to get his number for you?"

He grabs my head before I can get away and dunks me.

The chlorine water burns my eyes. "Watch it asshole!" I

sputter as I break the surface. "Payback's a bitch!"

I try to shove him under, but I should know better. He laughs as I try to knock him down. Matt is quick and strong. It's why he's such a good goalie. I lean all of my weight against the side of his head, but still can't get him to budge.

"He's enjoying that *way* too much." Mitch shakes his head and sends a splash of hot water flying toward me. And this is the jealousy from him that lets me know he still watches. That Rebecca hasn't taken him from me yet. At least not completely.

I glance down at my bare stomach that was just pressed into Matt's head as I slide back into the water. Both Matt and Chomps shrug like *of course it was enjoyed*. Boys.

There's a flicker of light from Bishop's porch, a lighter I guess, and my eyes rest there a little too long.

"Be nice, Pen. Invite the guy over," Chomps says. Trinna glances over her shoulder but keeps silent, like she usually does.

Inviting Bishop over is really the least I can do. I'm supposed to be *helping them like a hostess* as Mom would say. I stand in the tub and wave.

"Bishop! We got pizza! Come over!"

When I stop waving, Ditch is staring at me, jaw slack with our three pizzas. He was kind of a geek when he graduated, and not much has changed in the three years since. Maybe Matt's right and he has a crush on me or something. "You joining us?" I ask, trying to play nice. He did drive, like, an extra five miles for me.

"Uh…" His eyes hit my stomach, then my face, then my stomach, then my chest as steam from my body fills the air. "I'm on shift. Just wanted to drop your food off."

"Thanks." I grin. And then notice Bishop walking over, pulling a hat on. He looks pissed, which kind of makes him look hotter and me lose every coherent thought in my brain. It's one thing to wrestle with Matt, but it's completely another to try and be cool around a guy who sets my nerve endings on edge in a way I'm not at all used to. As Bishop gets closer, my mouth starts to dry out. This doesn't happen to me. Ever. I have to try to come up with the same courage I have on the ice. In about two seconds.

Chapter Five

Bishop

As I trudge through the snow with the stupid boots Gary bought me, and my stupid incognito hat, I still can't believe I'm going over there. First, this chick is crazy. I shudder when I think about how she violated my nose. And she lied to me about the delivery. Peanut butter and grilled cheese is getting old. I definitely would have liked some pizza the past few days, and here she is enjoying the takeout she told me doesn't exist.

No takeout. No laptop. No tablet. All I have is my cell phone, and since I'm ignoring Blake's calls, that doesn't count for much. He can't even get pissed at me about it, either. The guys in the band shouldn't be calling—Don's orders.

All this seclusion is killing me, though. I miss the buzz of the city. Miss never knowing who would stop by. Most of the people who know where I live are all cool and down for a good time. It was fun getting surprised by who or I saw or what I'd be doing each day.

I miss practicing with the band, and that pisses me off because they sold me out.

I stop long enough to put my cigarette out in the snow. I hate these things. I don't even know why I smoke them, but when you're with people who smoke 24/7 it's easy to pick up the habit. I've sorted out the pills I brought so I can have one or two every couple days. See, an addict couldn't do that. Plus, just because I have them, doesn't mean I'll take them. Gary's like a bulldog with my anxiety meds, so the smokes help take the edge off.

"Thought no one delivered?" The words rush out of my mouth as I walk up the stairs. There's the Snow Queen, two other girls, and a whole bunch of guys in the hot tub. I don't like the ratio. Not that I'm interested in anyone here, but still.

"Ditch only delivers for her," some dark-haired guy with a girl on his lap says.

"Ditch?" That's a fucked up name. Not that Bishop Ripe is much better. What I wouldn't give to go back in time and change that one, but now I'm stuck with it as my *code name*, as Gary has started calling it.

A guy raises his hand all eager-like. "I'm Ditch."

The dark-haired guy speaks again. "If you see him when we motocross, you'll know where the name comes from." They all laugh together. It's kind of freaky. I'm sure they're those kids who have grown up together, met when they played in the sandbox and haven't left each other's sides since. We moved around too much for that, not that Mom wanted to, but want and need aren't always the same thing. The only people I know even half that well are the guys in my band. And look what they did to me.

Blake tries to call every day…

I tell the voice in the back of my head to shut up. Since I'm the youngest in the band, Blake tried to take me under his wing in the beginning. Soon, he realized I didn't need it.

I cross my arms. Uncross them, trying to get comfortable. I haven't felt comfortable since I got here. Even since before that.

"So, I guess I owe you a slice. Go for it, if you want one." Penny nods her head toward the boxes.

Damn, I want one, but don't let myself move.

"Or beer."

My senses perk up. I'd love a beer. Would be a nice way to relax after all I've been through.

"She has a one-beer rule, and don't even think about trying anything else," her friend says. He looks a little shorter than I am. His shoulders are wide, and he seems like the kind of guy who has his hockey number tatted on him. He doesn't take his hands off his girl the whole time.

Damn, I miss girls.

The Snow Queen stiffens a little, the smirk I'm used to seeing on her face wiped away.

"Well…the rule is for good reason." The guy back-pedals and I can't help but wonder what that's all about.

"So, beer?" Penny stands up, steam rolling off her skin in waves, and water dripping down her body. Her very nice body. She looks soft like a girl should look, but toned, too. I have no idea how she can wear a two-piece in this weather, but I'm grateful for it. Did I mention I miss girls?

"Hello? You in there, Ripe?"

Ripe? Oh yeah. My stupid code name. Gary's so proud.

She grabs a towel and wraps it around herself. "It's cold. You've got about five seconds to decide before I get back in the hot tub."

My heart rate kicks up. I'm not sure if it's because of the bikini, the way the water makes her hair look even whiter, the cold, or the mention of alcohol. I haven't had a drop since "the incident." Besides the few pills, I've been a good little boy like they want. It's not like I'm going to get smashed or anything. She has a one-beer rule.

I try to see around her to catch a glimpse of my parole officer, also known as Gary.

"Five, four, three," Penny starts a countdown. The urge to snap at her hits me, but instead, I shove my hands deep in my pockets.

"Yeah…yeah, I'll have a beer." Then I'm kind of pissed because I'm sitting here feeling guilty over having a beer. It's one beer. If it's okay for these golden kids to have one, I can, too.

While she's gone, I find out the guy who can't keep his hands or mouth off his girl is really Mitch, and his attachment is Becca. The other guy, some huge blond who looks like the human version of a Mack truck with them is Chomps. Alaskans seriously have weird names. Chomps's girl is Trinna, and I can't remember the other guys' names.

The pizza guy leaves, and Penny hands me a cold beer without a word, then drops her towel, standing there just long enough that I know she wants to be watched, before sliding back into the hot tub with her friends. I open the top and down the whole thing, savoring the bitterness. I've missed this. The little twangy taste. Why does she have the one-beer rule again? I eye the door, wishing I could go inside and grab another one.

"Wow, holy beer-drinker."

Her surprise makes me feel a little strange. Like I have to defend myself.

"I was thirsty." I plop down in a chair. They have a firepit piled high with logs, burning in the middle of the deck, which helps to keep me semi-warm. When I pull, the tab comes off the can easily and roll it around between my fingers, knowing I should get up and go back to my cabin. I'm not sure why I don't.

The one guy, Chomps, asks me if I want in, which I refuse.

"You still hurting from the game?" Chomps asks Penny.

Game?

"Yeah, a little. No biggie though."

"What game?" I find myself asking.

"Hockey. She's our Lucky Penny!" Mitch grins.

Wait. "You *play* hockey? With guys?"

Everyone laughs, and I feel left out on some joke. Damn Alaskan sandbox kids.

"He thinks I 'help with the team.'" She does the air quote thing.

"And you let him live?" Chomps shoves her. These people are so screwed up.

"I shoved a tampon up his nose."

They all start laughing again, and I'm starting to get pissed. "You done showing off, Snow Queen?"

All eyes are on me like I screwed up big—like they can't believe I talked to her that way. News flash, I'm not going to fall at her feet like everyone else does. I'm Bishop Riley. I play the drums for a Grammy-winning band. I'm not kissing her ass.

Penny's jaw clenches and she shakes her head. She opens her mouth, probably to bitch me out, but gets cut off.

"So, umm…what brought you here?" Mitch asks. I can tell he's trying to defuse the situation and I let him, only it's the first time someone has asked me and I'm not sure what to say. Actually, I'm pretty sure Gary told me the story, but I didn't pay attention. I know *I almost OD'd and my mom and manager shipped me here* isn't the right answer.

"Gary…my uncle? He has some work to do, and I came with him to get away for a while."

"What's he do?" Chomps asks.

Shit. What does he do? I shrug. "I don't know. He works from home, but he wanted peace and quiet. To get away or whatever." Which is true. I know the stuff he writes for his magazine is done over the internet.

"Hmm," Penny says. "And you wanted to come with him? That surprises me."

"What is this? Twenty Questions?" I try to push a hand

through my hair, but then I remember I'm wearing a stupid hat. Are all Alaskans this nosey? The only thing I know about the state is it's cold, full of trees, and Sarah Palin can see Russia from here.

"So-rry." Penny says, her cheeks a little pink, making me feel like a jerk. There's no doubt in my mind it takes a lot to embarrass this girl.

Chomps breaks the tension when he starts to tickle her. Penny lasts about two seconds before she gets the best of him and they're all laughing. I sit back and watch them. From there, they launch into talk about hockey and school. I lose track after a while, and they don't try to include me anymore. Crazily, not answering questions becomes more annoying than answering them.

About thirty minutes later, I get up and walk away. I'm not even sure they notice I'm gone. My door is closed long enough for me to walk to the bathroom before someone knocks. I put some toothpaste in my mouth real quick before pulling it open.

"Aren't we the little joiner?" Gary teases. "I'm glad to see you're making friends."

"I'm not making friends. Can I help you with something?"

Gary actually says, "tsk, tsk," at me. "So grumpy. This Alaskan air isn't helping your mood at all." When I groan, he gets serious. "You feeling okay? You still haven't gotten sick or anything, have you? How are you sleeping?"

Didn't we already go over this? "Shit," I turn, stalk over to the couch, and fall down on it. "No, I'm not going through withdrawals or anything. I'm not a drug addict, Gary." Part of me wonders if I should tell him I can't sleep, but it'll probably make him think it's because I don't have pills. That's not it. I'm sure of it.

He walks over and sits down across from me. "I know this isn't easy, and I know you're pissed, but you can talk to me, okay?"

I groan again, and he holds up his hands before continuing. "I'm not saying you have to. I'm telling you the option is always here, okay? You know I've been through this years ago with Troy, but I'm not sure if you realize this is what I used to do. I can help. I *want* to help. Now, I'll ask you again. You okay? Do you need one of your anxiety meds?"

He used to *do* this? No, I didn't know that, but it explains why they sent him here with me. Makes me wonder how he went from therapist to writing for a magazine, though I don't know what kind of magazine he writes for. Maybe it does go together.

The shakes try setting in, but I don't tell him that. The more they think I'm okay, the faster I should be able to get out of this place. That beer should have helped me relax. "No, I'm cool. I don't need anything."

"Tomorrow's our chat day, okay? We can talk about anything you want. Maybe you'll have thought of something for you that's like Troy's trees were for him."

Yeah fucking right. Instead of letting those words out, I nod. Gary stays for a few more minutes before he tells me goodnight and leaves. Once he's gone, I pick up my cell phone and make a quick call to Maryanne. Maybe if I have her get me some stuff, I won't have to take my anxiety meds at all.

The rest of the night is spent trying to sleep, going outside and chain-smoking the cigarettes I hate, and wondering if Penny has drowned any of her friends yet. When I finally do fall asleep, I dream about climbing trees.

• • •

I'm standing on the porch the next morning, dreading my talk with Gary later, when I see lights going on and off in the big house. I figure it must be Penny getting ready for school. I probably slept a total of three hours last night. Every time I fell into a deep sleep, something forced my dry eyes open. They're burning today. Each time I blink, it's like someone rubbing sandpaper over them.

Soon, Penny runs outside and starts up her monster truck before heading back in the house. It's bizarre. I could never leave my car running in L.A. like that, or it would be gone. Or my motorcycle. Damn, I miss that, too. I have this friend Ryan I used to go riding with before things got crazy busy. Those were good times. *Is that when things were easier?* The question popping into my head pisses me off.

The truck. It's something I don't mind thinking about. Just like with her friends last night, the lack of security is new to me. This town is almost like one of those shows you see on TV that don't seem real. Where nothing bad happens, everyone is finish-each-other's-sentences kind of friends. I almost expect everything to be black and white. Like it takes place in the fifties or something.

Her truck continues to warm up, and I have the biggest urge to drive off in it. I don't know if it's just to teach her a lesson or if I hope I can run away and not come back.

When she comes out again, she's all bundled up and scraping the windows. Her hair is hidden under a hat and another screwed up urge hits me. This time I want to take the hat off so I can see her hair. It's such a killer color.

"Hey!" she yells to me and waves. I'm still kind of pissed off about last night so I don't do anything back. Penny shakes her head at me before climbing in the truck and pulling away. Her hand shoots out the window and she flips me off before she's gone.

I can't help but chuckle. That girl is no joke.

• • •

"You have something hanging out of your lip."

The old man smirks at me. He's got long gray hair and a long gray beard, and I am pretty sure if there are bodies in the freezers, he's the one who put them there.

"Thanks for letting me know." Penny left about twenty minutes ago, and I still haven't managed to leave the porch. I really don't want to be a jerk to some old man, but I'm not in the best mood, either. I look away from him.

The old guy laughs. "I'm giving you a hard time, Rookie. It's nice. Think I could get one?" My head snaps his way, and he winks at me. It's crazy, but I don't doubt this guy for a second. He would totally get his lip pierced.

"Got any plans today?" he asks me.

"Nope." I pull out another cigarette and light it.

"You afraid to get your hands dirty?"

"Huh?"

"Nah, I don't think you are." He laughs again. "Know anything about cars?" He's practically bouncing on the balls of his feet.

"Yeah. A little." A lot, actually.

"Wanna work on one with me?" This guy is all huge eyes, crazy beard, and twitchy movements. It's like he's high on something, though I highly doubt he is.

My body perks up a little, suddenly not tired anymore. If he wants me to work on the Corvette I saw the other day, the answer is hell yes. Actually, I'd pretty much jump at the chance to work on any car. My hands itch to keep busy. "I guess."

He holds his hand out to me. "I'm Gramps."

"Bishop." I shake his hand and then follow him. He leads me to the Corvette. Without Penny here, I get the chance to admire it even more. It's buffed smooth but mottled gray, primed and ready for paint. I'm almost positive it's a 1975. It's—

"A beauty, isn't she?" Gramps says. He sounds like a kid he's so excited.

"She's awesome. I love cars like this." And I can't believe I actually get to work on her. Not just because she's incredible, but because I have the time to.

Gramps and I dig in, leaning over the engine. He tells me about some trouble they've been having with the engine and getting the wrong carburetor, so they're almost at a standstill aside from some minor gaskets. I guess Penny has some huge plans for fixing her up. "This is Penny's ride?"

"Yep."

"And she works on it?"

"Yep, but don't let her hear you sound so surprised. She has a bit of a temper."

Yeah, I already made that mistake with hockey. "No shit," accidentally slips out of my mouth. I brace myself because most old guys I know get all pissy when I curse, but Gramps just laughs.

"She's a tough one, my Lucky Penny."

She is. I kind of want to tell him, but realize it's ridiculous. I don't know her.

We're quiet for a few minutes. Gramps hands me a wrench. The first gasket is an obvious one, and the new package is resting on the edge of the engine. "What about you? What're you into?"

Surprisingly, it only takes me a few seconds to answer. Gary and Troy's stupid fucking trees pop into my head. "Drums, but cars are cool. Working on them gives me something to do with my hands. I like that…keeping busy."

I'm not sure why I said that, but he seems to get it. I think he'd probably get a lot. He doesn't reply, and we get to work. When he asks me questions about cars, I know all the answers. I even point out a few things to him, too. I hate to admit it, because I don't want anything here to be cool, but it feels good.

Troy built a tree house to keep from going crazy in this town. Maybe the car can do that for me.

Chapter Six

Penny

I pull up in the driveway, exhausted. My body feels like Jell-O after practice. I'm frustrated because the team from up north in Barrow—the ones we're supposed to play for State Semifinals—are snowed in and our game's been moved back a week or more. I hate postponements, but it *is* Barrow, and it *is* still winter.

When I get out, I see Gramps and Bishop in the garage, *leaning over the engine of my Corvette.* I can't believe that cocky prick has his hands on *my* car. I tried to be nice this morning. Well, until I flipped him off, but seriously—I was trying to be nice by waving at him, and he just stood there.

Cocky. Prick.

Oh. And that's *after* I got him a beer, offered pizza, and he just took off while we were all hanging out. No good-night. No thanks. No nothing.

I jump out of my car and resist the urge to run into the

garage. "Hi Gramps." I give him a kiss on the cheek as he leans out from under the hood with grease on his hands.

"Bishop and I got all the gaskets changed out today." Gramps pinches my nose with a grin.

"I can change gaskets." It comes out snappier than I meant. But really, Gramps knows how picky I am. I don't want some *amateur* working on it.

"I should take off." Bishop grabs his coat from a stool and heads for the door.

"Oh!" Gramps steps toward him. "Penny can take you to get drums."

"I can *what*?" I don't want to take this guy anywhere. Especially after he messed with my car.

"No." Bishop shakes his head. "I'll take care of it."

Gramps chuckles. "But Pat doesn't have a crush on you and might not give you the same deal Penny will get."

"It's fine." Bishop shakes his head and moves toward the door. "Thanks anyway."

I open my mouth to say *see ya*, but then I remember that the *he had his hands on my car*.

Gramps leans over, and I almost lean away because I know right now what he's going to say.

"These guys are paying your mom a lot of money for two cabins and no work on your part. Grow up, be nice, and take the boy to town. Wouldn't hurt if you were a little extra nice to Pat, too."

Only Gramps could talk to me like this and still make me smile. His voice is quiet but all happy. Bishop's almost to his cabin.

Hell.

I jog outside. "Bishop!" I even use my best cheery voice. "I'm heading to town anyway, and I'm sure Pat can get you a deal. If you need drums, we should get you drums. You've got to be bored out of your mind." *Because you don't do anything except go for walks in the snow and smoke.*

He pauses, and he flicks his gaze toward Gary's. "Just a sec."

Like he did last night, he shoves his hands in his pockets, looking everywhere but at me. It's not like I asked the guy to marry me or something.

"Listen, if you don't want—"

"No!" he practically shouts at me. "Just give me a minute." Still, he looks like I'm trying to pull his teeth, not take him to get something he wants.

Bishop turns and walks away. His hotness is seriously seeping away with his crappy attitude.

He knocks on Gary's door—I'm not totally buying that "Gary's up here for business" thing—and I realize he's asking him if he can go. So. Young enough to need permission, but old enough to not go to school?

What's going on with them?

Since I'm trying to be all accommodating and want Gramps happy with me, I head to my truck and climb in the driver's seat to wait.

When Gary's door closes, I start my truck and wave at Bishop to come over. He holds up a finger, runs into his cabin, and comes out wearing another hat.

Bummer. I like his hair. Not that it matters what he does with his stupid hair.

It's a ten-mile drive to town on icy roads, and already close to six. I'm pretty sure the music store closes at six. That's not good. I dial Pat as Bishop opens the door.

"You sure this is cool?" Bishop asks, and the uncertainty in his voice makes me pause.

"I'm on the phone with Pat. Get in." I force my lips into a smile. Bishop frowns again. The boy's got some serious damage. He needs to get over it. Whatever "it" is.

He slides into the car, and I look over him again. Nice eyes. Good build. Something like fluttering hits my stomach before I snap my brain back into focus and start out of the driveway. My reaction is because Bishop is new, that's all.

"Penny!" Pat sounds way too excited for a simple phone call. I'm not stupid and kind of know he watches me, but I'm a girl guys watch—not a girl anyone actually asks out. It sucks because I've only ever kissed Mitch, and it was just the one time.

"Penny?" he asks.

Focus, Penny. "Hey, Pat. I'm calling for a favor."

"Of course you are." He chuckles. "What do you need?"

"There's a guy staying in the cabins who needs a set of drums. I told him you could hook him up, but we're just leaving my house." I hit the gas at the end of the driveway, just to spin Bitty sideways for a bit.

Bishop's jaw flexes, but he doesn't flinch. I'm impressed. I let Bitty slide back to my lane.

"So you want me to stay at the store, is that right?"

"We'll just be a couple minutes. Promise."

He laughs. "I'll stick around. See you in a few."

I flip my phone off and shove it in my pocket. "He's open late."

A corner of Bishop's mouth twitches. It's the first emotion I've seen from him that doesn't involve his scowl, and I like it enough to know I'll be trying to make it happen again. "Of course he is."

· · ·

So. Pat only has a three hundred dollar set and a two thousand dollar one. Bishop is behind the two thousand dollar one, making me wonder what kind of computer work his uncle is into, if he's actually into computer work at all. Pat grins from ear to ear while he watches Bishop adjust the drums. They exchanged a few whispers when Bishop sat down that made Bishop look a little sick. Later, I'll have to ask Pat what that was about.

Bishop's got a behind-the-counter set of sticks that he flips as if they're part of him. The muscles in his arms flex in a practiced rhythm as he continues to spin the sticks. I sit on a stool under a row of guitars, and he drops his baseball hat before adjusting himself on the seat.

Suddenly, he doesn't look sick anymore.

Bishop's eyes close just longer than a blink. I hold my breath in anticipation and really take him in. Slightly long hair, perfect nose, strong and muscled but not huge, just…lean. His eyes open, and I swear he's in a different place.

Okay. I love music as much as the next person, but I never pay attention to the drums.

Until he starts to play.

For the rest of my life, I will pay attention to drums. It's unreal. The rhythm. Everything. It's like there's too much to take in at once. He can't be thinking, just feeling. Pat's grin spreads even wider as Bishop keeps playing. His hands fly so fast I can hardly see them. Every once in a while his eyes close, so lost in what he's doing that all I can do is stare. I'm not an expert, but this guy has to be some kind of genius or something. I'm frozen on this stupid little stool made for people who play guitars, just staring at the guy. I know exactly how he feels right now. He's in the zone behind the drums, just like I am on the ice.

The rhythm stops, and the room feels empty and flat, like I do when someone knocks the wind out of me. And I now understand why girls think guys who are in bands are hot. Watching the guy work, his head lost in what he's doing, and something so amazing coming out of it? Hot.

He's sweating when he stands up, his hair sticking to his forehead a little bit. "I'll take 'em."

And then, Bishop actually *smiles*.

Pat moves to the register, and Bishop follows. He writes up a slip, and Bishop shifts his weight back and forth a few times, glancing over his shoulder at me. He went from happy to twitchy in about three seconds.

I move for the door, ready to be home. "I'll back up the truck."

Bishop snatches his credit card off the counter, but it slips from his fingers and drops to the floor.

You'd think he'd be more relaxed after drumming, but when I lean down to pick it up, Bishop half-falls onto the credit card, snatching it just before I grasp the edge.

I stare at him just long enough for us to both know that was odd. He breaks eye contact first without a word and shoves his card back into his wallet with shaky hands.

Something weird is definitely going on.

• • •

We pull out of the music store lot with a two thousand dollar set of drums in the bed of my truck. How can a guy my age just hand over a credit card for two thousand bucks?

Bishop's gone quiet, staring out the window, his leg bouncing.

"You're not like…in some kind of weird trouble or anything, are you?" I ask.

Bishop's brows go up, and he's looking at me a little like I'm crazy, but there's unease there, too. I think. "Weird trouble?"

I start to ask about his card and his twitchiness, but as the words begin to form in my head, it sounds kind of stupid. "Never mind."

He slumps a little lower in the seat.

I reach out to poke him, but stop because I don't look for

ways to touch guys who aren't Mitch. And anyway, I just made the mood in the car strange, when it should be fine. "Looks like you found yourself a fan back there."

Bishop pulls his hat down another inch. "He just appreciates mad talent."

I snort even though I can't even argue with his talent remark. My stomach rumbles, it's black outside, and I still have stuff to do. *And* I can't get the picture of Bishop playing drums out of my head. He's definitely a puzzle. Who's his uncle? Does he have rich parents? Is he some kind of prodigy? If he was in a band, he wouldn't be here, but if he's not, wouldn't his talent be wasted? Or maybe it's just a sideline to who he really is.

Or maybe I'm spending too much time thinking about a puzzle that really isn't one.

"You've played a while?" I ask, wondering if he'll volunteer any info without me tossing out another stupid question like *weird trouble*.

He nods. "A while."

Frustration bubbles inside me at how perfectly vague he's being. "You in school? Homeschool or something?"

"Homeschooled. Graduated." He sounds bored, but his jaw is tight as he stares out the window.

I guess I really won't get any info from him. Fine. I'm not fishing...at least not to his face. I'll try Mom for information next. If we ever end up being home at the same time, anyway. I wonder again if money is tighter than I think it is because she's been doing nothing but work for weeks now.

"What time is it?" I ask.

Bishop stops flipping his sticks just long enough to check his watch. "Seven."

"Cool. Jeremy's working the window at McDonald's, which means my food's free. I gotta stop. You want something?"

He pushes a strand of brown hair out of his face, showing off his eyes. He's got a nice profile. Masculine. And after hearing him play, he's a lot more than the guy with a crap attitude.

"You've gotta be kidding me," he says, and shakes his head.

"What?" Only I know what. And I might be showing off a little, but it's been a long time since I asked a favor of Jeremy, *and* I showed him how to change his oil without making fun of him. I figure he owes me.

"You have a way to get everything you want. You're, like, Miss Alaska or something. It's sort of ridiculous." For once, there's no attitude in his voice. The guy is still lighter from just a few minutes on the drums. I actually get that—it's why I play hockey. And ride snowmachines. And dirt bikes.

"If you compare me to a beauty queen again, forget the tampon, I'll use one of your drumsticks." I grin and bat my eyelashes. "And I get what I want because I'm nice to everyone."

Since I know I don't want to leave Alaska, it sort of changes how I act. Like these people are the people that I'm going to spend my life with. The weight of leaving for college settles over me again. I'm supposed to want to get out of here and go to school. But I don't want to. Not yet. Maybe never.

"You? Nice?" The corner of his mouth turns up.

"It all depends on who I'm dealing with." I narrow my eyes, only half-teasing, and nervous flutters start low in my stomach. This time, they don't go away when I will them to.

"Oh. I see." He's still wearing his *half*-smile, like he's not ready to give in yet and admit he's having fun.

"You think I don't see how you look at my house? At my friends? At where I live? It's like you hate everything about the place that I love. You're not better than me, and you're not better than this place. So, yeah. It pissed me off a little. At first." I keep my voice light, but it's harder to breathe when I'm being honest like this, especially now that I'm trying not to think about how close and alone we are. I flick on my turn signal and join the line at McDonald's. With only two fast-food restaurants in town, this place gets full.

"You don't hold back, do you?" He twirls the stick between his fingers and I wonder for a second how he got to be so good. "I don't think I'm better than anyone. I just know I don't belong here, and I don't want to. I have a life somewhere else. Plus it's not like you didn't look at me the same way."

"I don't hold back *most* of the time. I've known these people forever, and we can say almost anything to each other. And it would be that way with Mitch, too, if he—" The words are out before I can stop them, and I'm shocked because I never say things I don't mean to.

He chuckles. "Lover Boy?"

Lover Boy? How the hell would Bishop know how I feel

about Mitch? My stomach tightens, and my mouth gapes open—both aren't like me. At all.

"He couldn't keep his hands to himself." Bishop chuckles. "Not that I blame him because his girl is—"

"Okay," I interrupt, because the Lover Boy comment was because of *Rebecca*, and not because of *me*. Which actually feels worse than him realizing how pathetic I feel over Mitch. "Let's not talk about Mitch and Rebecca. Cool?"

"Hit a bad topic?" Only his voice doesn't have enough snark in it for me to fight back.

"You got your discount drum set, and you're about to get free fries. I think we're good on being nice for the night." I give him a smile, so maybe he won't take it as seriously as I mean it. Gramps was right. I need to be nice, even though Bishop just pointed out something I already know. I really am losing Mitch.

"Drum *kit*. And fair enough."

Somehow him agreeing that we're okay not being nice makes me want to be. I start to talk three times before I find words because Bishop looking as good as he does, and playing drums like he does, and being new, and the crazy butterfly things I can't shake from my stomach…I'm just in a different kind of territory with a guy, and it's territory I don't know how to deal with.

I can feel the twinges of nerves pushing words out faster than I know I'll want them to come. "Our game got pushed back because the kids who live in Barrow can't fly out until the storm passes. I'm going snowmachining with the guys tomorrow. You like to go fast?"

"Yeah. Maybe."

His "maybe" gives me some relief, making me wonder what my problem is. Why would I care if he wanted to come or not? "I'll give you a knock after school. I have extra gear and stuff. I'm tall so it's all for guys."

"No pink snow pants?"

He's actually teasing me. I can't believe it, and now I'm actually looking forward to doing something fun with him. Finding another way to make him relax a little. Maybe even actually smile again.

I'm grinning, searching his brown eyes in the darkness of my truck. "Definitely no pink snow pants."

• • •

When I jump out of my truck to head for Bishop's cabin, all I hear is drums. The guy is crazy good. Definitely good enough to join a real band. Not like the guys who hang at the music store, making up band names for a group that would rather get high than practice.

I bang on Bishop's door, even though part of me wants to wait until his song finishes. That could take forever. The guys'll be here any minute, and I have to be suited up and ready to go or they'll get ahead on the trail. I'm not following any of those pansies down *my* trail. I knock again and Bishop doesn't answer, so I step inside. "Come on! You're not wimping out on me are you?"

Bishop stops playing with a murderous look on his face.

I choose to ignore it, even though there's something to be noticed about a guy who feels so much. Good or bad. "The drums will still be here when we get back, but your chance to go for a ride and watch me make asses of the guys on my team happens now."

"What if I was playing naked?" He wipes his hand across his forehead—damp with sweat like it was yesterday. His expression is unreadable.

A lump forms in my throat at the thought of what he'd look like playing the drums with no shirt. How his body would move without conscious thought. The way the muscles in his chest and abs and arms would flex. Something foreign washes through me with the idea of it, making my legs jelly for a second.

Whoa. This is new. Mitch doesn't make me feel *that.*

Silence presses in until I find my Penny mojo and roll my eyes because I can't feel all this weird newness around him without it backfiring. "It's nothing I haven't seen before. All my friends are guys."

His scowl is replaced by something almost like a grin. "You're nuts." He shakes his head, still partially grinning.

"Come on." I step back, needing to be out of the small room. "Let's get you suited up."

Bishop grabs his coat, shoves his feet into his boots. "I have to talk to Gary real quick."

He jogs to the other cabin and knocks. Okay. Strange. I don't have to tell anyone when I snowmachine. Maybe it's a city boy thing.

A minute later, we're at my house. As soon as I step in the door, I start tossing outdoor gear his way.

"What am I supposed to do with this?" His brows pull together as he watches the pile at his feet grow.

"Put it on?" I suggest as I finish suiting up and reach for my boots. Still not looking at him after his naked comment.

He lets out a breath, but I see a hint of a smile as I look at through my hair. I almost offer to help him with the snow pants, which have some crazy straps, but he figures it out before my boots are laced.

He's so quiet. I start to wonder if he's always this way. I'm not, so quiet people unnerve me. What's he thinking? What does he want? Why won't he talk?

I open the door to the part of the garage with the two snowmachines. Gramps has money, Mom just doesn't want him to use it. But he does once in a while—hot tub, new snowmachines, my truck.

I point to Gramps's favorite machine. "You can take that one. It's an 800, so you'll be able to keep up."

Another small smile hits as he sits on the seat. He scans over the black and orange cowling covering the engine, at the two skis in front and then underneath him at he checks out the thick rubber track. "Anything special I should know?"

I stand next to him and point to all the important pieces. "Gas. Brake. If a tree is smaller than my wrist, you can drive over it." I hold up my hand.

He cocks a brow.

"When in doubt, always hit the gas."

He nods once and again almost smiles. "Nice. I miss riding my bike in the city. Maybe this will be close."

"Trust me. It'll be better. And I know this sounds crazy, but we're headed to Matt's parents' hayfields, and the snow is deep. If you really want to play, turn the handlebars the opposite direction you want to go, hit the gas, and lean the direction you *do* want to go. It'll lift up the side of the machine, turn you around, spray snow, and make you look like you know what you're doing."

His brows go up, and I'm noticing his eyes again.

"You're not going to make me look like an ass, are you?" Bishop wrings his hands together as though he doesn't know what to do with them.

I shrug and try not to laugh. "Try it for yourself, and you'll find out."

"Are you always like this?" A corner of his mouth goes up, and my stomach tenses just a bit at the way he's looking at me.

"Are you always so quiet, grumpy, and introspective?"

He shrugs. That, to me, is an affirmative.

I toss him his helmet. "See you on the trail."

We start the machines just as Mitch and Matt pull up, and I won't be behind them, so I grab a handful of throttle and rocket out of the garage to make sure I'm in front. Bishop's right behind me. The guy catches on quick.

In seconds, we're flying down the trail at close to seventy. We hit Matt's hayfields ten minutes of speed later. Mitch raises his hand in the air and makes a circle—snowmachine language for "we'll all play here for a while."

Bishop pulls up next to me

I have to yell over the sound of the machines. "We're all just screwing around. Do what I told you with the skis, worse that'll happen is you'll fall off in a pile of snow and have to climb back on."

"Okay." More than just the corners of his mouth are turned up now. It's an actual freaking smile on the king of grouchy.

I'm so good.

Chapter Seven

Bishop

Adrenaline races through me, making me feel higher than any drug ever has. I've ridden bikes, dirt bikes, four-wheelers, but this? This feels different.

Cold air whips around me the faster I go, but I can't make myself slow down. I don't want to. I do what Penny said, turning the handlebars the opposite direction and leaning the other. The shit actually works. Snow flies out from under the machine as I whip around in a circle. All these other guys out here can't keep up with me. The only one who can is Penny.

Part of me wants to try and show her up, but the other part—the stronger half—is having too much fun to turn it into something else. I just want to keep going, enjoying the freedom that I'm not sure I've ever felt. It's like nothing can catch me here—not my psychotic dad who I pretty much had to pay off to get him to leave us alone, not fans, my anxiety, my manager…not even my personal guard.

I don't know how long we're out here when they all pull up together in a circle. I'm not ready to go back—not sure I ever want to stop but know I have to. I rev up the engine before flying over to where they are, spraying snow all over Penny before coming to a stop.

"Think you're pretty cool now, don't ya?" She rips her helmet off, her white hair flying free.

"Don't think. I know. I owned that." My eyes don't leave her. She's so wild, this girl. I've never known anyone like her.

"Didn't own me." She turns her attention back to her friends. And she's right. She showed all the other guys up. I have a feeling no one has ever beat her at anything. "You guys ready to head back?"

I watch them, the way they all keep their eyes firmly on her all the time. I wonder if she knows half these guys are in love with her. Or maybe not love, but they definitely want her. And respect her.

Or maybe they're scared of her.

"Yeah, I've got stuff to do. I'm supposed to go to Becca's," Mitch says, and Penny rolls her eyes.

She opens her mouth to reply, but I cough and say "whipped" at the same time. Mitch scowls at me, but Penny gives me a smile. It almost looks…appreciative? And I realize that's why I did it, which is pretty fucking weird. But then, I guess I owe her for showing me a good time today and helping me get my kit.

"Race you back!" She shoves her helmet back on and is speeding away before I realize what's happening. All the other guys start shoving theirs on, but I'm faster, pushing the damn thing on my head and hitting the gas. I don't know where the rest of them are, all I know is I'm catching Penny.

The trail from the fields is smooth and fast, but each little bump makes me feel like I'm floating before the track catches again. This is seriously like flying, and I'm after that taillight in front of me, determined not to let her win. I can't even explain how it feels. As good as it does when my sticks are slamming down on the drums over and over. Maybe better than that, too. It makes me forget everything else.

The stupid chat I had with Gary that didn't do much of anything.

Why I'm here.

That no one is supposed to know.

Pat figured it out—there was no way to keep it from him when I bought the drums—and if he tells, I'm fucked. There was no denying it, though. He's as into music as I am, and he *knows* me. Or he knows Burn, I guess. Penny could have easily found out when I dropped my card. None of that matters, though. Not while I'm flying over the snow.

We both slide to a stop at almost the same time. I'm only a few seconds behind her. I'm panting so hard, I feel like I've been playing my drums for days on end. "Dude, I'm fucking awesome." The words are broken up since I'm out of breath.

"What?" Her cheeks are all pink and a little sexy. Whoa. When did I start noticing her cheeks? "You didn't win. We tied."

"Yeah, but you cheated. You started early, we stopped at

the same time, which technically means I beat you."

"Are you seriously trying to win on a technicality? What is this, CSI?"

I start to laugh, but I don't reply as the hum of the other machines gets closer and closer. I'm still breathing hard, watching her straddle the machine across from me. I kind of want to thank her for bringing me out, but I don't really know how, so instead I say, "Whatever, I'll give you this one, but we're having a rematch."

I suddenly can't wait for it to happen. Then, I do the strangest thing. I take a deep breath, smelling the cold like I did with Gary, and thinking it might be something I'll try to remember.

• • •

My body actually hurts when I get out of the shower. It's the good kind of hurt, though. I haven't done something like that in…hell, I can't even remember when. I'm wearing sweatpants, a sweatshirt and socks as I fall onto the couch and kick my feet up. I'm out of cigarettes but don't know if I'd have the energy to go outside and smoke anyway.

I look over at my drums in the corner and remember the new beat I played today. It reminds me of the song Blake was working on when I left. He writes just about everything we do, but sometimes I help. I miss that.

Suddenly, I feel like talking to him, even though I've been the one ignoring him. I hit the button on my cell to give him a call.

"B.R.!"

I laugh at the way Blake answers the phone. He's always got a ton of energy. He said he had ADD when he was a kid, but it got better when he started singing. I'm not sure if that did it or if his energy just got redirected. That's kind of what happened with me. When I started playing drums, it helped me forget my asshole dad. "What's up?"

"What's up? I've been trying to call you, you've been ignoring my ass, and all you can say is 'what's up?'"

I want to tell him I feel like he betrayed me. That he should have had my back, but I don't. Instead, I just say, "Don't want to go there. We aren't supposed to be talking anyway. What ya been doing?"

He leaves it at that, which doesn't surprise me. He knows me, and he doesn't ever really expect me to talk more than I want to. "Not much. Chillin'. How's Alaska?" He chuckles when he asks.

It feels kind of cool to talk to him again. "Fuck off. It's Alaska. How do you think it is?" Flashes of riding today flash in my head. Some parts of it are pretty cool, I guess. "Actually, I went out snowmachining today. It was awesome. Those things go fast as hell. I want one." Not that I'd have somewhere to ride it, but still.

"Nice. Who'd you go with? Don't tell me Gary's taken up extreme sports?"

I laugh because that's the most ridiculous thing I've ever heard. "Yeah right. He spends all his time making me go on walks with him, working, or talking to Troy."

"So who?" There's some noise in the background and then Blake yells at someone to shut up. It bothers me for a second because I'm sure he's with the guys. They're all together at home, and I'm out here, but before I can dwell on it much, I remember what he asked me.

"Some chick named Penny. She's like the Alaska Hockey Queen or something. I haven't seen her play, but she kicks ass on the machines. Got a '75 Corvette too. It's nice." Shaking my head, I realize I sound like I'm bragging on this girl or something.

"You're hooking up with an Alaskan chick? That didn't take you long, man."

"What? I'm not messing around with her. Though she is kind of hot…" Actually there's no *kind of* about it. "I'm not here for that, though, remember? You helped send me here. I'm just getting by until Don gets the bug out of his ass and lets me come home."

He ignores part of my comment and says, "So? You can't get some while you're at it?"

His question annoys me because Penny's not like that. Then *I* annoy me because his question shouldn't bother me at all. "I didn't call to talk about Penny. I bought a new drum kit. Played around and I have a killer solo that would go with 'Break Out.'"

"Really? Nice. I'll tell the guys. We've been screwing around with it, but I can see if they're cool with setting it aside till you get back."

His words hit me the wrong way. They're working on our

songs without me. He'll *see* if they *mind* waiting for me? My body tenses up. "*See* if they're okay with it?" There should be no problem with waiting for me. Everyone's supposed to be on vacation right now, not only me. "We're still a band, right? It's not like I'll be here forever. I'm doing all right. I'm thinking about bailing and coming home anyway." Am I? Why not? If I can get the guys behind me, Don won't be able to say no to all of us.

"B.R, you know that's not what I meant, and…I don't know if that's such a good idea…I mean, you're there for a reason, ya know? It's not like —"

"Fuck off, Blake. Don't try and play that holier-than-thou crap with me." Fucking anxiety. My hands start to shake. They know me, so they should know I don't have a problem. I'm not on anything right now, and I was fine before he started in on me. Actually, I was better than fine. Maybe even good.

He sounds concerned when he says, "I'm not trying to be a jerk. We all party. Hell, Chase likes to have a good time almost as much as you, but it's different. None of us end up in the hospital. We make meetings and don't get lost in other countries. You scared us, man. If Maryanne hadn't been there…"

Yeah, Maryanne who was the one who hooked me up in the first place. "Speaking of Maryanne, I'm going to go and call her. At least she doesn't give me shit when I talk to her." *She* knows I don't have a problem. She doesn't even have the same crazy schedule as us, but she gets why I do what I do on the rare times I do it.

"That's because she's a pill-popping groupie! She wants in your pants because she wants your money and because—"

I don't know what else he says because I hang up the phone. Screw him. Screw all of them. They don't know what they're talking about. Patting my pockets, I look for my cigarettes before I remember I'm out. I shake my hands, hoping it will make the trembling stop. This time, when I pick up my phone, I call Maryanne. She answers on the first ring.

"Hey, Bishop."

"Did you send it?"

She giggles. "Yep."

I fall back, not even realizing I'd sat up, already feeling a little better.

• • •

"I got you a laptop." Gary walks in front of me and glances over his shoulder.

I suck in a breath of cold air. "You did?"

Gary nods. "It might come in handy. You never know."

We're silent for a few minutes as we keep walking. *Thank you, tell him thank you.* I tense a little as a car passes us. With the snow piled next to the road, and no shoulder, there isn't a lot of room for walking.

Gary shoves his hands tighter in his pockets. "Do you like working on the car with Gramps?"

"Obviously, man. You know I like cars."

He glances at me before his gaze shifts back to the icy road. "I did? Hate to break it to you, Bishop, but I didn't. I've never even heard you talk about cars until we got here."

That's stupid. Or maybe I just didn't talk about them with him. "I have a Ranchero at home. I plan to fix her up. I'm thinking I'll get started if you guys ever let my ass out of here."

That remark earns me a smile, but I know Gary won't offer to let me out early. "When I was in college, things were crazy busy. I was working with Don some of the time and you know how much of a slave driver he is. Kind of like with our walks, though, I set out a certain amount of time where I could just do what I wanted—something I loved. Not work, not school, just something that was happy-Gary time."

Here we go again. With my top lip, I play with my piercing before answering. "That's not always easy to do on the road."

We take a few steps in silence, and I like it when this happens. Like he's actually listening to what I'm saying and taking it in instead of jumping in with some random slogan to help me feel better. "If it's important, you find time. If you don't look out for yourself, Bishop, no one else will. I'm not stupid. I know you can't work on a car on the road, but you can read up on them. Make plans for what you want to work on next. Or cars can be your home thing and you can find something else—something *good* for you that gives you that same feeling to do on the road."

Without thinking, I nod. That kind of makes sense. There have been so many times I thought I would go crazy on a plane or in a hotel room. It might be kind of cool to have something planned to do during those times.

At some point, Gary must have slowed down or I sped

up because we're walking together now. "Troy is a planner. He drives me bat shit crazy sometimes. He keeps calendars all over the house and his phone beeps every five minutes to remind him of something. And God, don't let him miss his time in the gym because then I actually want to strangle him, but the point is, it's what works. His activities give him something to look forward to, and his schedule helps him feel grounded."

Gary pauses, leaving this conversation similar to the one he did about trees. "What keeps you grounded, Bishop Riley?"

I don't know.

. . .

Schedules. I have one of those, too. A pill schedule and one with Gramps.

For the fifth morning in a row, I check with Gramps to see if I got any mail. I've been holding out, keeping my pills to only take every few days, and it's working okay. Still, when he tells me no, it freaks me out a little. Mail shouldn't take this long.

Like every other day, we get to work on the Corvette. He calls me "Rookie" all the time, which I would have thought would be annoying. When, coming from him, it's not. It's a blast working on the car with him. He's a nutcase, with his crazy beard and crazier jokes, but a cool one and we're actually making some progress with her.

I hardly see Penny. Gramps says she's been practicing late or something. She definitely takes this hockey stuff seriously.

Sometimes, Gramps and I are quiet almost the whole day. Other times, he tells me stories about when he was younger, about wars, traveling, and even girls. Gramps likes to talk about girls, which I think is pretty cool. He doesn't sugarcoat anything and even though I'm quiet most of the time, I have a feeling I could tell him anything.

I kind of think he might *know* everything already.

Once in a while, he'll act a little strange, mumbling about weird stuff or something, but the guy is old as dirt. I figure that's got to be normal. I'd be insane right now if it wasn't for him and this car, I know that. Twice Gary has taken a break from working and reading to come out and watch us. He gets a kick out of Gramps, and Gramps definitely knows Gary is a little loony. Okay, maybe not loony, but mushy as hell. He got three calls from Troy the other day, and he'd get all smiley each time. Every time Gary turned his back, Gramps would put his finger to his temple, spin it in a circle, and mouth "crazy" at me.

He's awesome.

The nights are killing me, though. It's almost like I'm transported back to the stage. Or maybe not even there, but an empty room where I can still hear the people calling for me.

This town is enough to drive anyone crazy. It gets dark too early. I'm stuck inside the cabin with nothing but Gary, two TV channels, my drums, and now a laptop. How do they think this helps? It's making me go nuts. My shaking is getting worse. Every time I try to sleep, my head is suddenly flooded with stuff that doesn't matter. It sucks.

After hours of lying awake in the dark, I get up and

turn on my laptop and look up the first thing that pops into my mind. It doesn't take me long to find a couple online car magazine subscriptions to buy. *Now what?* So, I pull up an empty document to type but my fingers struggle on the keys, a little of the trembling coming back.

I slam the laptop closed and fall back against the couch. What the fuck kind of schedule could I make for myself anyway?

If Maryanne's package would get here, it would help take the edge off. That's all I need, a little help taking the edge off…

• • •

It's late one night when I notice Penny sliding into the hot tub, that white-blond hair all shimmering. Damn, the girl is hot. I'm not sure if she realizes how hot she is. Or maybe she does. Spur of the moment, I shove my feet in my boots, grab the jacket I'm getting tired of wearing, and go outside.

"Hey." I walk up the stairs. She has her head leaned back, resting on the deck.

Penny doesn't even bother to open her eyes. "Want to get in?"

"Nah."

We're both quiet for a minute, her staring at the back of her eyelids and me staring at her. There has to have been a reason for me to come out here, only I can't think of it right now. "So…the mail? I have a package coming. How long does it usually take?"

Finally, she opens her eyes and turns her head a little.

"Depends. Priority or regular mail?"

I can't believe I didn't think to ask. "Not sure."

"If it's regular mail, it can take forever. Sometimes a couple weeks."

A couple weeks? "Tell me you're kidding."

She rolls her eyes like I'm an idiot. "Bishop, you're in *Alaska.*"

Panic starts to set it. Wait, panic? No, I just don't want Maryanne to get caught mailing that stuff. It's not like I'm totally jonesing for it. "Yeah, Alaska, not the moon. A couple weeks? Remind me why anyone would choose to live here?"

The scowl on her face tells me I said the wrong thing. "There's nothing wrong with *here.* I don't get why everyone thinks that." She closes her eyes again, ignoring me. Obviously, I hit a sore spot.

"Sorry," I mumble, a little surprised that I apologized to her. "If you like it so much, why are you leaving? Gramps says you have a ton of big colleges who want you. That you're just deciding where to go."

Her eyes widen before her face pulls into a frown. "You don't know what you're talking about."

"What? Are you scared to leave?"

The look she gives me tells me that was definitely the wrong thing to say.

Chapter Eight

Penny

"*Scared* to leave? I'm going to pretend you didn't just say that." I need time to think about what to say so I slide down until the water covers my head before sitting up and wiping my face. But I still don't know if I'm going to give him a real answer or not. "It just...It doesn't matter. I don't know where I'm going to college, okay?"

Bishop will agree with the rest of them and tell me I need to go. *Take advantage of the opportunity.*

Just because the college teams might want me doesn't mean I want them. Irritation washes through me in full force as I think about how even my team is pushing me. The guys were all slapping my back after two more colleges contacted Coach about me this week. It's not like I'm the only one of us getting offers—I'm just the only one who hasn't decided.

Why does everyone want me to leave?

Bishop shrugs. "Figured it was a big deal that so many

people wanted you."

"Why?" I snap. "'Cause I'm a *girl*?"

His brows rise a bit. I can feel myself being a bitch, but I can't care right now. Chomps slammed me hard in practice today, and my whole body aches. My brain hurts from the pressure of our games and school and Gramps and another day of Rebecca making kissy faces at Mitch, and I just need to be alone for a bit.

"Hell, no." He chuckles. "That makes you more scary."

He's even being nice.

"Semifinals are in three days. I'm wound up." I'm almost… apologizing. Crazy. "I'm going to take a handful of Advil and drop into bed."

Something in Bishop's expression tightens before relaxing again. "Yeah. Okay."

Neither of us moves, but I hate the tension between us. The ride home from Pat's, snowmachining—Bishop is fun in a way I never expected.

"Shit. I'm sorry." I pull my knees to my chest while I put my thoughts together. "I already know what I want. I want to go to UAA or UAF, and apparently that's not big enough for someone who's wanted by some of the best women's college hockey teams in America."

Bishop stares at me long enough that I swear I start to shrink. "After all the shit I've heard come from your mouth, I can't believe you'd let anyone talk you into anything. You're stronger than that."

"I don't…" I blink a few times at his compliment. Stunned

by what sounds like concrete belief in me and what I want. "It's hard when so many people expect so much."

He fingers his lip ring for a moment, making me wonder what prompted him to get it. The silence between us this time is relaxed. "That's definitely something I can relate to."

I watch him for any sign or hint that he might tell me something about himself, but he just keeps playing with his lip and staring across the water. For some reason, him being someone I don't know well makes it easier to talk. "I should be thrilled to play on women's teams. But knowing I can stay in a place I love and keep playing with guys who I actually know how to get along with and talk to...I don't see the point in giving that up. Especially when I'm not even sure what I want to study."

Bishop scoots closer, searching my face in a way that twinges the feeling of want inside me again. "Penny, you're probably the toughest chick I've ever met. You'll figure it out, and once Gramps and your mom see you happy, they'll get it, too."

"Maybe." I roll onto my stomach to face him more directly and rest my chin on my arms. It's so strange. It's almost like he understands me. "But right now, I feel like the hero, and if I do what I want, I might..." *lose it.* They might think I wimped out. Was too scared to go.

"If you talked to Gary, he'd feed you some bullshit line about how sometimes we have to hit bottom before we figure out what we want. But you don't need that. You know what you want, and it's something that's cool. Do what you want

Penny, because *you* want to do it. No way in hell, with your track record, that it won't work out."

A corner of his mouth pulls up in a half-smile, and I stare at his lips. Now the silence feels awkward because there's a small part of me that wonders what kissing him would feel like, what the ring would feel like pressed against my lips, and the longer I stare the bigger that part gets.

Snap. Out. Now.

"You're a lot less of an asshole than I figured you'd be when you first got here."

Bishop snorts as he stands with a real smile this time. "Only you, Penny. Get some sleep."

I give him a salute and even return his smile, which feels like maybe something new for me. And it might be big.

. . .

I swap notes on the kitchen table with Mom.

> Penny – Sorry, it feels like I haven't seen you in forever. I should be here and hopefully still awake when you get home from school. I see we have three more possible scholarship offers to talk about! So proud of you! Love, Mom

I flip her paper over and write my own.

> Mom – All's good. No worries. Miss seeing you around. Love, Penny

That's easier than trying to spit out everything that's on my mind. Mom and I haven't talked for real in way too long. I definitely don't know how to start with a note.

• • •

School is just school. I do it so I can play hockey. The guys and I are all wound up tight, and Mitch and Rebecca are more attached than ever. Apparently, her dad walked in on them having sex one afternoon and isn't letting her out of his sight aside from when she's at school. So. They're trying to make up for lost alone time…in the hallway.

I've definitely been pushed aside for Rebecca because Mitch and I have barely spoken since this whole mess went down a few days ago.

Coach takes it way too easy on us again. We need to really skate, not glide around like figure skaters carrying sticks. *Beauty rest.* What the hell is that?

I need distraction. When I leave school, I head straight home. I might work on my car or see what Gramps is up to. But with my car comes missing my dad, and some days it's hard to see Gramps be confused. Some part in the back of my brain wonders if Bishop will be bored. If he'll be playing drums, or if he'll be hanging on his porch. Maybe he'll be up for something.

When I pull up, Bishop's on his porch, smoking again. I hate cigarettes. They stink. And they make everything else stink. But I'm still glad he's out here because it makes me feel less stalker-ish in asking him to do something with me. And the weirdest thing happens because I freeze as my hand hits the door handle. What if he says no? I can feel each heartbeat and hate that he's affecting me and making me feel weak. This is stupid. I'm Penny. I can handle some random guy.

"Hey," I say as I jump out of my truck. "If you wipe that cigarette smell off, wanna come with me for another ride?"

Bishop glances at the newly started cigarette in his hand and drops it to the ground, frowning. He stares at his hands for a moment before meeting my eyes.

"Well, shit." I fold my arms. "Grumpy Bishop is back. What's up with you?"

"Some shit with the ban—" He shakes his head. "I don't know…Maybe another time, or…"

"Come on." I grin, hating how grouchy he is. But he saved me from myself the other night in the hot tub, so maybe today I can save him. "You know you're curious. Go brush your teeth, get your ass in your snowmachine gear, and come play."

He pushes out a breath. "Give me a sec."

He disappears into his cabin, and like an idiot, I'm holding in a smile because he said yes.

• • •

"So, what does the mighty Snow Queen have in store for this evening?" he asks as he steps into the garage, smelling like mint toothpaste and cigarettes. At least he tried.

I let the stupid queen name pass because it looks like his day was worse than mine. "A ride somewhere cool."

"Where?" he asks as he sits on the machine next to mine.

I stare at him for a moment, wanting to do something to get the frown off his face. "Trust me?"

He gives me his hot half-smile again which sends a rush through me. "Hell, no I don't trust you. But I'll follow you out of here for a while."

I bite my lip to hold in a grin and hit the gas so hard that the front of the machine floats for the first hundred feet or so.

No matter how fast I go, I can't shake Bishop. He's not moving ahead, because I've taken two turns on the trail, but he wants to make sure that I know there's a chance he could beat me if he knew where we were going. I can totally appreciate that.

We hit the edge of the mountain and start the climb. He's going to love this, and as I keep my thumb on the throttle and we keep climbing, I'm even more glad he was on the porch when I got there.

Once we pass the abandoned-mining-house-turned-abandoned-lodge, it takes me a few minutes to find the exact spot. As his machine sprints in front of mine and then waits, I know he's impatient.

Boys.

Finally, I find the entrance to the old mine and turn off the machine. It's dark out now, and I'm really glad I know the way back home because there will be no light left.

"What is this?" he asks as he pulls off his helmet, eyeing the black hole that is the mining tunnel entrance. The only reason we can see it this late is because the snow always finds some light to reflect, and there's obviously no snow over a man-sized gap in the mountainside.

I toss him a small flashlight as I turn mine on. "Come on."

Bishop grins in the faint light, which is the exact look I wanted to get from him after I saw him frowning on his porch.

The temperature warms drastically as we step inside. "Caves stay constant, so they're warmer than outside in the winter and colder than outside in the summer."

The gray walls are rough, wet, and close. I can touch both sides when I stretch out my arms, and can just barely stand upright. Even our flashlights don't push away much of the darkness.

"Is it safe?" he asks.

"Are you scared?" I lightly punch him in the chest, suddenly very aware that it's only the two of us, and he's a bit close. And has one sexy smile. Flits of nerves hit again, and I step back, not having any idea what to do about them.

He makes his scoffing noise, but I'm not totally buying his bravado. "No. I just don't want to die inside a mountain in Alaska, that's all."

I spin and light up his face, making him squint. "So, where *do* you want to die?"

He laughs and pushes my flashlight away. "Warm, happy, on a beach, with a hot girl. Or a few."

A bubble of happiness fills me because I got Bishop laughing. "Of course."

We're in about fifty feet in from the entrance now and the rusted rails for the mining cars appear out of the dirt.

"Holy shit." He looks down. "Is this an old mine?"

"Yeah. I love this place. It hasn't been used since the forties, but they did tours when I was little. The lodge we passed was open when I was a kid. We used to snowmachine up here with my dad to get burgers."

Bishop opens his mouth, I'm sure to ask about Dad, but closes it again. I don't realize I'm holding my breath until I let it out. Bringing up Dad isn't a good idea in front of someone I don't know well. Or, really, anyone.

"Anyway. It makes me sad that the place shut down." I sit on the dirt, which feels bizarre after snow being on the ground for so many months.

"This has to be a big party spot, huh?" he asks continuing to walk ahead.

"Too far out." I shake my head. "And a kid got lost in here about four years ago, so it turned into one of those crazy ghost stories that scares the shit out of everyone." I shine my light on Bishop's back as he keeps walking. "And after that first kid disappeared, every time we came out to party, we lost someone."

He stops. "Really?"

"No." I laugh which sounds sort of like a weird, girly giggle before I make myself stop. "I'm messing with you, California Boy."

He shakes his head and turns toward me. "You can't help yourself, can you?"

"Nope." I stand. "Wanna see the lodge?"

"Can we get in?" He starts to move back my way.

I'm biting my lip again to hold in my smile knowing what

his reaction will be. "Garrett's the realtor, and I know him, so I know where the key's hidden."

"Of course you do."

• • •

I both love and hate walking through this old place. I see my dad in here, laughing with Mom, feeding her fries over the table. Ten is too young to lose your dad.

Our flashlights make crazy shapes on the walls as we move through the tables and chairs covered in dust. The windowpanes are so filthy that our light barely reflects off them as the beams follow lines on the walls.

I've never gone to the rooms upstairs—the empty place is a bit creepy—especially in the dark.

"This could be so cool." Bishop turns around, letting his light shine across the wooden bar, the chairs, and tables.

"Could be," I agree. "It was."

"You could have a small stage over here, you know, musical talent and stuff." He's picturing it all right now. Differently than I am because I'm thinking about what it used to be, and he's thinking about what it could be.

I turn to see where he's looking. There used to be a jukebox there. An old one.

"And rooms upstairs?" He points his flashlight at the ceiling and looks up.

"Yeah. And then"—I point to the far wall—"there's an owner's house back there. It isn't much, but it would be awesome."

"Another piece of Penny Jones falls into place." Then he looks confused like he doesn't like that he's figuring me out. "You really love it here in Alaska, don't you? I mean, I know you said you wanted to stay, but it's deeper than just a want for you." His flashlight beam hits me in the eyes, blinding me.

I cover my face until he points it away.

He gets it. It's so crazy how he understands what people I've known my whole life don't. "I do love it here." I nod. But I'm getting this edgy feeling in my chest, like our conversation might go too far. Maybe I could just redirect. "So." I turn to face him in the dusty dining room. "Who are you?" Maybe he'll answer a direct question since all my sideways ones don't seem to work.

"I'm Bishop." His voice sounds serious, and his eyes don't leave mine. And even in the dim light made by our flashlights, and the odd shadows moving around between the chairs, his dark brown eyes are deep. And I bet he feels deep, too.

"Yeah. I got that part. Bishop Ripe from California." I'm settling into the fact that this guy is a bit of a mystery, and it doesn't bother me as much as it should. Maybe it's that he's temporary, so it doesn't matter. Maybe I'm actually mellowing out.

"Yeah," he answers.

Or maybe I'm not mellowing because I *really* want more information and everything's turning up in dead-ends. "*That's it*?"

"There's not a lot to know."

This cool tension in the air has become an interesting part

of being around Bishop. "There's more to you. And once I decide I need to know, I'll figure you out."

Whatever hint of a smile he used to have is gone. "I don't doubt it."

I spin and move back toward the exit, feeling a bit like we've talked a step too deep on both ends, and I don't think that's what either of us wants today.

"But Penny?"

When I turn to face him, he actually looks vulnerable. I stop and suck in a breath, afraid to speak.

"Don't dig, okay? Not yet." He swallows once and the air between us is so still that I hear his weight slowly shift. "Please."

I wasn't expecting the "please." The look on his face softens everything in me. What could be so bad? Why is he hiding? I want to make some smart remark, but even I know now's not the time. "Okay."

"Thanks."

The sudden seriousness between us isn't what I wanted tonight. The handle is still frozen cold as I pull open the door. I need to do something to lighten things up, but I don't know what to say. Not after he laid himself out like that.

I glance over my shoulder, suddenly knowing exactly how to handle this. "Now you can try to keep up on the way back."

"Or since I know the way—*you* can try to keep up with *me*."

Despite his grouchy exterior, I think I'm starting to like him.

Chapter Nine

Bishop

Penny is nuts.

Badass and gorgeous, but she's totally nuts. It's wild that I like that about her, but she's fun in a way I don't ever remember having. Things are simple with her, and even though I didn't realize it before, I think I might need simple. *When were things simple for you, Bishop Riley?*

Working with Gramps pops into my head. And riding with Penny. Even my lame nature walks with Gary. If he asked me that same question in this moment, I think I would tell him right now. Right now is when things are simple.

Thoughts like that send shivers down my spine. Easy, yes, but easy isn't *better*. L.A. is fun. I like fun.

The only reason I'm doing okay here is because I like giving Penny shit. I don't know who else I would have enjoyed beating as much as I liked winning our race back to the house the other night.

Yeah, that's right. I won. Not by much, but a win is a win. And damn it felt good. As good as I can remember feeling in way too long.

My mind flashes back to the lodge—watching her practically break into the place. Key or no key, I'm pretty sure we could have gotten into trouble for being in there, but like everything else, she pushed in with no fear. I wonder if she's scared of anything. Well, except maybe leaving home.

My cell rings and I hit the button without looking at who it is. "Hello?"

"Bishop. Hey, sweetie. How are you?" Mom's voice sounds uncertain, and nausea replaces the calm I just felt. Every time I talk to her, I feel like shit. Hate that even though things aren't as bad as she seems to think they are, I'm disappointing her. She always believed in me, and it sucks that she doesn't anymore.

I could have almost died…Would Dad still leave her alone if I wasn't around?

I shake those thoughts from my head. I didn't die, and they were probably exaggerating. "Hey, Ma. What's up?"

"Nothing. Do I need a reason to call my son?"

"No."

"That's what I thought." There's laughter in her voice. "I miss you, Bishop."

"Then let me come home." The words automatically pop out of my mouth, and then I feel guilty. I don't want to take anything out on her, plus, well, I'm actually having a little fun right now. The thought of going back to Don's demands, the band, all the traveling…Maybe I *can* look at this like a little vacation. But then considering Dad called before everything went down, I should be with her instead. *Relax, Bishop. Don will help take care of her, like he does when you're on tour.* "Sorry. I didn't mean that. I just woke up from a nap, so my head's a little foggy."

She sighs. "That's okay. I talked to Gary. He says you're doing well. That you've made some friends there and you've been snowmobiling. That's good, Bishop. You could use that. Friends, fun."

Snowmachining. It's snowmachining. I scratch my head, not sure what to say. "I have friends and fun at home."

"Do you?" There's no doubt in my mind what she means by that question. She's asking if Maryanne is really a friend. The guys don't seem to think so. Are *they* really my friends? I mean, we're cool. We've been tight for a year and a half, but none of them except Blake came to me before telling Don they thought I had a problem. Blake was always calling and checking in with me.

"I wonder if I did the right thing." Mom's voice is soft, unsure. "If I should have let you join so young. If it would have been better if you finished school first instead of just getting your GED. Maybe things would have been different if you'd been older."

My chest tightens. "Everything's fine. I would have fought you over it if you tried to stop me. You didn't do anything wrong. Plus…it helped. It got Dad off our backs."

She makes a soft sniffing sound, and I know she's crying. I

hate that sound. The need to wipe it away takes me over. "And this? The Alaska thing? I'm actually having fun. You did good, Mom. You did good."

• • •

I'm a little on edge after my conversation with Mom. On reflex, I pick up my phone and call Pat. I called him to ask about some drumsticks, and we've kind of kept talking since. His love of music is unreal. He's pretty cool for not telling anyone who I am.

When he doesn't answer, I toss my cell on the table. My package from Maryanne still hasn't come, and I've been out of pills for a couple days. Which has been okay. I've been so busy with Gramps and snowmachining and stuff, I haven't even thought about it. Much. And I'd still be okay now if it wasn't for talking to Mom…and the game tonight. I'm sketchy that someone's going to recognize me. I don't want to, but I know I need to go to Gary.

It takes about thirty seconds to get to his cabin. "Hey." He pulls open the door. I'm surprised when I walk in and see Troy's here. Nice. Gary's getting a booty-call while he's supposed to be helping me. And maybe I should hate Troy, because he's the reason I'm in Alaska instead of a beach for my *vacation*. But then I think about Penny and the snowmachining and Gramps, and I realize I might not be as pissed as I used to be.

"What's up?"

Troy nods his head at me from the couch. "How do you

like my hometown?"

He's always been quiet, and I'm wondering if this is the first time I've heard him speak.

"Yeah…It's good…I…"…have no idea what to say to him. *I heard you like to climb trees* doesn't sound real good.

Luckily, Gary saves me. "Bishop Ripe. How are you this fine day?"

I shake my head. "Funny. Listen, I'm…" I look over at Troy to see if he's watching us. It's embarrassing as hell that I can't even take my doctor-prescribed anxiety meds without my babysitter's permission.

With a lowered voice, I lean toward him, "I'm not feeling too hot. Can I get one of my pills?"

Gary looks at me, his eyes crinkling a little around the edges. "Yeah…sure. Come with me." I follow him to his room, and he shakes one pill into my hand. I put it under my tongue and it starts to melt. It tastes like shit but works a lot faster this way.

"Thanks, man." I pause for a minute, words struggling to come out. "So you really used to do this? Help people who have a problem? I mean, I don't. I think that's pretty obvious, but it was your job?"

Even though Gary and I walk daily, and we have our weekly chats, he doesn't talk about his job. All the articles he writes are about his experiences in helping people. Up here, it doesn't feel like he's really working, sometimes.

He nods, studying me. I think it's the most serious I've ever seen Gary. "I did. It didn't last very long. It's tough work.

Rewarding and I loved it, but hard. It suits me better to write about it, I think. Listen, I know there's more going on in that head of yours than you're sharing. I've been easy on you, but maybe we should dig a little deeper next time we talk. It will help. I want to help—"

I cut him off. "I'm fine. I'm heading over to work on the Corvette with Gramps for a while, and then I'm going to Penny's hockey game." I'm eighteen years old, and it's ridiculous I'm practically asking for permission.

"Do you want Troy and me to go with you? Or Troy wouldn't mind staying here and you and I could hang. It'd be fun."

Nope. Definitely not my idea of a good time to have my babysitter go with me. "No. I'm good."

More eye crinkles before I get a simple nod. "Check in with me before you go and when you get home. I'll also be calling you, and I expect you to answer within two rings. And what I said about our next chat—it's important and it's happening."

Anger pulls and tugs at my insides, but I bite my tongue before nodding, then I turn. I'm almost to the door when Gary calls out, "Hey, Ripe. I'm proud of you. You're doing good."

I give him a nod before walking out. He's the second person who said that to me. I actually feel guilty. He wouldn't be saying it if he knew about the beer I drank and that I'm waiting for a package of fucking pills to come in the mail.

• • •

I've been working with Gramps for a few hours when he thumps me on the forehead.

"What the hell was that for?" I jerk back, rubbing the spot.

"What's going on in that head of yours today, Rookie? You're not being your usual charming self."

I almost crack a smile at the nickname. Instead, I stand, crossing my arms, not caring that I'm getting grease all over my clothes. "Me? Charming?"

Gramps doesn't laugh the way I want him to. He's right. I'm feeling on edge, and I don't know why. I keep thinking about Mom, Gary, pills, hockey, Penny, the band, Alaska, Maryanne, and whatever else I can jam into my over-packed brain. My thoughts are being tugged in a million different directions, and it makes me want to crawl out of my own skin.

"You might fool some people, but not me." He walks over, falls into a chair, and I do the same. "How you doing, kid?" It doesn't bother me, like it does with Don, when he calls me *kid*.

I shrug. "Okay, I guess. I mean, I'm good, I…" I what? I don't even fucking know what's wrong with me.

"Did I ever tell you I was in two wars?"

He has, but I don't want to embarrass him by pointing out we've talked about it a lot. "No, but being as old as you are, I figured."

This time, Gramps laughs.

"Smartass. Like I was saying, I was in the war. Tough shit, it was. People think they know, but they don't. If you weren't there—in any war, there's no way of knowing what soldiers go through. I think that's the way it is about most people. It's easy to sit back and think you know what they're dealing with, but you don't. Not unless you walk in their shoes, and most people aren't willing to borrow someone else's."

I nod, wondering where this is going, but knowing he's right.

"When I came home, I was all screwed up in the head. Drank a lot, trying to deal. Of course, that never works, does it? I wasn't nice to a lot of people. Blamed a lot of people. It was a hard coupl'a years. But then I met a woman—no, not just a woman, the *right* woman, and she woke my dumb ass up. I got better, not just for her, but for me. I know what it's like to struggle, Rookie."

My leg is bouncing up and down like crazy. My vision goes blurry. He knows. Well, not that I have a problem, because I don't, but he knows why I'm here. That everyone thinks I need it. Fear that he'll ask me to leave scrapes at my spine.

"I'm not saying I know what you've been through. Not sure your shoes would fit, but what I am saying—" He rubs his long beard. "I'm here. You ever want to talk, scream, whatever. I'm here."

He doesn't have to offer that. I'm not Gramps's responsibility like I'm Gary's. My mouth opens. Closes. I should want to tell him I'll never need to talk. That I'm fine. The urge to thank him ghosts through me as well. It's strange because I sort of want to talk to him, but I'm not even sure what about. There's no reason. I wasn't in a war, never been through something really bad. I'm just me.

Amazingly, Gramps seems to know I'm not ready. He stands back up and claps his hand down on my shoulder. "I know about that damn band of yours, too. Think you're so tricky, but no one gets anything past me. Now get your butt back over here and help me finish before that hockey game starts."

Panic squeezes me for a second, but then…just lets go. I trust him. Really trust him. Without a word, I do what he says.

• • •

The arena is packed with people squeezed in so tight I can hardly breathe. Christ, I'm not even on stage, the crowd isn't even for me, and it still makes me want to lose my shit.

This is pretty cool, though. I've never been to a hockey game before, so I try to focus on the ice and not the people screaming around me. Try not to hear them chanting my name when I know they're not.

When the players come out, I try and figure out which one is Penny. Gramps sits between me and Penny's mom and points Penny out to me right before they toss the puck and all hell breaks loose.

No joke. All. Hell.

People are flying around the ice, pushing and shoving at each other. I've watched hockey on TV, but it's nothing compared to seeing it in real life. They slam so hard that the plastic vibrates. I kind of want to jump out there and remind them there's a girl out there with them, but then I think about

Penny and know if I did that, she'd be going after me with her hockey stick.

She's no joke, either. She can take these guys. They should be the ones who are scared.

So instead of making a fool out of myself by busting out on the ice, I pull my hat lower on my head, hoping it'll help make it so no one recognizes me. Penny gets shoved over, hits the wall and after falling on her stomach, doesn't even pause before getting up. Four minutes into the game, she gets put in the penalty box, and Gramps stands up and yells, "That's my girl!"

She's fast. Faster than any of the guys out there. It's awesome.

I forget about the crowd, pills, Mom, Don, Gary, the band, Maryanne, and everything else. There's no room for anything else in my head right now. I don't want anything else there. I just stand here and watch her fly.

Chapter Ten

Penny

We win 2-1, and the crowd goes insane as we skate toward the exit. One of those goals was mine in the first, just after I was let out of the box. The other was Mitch's in the second. Those Barrow kids were out for blood. I'm going to hurt tomorrow. It's a good thing we have a couple weeks before state.

The guys are still smacking each other, and I rip off my helmet so I can breathe. My hair sticks to my face and neck. I'm hot and need out of my gear, but people press in close. I'm shaking hands and nodding and smiling like I might actually be absorbing some of what people are yelling over the noise of the crowd.

"Lucky Penny!" Chomps kisses the back of my sweaty head and half the team follows suit.

Matt deserves some high-fives as well. He kicked ass tonight.

I turn to see Mom and Gramps making their way through

the crowd of tightly packed people, and my high slows.

"Mom. You're in scrubs?" I ask. "Are you ever not working?"

It shouldn't matter, I'll be going out with the guys tonight anyway, but still.

She pulls her mouth into a small frown. "I'm sorry, but I'll be home tomorrow, and I should be awake in the afternoon."

I'm straining to hear her over the noise. "Okay."

Mom glances behind her again, but there are people everywhere.

"Nice job, Penny." A guy reaches around Mom to shake my hand.

"Yeah, thanks. Ben, right?" I think I remember this guy as someone Mom and Dad went to high school with or something. He starts to speak, but there are voices shouting and music playing over the loudspeakers, and it's all too much.

Mitch grabs my waist, pulling me backward, and I scream in surprise. In seconds, I'm also pushing off Matt and Chomps and half the team as I head for our bench and my skate guards.

"We'll see you at home! Love you!" Mom calls as I'm buried in guy smell, hockey gloves, and sweaty gear.

I slide on my guards when I see Bishop looking a bit wide-eyed and twitchy off the side of the rink. I get two more slaps on the back as I head to the corner Bishop's in. Only there's still a sea of people in here all telling me congrats, and I'm starting to feel like I just need to get to him.

"What's up?" I ask, when I finally make it to where he's half-plastered against the wall, knowing something big is definitely going on.

"I need air. I mean out. Air." He gestures with his hand and won't look at me.

"Uh…I need a shower," I tease, but he doesn't react, so maybe this is not a teasing kind of thing.

He looks all amped up on something. His eyes won't focus on anything, and he can't stand still. "It's cool. I'll…" But it's obviously not cool.

"Let's get out of here." I take his hand in mine, and he squeezes me with a death grip. I'd never tell him that, of course.

"Yeah. Thanks." He hardly gets the words out.

I lead him out the back door. The first thing he does after relinquishing my hand is light a cigarette with shaky fingers. I nearly try to hug him to see if it helps, only Bishop and I don't touch that way. I have no idea what to do.

We walk in silence toward my truck, where it's parked in employee of the month parking because I know Rick, and he's almost always employee of the month and doesn't mind.

Bishop drops his half-smoked cigarette in the snow, gets in the passenger's side, jerks off his hat, and immediately slumps in the seat with his eyes closed.

Holding onto the open door, I wait for him to say something. He's starting to freak me out a bit. "Are you okay? You're not going to hurl in my car, are you?"

"Shit. I just needed out. Air. Crowds." He does this weird breathing thing. *In. Out. In. Out.*

I still want to touch him, but I'm afraid to. I reach in like three times until I remember what works for me. "Punch something. That breathing shit never works."

He shakes his head like he's trying but still doesn't look at me. "Damn…You're something else."

A few random shouts and the sound of car engines starting swirl around us. Neither of us speaks for long enough that it's starting to get weird, and I get this need to break the silence.

"Crowds freak you out?" I ask slowly.

"I'd rather not use the words 'freak out.'" His eyes close again, and his hands tremble in his lap.

It's awkward to stand in all my gear, but I also can't leave him. "Is this where you tell me who you are? Why you're up here renting out all the cabins even though they'd be empty anyway?"

He lets out another desperate sounding chuckle. "No."

"I'm going to shower so I don't stink up the truck. Oh! These were dropped off at my school. They're from Pat." I dig in the side pocket of the passenger door for the drumsticks and hand them over.

Bishop takes them and immediately starts twirling the sticks, still with his eyes closed and still with the weird breathing. "Nice of him."

"I think he has a crush on you," I tease.

"He's cool to talk to. We're both into music."

They talk?

He spins the sticks a few more times before blinking and then closing his eyes again like he's not ready to see the world. "You were wild out there, Penny. Fuck, that's crazy, you know?"

The high from my game slams into me again, and with it comes the thought that he gets it. Or is maybe trying to. "It's why I love it."

He nods and keeps twirling, eyes still closed, breathing still regulated, and starts beating soft rhythms on my dash. At least he knows better than to slam those things onto Bitty.

Finally, after what feels like forever, he looks at me. "I get it…why you wanna play here and why you want to be on a guys' team. You're good." And then he quickly turns away as though he said too much while I'm dying inside. He *gets* it. This guy who barely knows me gets it when no one else does. I don't know what to say.

"Give me ten minutes to shower and get my gear. K?"

He stares at his drumsticks, letting out another slow breath and attempting a smile that looks more like a grimace, but at least he's trying. "Want any help with that?"

I get a flash of what it would be like to have him helping me. His fingers on the skin of my shoulder, and his dark eyes staring into me the way they did the night I sat in the hot tub and he told me I could do anything. There's a tension and a want in the nerves that course through me at my over-active imagination that I don't know how to deal with. My cheeks flush before I can find words. "You must be feeling better."

His eyes finally meet mine, and vulnerable Bishop is back. The one who makes my legs go weak. "Thanks."

I have to exit the situation because it's suddenly so intense

I don't know what to do. Having a guy crush on me is one thing. Having him get me and my decisions is something else entirely. This wasn't part of my plan. "See you in ten."

· · ·

Since dropping Bishop off at his cabin, I've done nothing but try to redirect my thoughts with the help of some ridiculously loud music. I don't want to be thrown off by someone I just met. I know what I want. I want the future I've always relied on, and some of that future depends on a guy at this party, not a guy I don't know. By the time I pull into Matt's, my head is relatively clear, and I'm finally ready to celebrate instead of over-thinking about someone I shouldn't.

I find Mitch, and my stomach starts twisting with a sense of urgency that hits me hard. I have to do something. Say something. We graduate in a few months. He'll leave for college. It looks like I might leave for college. My heart hits harder with each thought. With how my future suddenly feels so uncertain.

He's rehashing some part of the game, but his words get lost in my thoughts and the pounding music.

"And then this girl." He grabs me from the side and hugs me to him, kissing my forehead. Chalk one more action up to confusing. "Made that insane goal in the first—" His voice fades out as I breathe him in, only…Only it doesn't feel like I thought it would. Not tingly and exciting.

When Mitch's hand drops from around my shoulders, he hands me the bag of keys. He knows the drill—he got here first, so he picked up keys. Routine. Safety.

"Thanks," I say blinking stupidly at the mesh sack in my hand.

The guys keep going over plays, which I normally love but I'm still staring at the bag of keys like I know something's *different*, even though I can't put my finger on it yet.

"Holy shit! Becca! How'd you get out?" Mitch sprints to the front door, leaping over the couch on his way, and scoops her off the floor.

He walked away from me without a second glance and is now looking at her like...like...like I know he'll never look at me. It feels as if someone punched me in the gut because it seems official now. He's left me for her. And I guess...I don't even know what to think about it because it feels both easier and shittier than I expected. But maybe that's the point. I *expected*. I'm not even sure why this is different from yesterday when he held her or the day before. If it has something to do with me, or with them, or maybe it has to do with the fact that Mitch's future is looking more solid all the time, and I'm not sure how much a part of it I'll be. That's the part that's sucking the air from my lungs and feels so horribly unexpected.

"What's *that* face?" Chomps pushes my shoulder.

"Just need some air. I don't think everyone in here actually showered," I try to tease, but my voice comes out weird.

The cold air tingles on my skin as I step onto the porch, and the voices and music lower to a steady, unrecognizable hum. Before thinking, I go to the cooler on the porch and grab a beer for something to do. No ice in here. At these temps, it's more a problem of them all freezing. Sort of funny that we use coolers in the winter to keep stuff warm. I'm pathetically trying to distract myself from the gnawing at my insides over…what…change? No, not change. *Confusion*. It's confusion and not knowing what to expect about anything, which is stupid. Whatever's happening or not happening between Mitch and me isn't everything. It's *one* thing. It's just that Mitch was one of the few things that I thought I'd always be able to count on.

My gaze goes to the window again where I expect to see Mitch and Rebecca in some corner, trying to eat the other's faces, but instead they're dancing. Slow and awkward because Mitch wouldn't know how to dance any other way, but he's holding her like she's everything. Eyes closed, knowing the team's going to give him shit for it later. There's an odd sort of detached realization that I don't want to be standing in Becca's place, but also that I don't want to be ignored by my best friend. I have no idea how to reconcile my feelings yet. How to really want one without the other.

I slide my fingers over the tab on the top of the beer, but all I can think about is Dad. How I lost him because some stupid asshole wanted to get wasted at a party. My hands feel shaky as I set the beer in the cooler and push my way back inside.

I shove the keys at Trinna and Chomps. "I have to go."

"What?" Matt grabs me in a sideways hug. "You just got

here!"

"Yeah. I know." I glance toward Mitch again. He doesn't even see that I'm leaving. That I'm upset. The guy who answers my texts the second I hit send probably won't know I left. I shove Matt off and head for the door, needing out. Home.

. . .

My chest sinks when I pull into the driveway, and Mom's car isn't here. Again. I feel even stupider because I knew she was working when she showed up to the game in scrubs.

I keep trying to pull in a full, real breath. Like air will somehow stop all the mess inside me.

It doesn't, but it does slow it down.

I'll say goodnight to Gramps and then crawl into bed. I can do this.

As I get closer to the house, I hear *my* music playing instead of Gramps's country music. That's…odd. Since when does he like rock?

The lights in Gramps's trailer are on, but the door's open, so I don't think he's in there. I jog up the stairs, and panic seizes my chest. Gramps is dancing without a piece of clothing on. His droopy butt cheeks wiggle with each move, and I'm just thankful his back's to me. This is new. And definitely not good.

What am I supposed to do? My body starts to go numb because I realize this is all going to be my responsibility. The reality of this situation grips at my chest, and all I can think is *please don't let him remember this.*

I fumble with my phone as I pull it from my pocket and dial Mom. Her voicemail picks up. *No. No. No!*

It actually hurts to even type the words. GRMPS DNCING NAKED. WHAT DO I DO?

My phone buzzes in a call.

"Mom?"

"I'm so sorry, honey. I'm one of two nurses in labor and delivery, and we have two women in here. There's no way I can leave. Not right now. Try to get him to take a sleeping pill, cover him up, and I'll get home as soon as I can…" I hear muffled sounds in the background before Mom comes back on. "Hold on a sec."

"Um…" I don't want to try to give my naked Gramps a sleeping pill. I keep Mom on but go to Messages on my phone.

I send Mitch a quick, desperate text because I don't want to do this alone. NEED HELP W GRMPS. PLSE COME.

I choke as another sob tries to work its way up. I have to be stronger than this.

"I'm back," Mom says. "Let me call someone to help, okay?" Guilt is all over her voice.

"No, no. It's cool," I lie. "I can do it. Mitch will come."

"Penny, honey. Really. I'm so sorry." Mom pulls in a breath and starts talking again, but Gramps spins to face me, his eyes as big as his smile.

"Lucky Penny! How are you?"

"Gotta go, Mom." I stuff my phone in pocket, my insides shaking again, and try to find something in me that can deal with this. And to not look down too far.

Still no text back from Mitch.

Now what?

Chapter Eleven

Bishop

I'm officially a loser.

What kind of guy loses it at a hockey game and can't even hang out afterward? But I knew going to the party wouldn't have been a good idea. Gary would have freaked out.

Penny's truck pulls in front of her house, and she runs inside. I don't know what it is, but there's something pulling me to her house. It was cool of her to try to get me to hang out with them, and the way she tried to help when I lost it. Gramps would expect more of me, bailing the way I did again, and I don't want to let him down. He's keeping my secrets and well—shit, I want to see her. I'm lonely, so fucking lonely in these tiny walls, my friends a thousand miles away. Gary next door with Troy. I even called Pat again when I got home from the game. He offered to come get me after my bullshit excuse of no car, but I told him no. Now I wish I hadn't. It feels like everyone in Alaska has someone to be with but me.

Which is probably my own fault, but still.

I reach for my cigarettes but decide against them before I head for the door. It's late—well, not late if you consider the fact that she went to a party tonight, but late enough that I shouldn't be going over to her house. Still, she just got home, and I'm sure Gramps won't care. Her mom's car is gone, so I think it's okay.

Music blares from inside the house and for a minute I wonder if they moved the party here before—oh, shit. They're listening to *me*. Not just me, I guess, but my band. Thinking of how she'll react if she knows makes my gut ache. Everything will change if she knows. It'll suck if she starts treating me the way other girls do. Will she not give me shit and ride snowmachines and stuff with me if she knows I'm Bishop Riley, pill-head and drummer for Burn instead of Bishop Ripe, moody guy from California?

Wait. Pill-head?

"Gramps! Come here! You can't go out there!" Penny screams fanatically. The sound of her voice, the hitch of pain in it makes me shove the door open. I'll probably regret it when she yells at me for walking into her house, but something doesn't feel right.

Gramps runs around the corner toward the door, buck-naked. Like seriously naked, and I definitely don't think I should have walked in, but the wild look in his eyes isn't the Gramps I know.

"I'm a grown man! I know what I'm doing." There's a hard edge to his voice I never expected to hear from him.

Penny rounds the corner next and her red-rimmed eyes catch mine. All sorts of things flash across her face: pain, embarrassment, fear, anger, and it doesn't even bother me that I can read her because this? This is serious. Something is wrong with Gramps.

I'm frozen, not sure what to do, standing in their open doorway, cold air flooding inside. My music pumping through the speakers with a naked Gramps and a broken Penny standing in front of me. No, not broken, but cracked. I don't think anything can completely break her.

"Get out!" She stomps toward me. "This isn't your business." She's right in front of me and I'm still stuck in the same place. I see her chin quiver and then Gramps's head drops like he's confused.

"Pen—"

"Please?" Her voice cracks as she speaks. "I don't want you to see him like this." One tear, just one brims over and trickles down her face.

I want to wipe it away.

I want to fix this, in a way I can't fix anything else in my life.

"Let me help. You shouldn't have to do this alone." There are so many questions shoving their way into my head right now: what *is* this? How often does it happen? But right now, none of it matters. The only things that do are Gramps and Penny.

She wipes her eyes, even though there aren't more tears. I wish I knew how she does it. She's like a brick wall, so strong and sturdy. "He wouldn't want you to see him like this."

She right, but it's still not okay to leave her with it. "And like I said, *you* shouldn't have to deal with it alone." My hand is shaking, but this time not because of anxiety or the need to be medicated, but because I want to touch her. Feel the soft skin that holds in so much strength. I've spent weeks here, and I never would have imagined she lived with something like this going on.

"Don't talk about me like I'm not here. I'm not a damn kid! If I want to go outside, I can damn well go outside." Gramps is coming our way now. I don't wait for Penny's permission and step around her to head him off.

"Where ya goin' old man?" I try to tease but it comes out flat. Hopefully, he doesn't catch on. "It's cold as hell out there. You wanna go out, we'll go out, but let's get your working clothes on. That engine is way too greasy." I have no idea what I'm saying. If I sound like an idiot or if it will do any good, but it's all that comes to me. "And what's this shit you're listening to? I thought you had good taste in music." It's a risk, bringing it up, but if the Gramps I know is in there, it'll work.

That secretive, cocky Gramps grin curves one side of his mouth, and I think he's in there. Whatever's going on, the Gramps who works with me on cars realizes this is funny — knows there's something familiar and a private joke that he's in on.

"Don't call me old man, Rookie, and you're right... the music *is* shit." He laughs and the fist squeezing my chest tightens slightly.

"It's not *that* bad. Maybe you need to get your hearing aids changed. Now show me where your room is so we can find your stuff and go work on the car."

He wraps an arm around my shoulders, and I try and forget the fact that I have a naked old man next to me. While we walk, I turn my head, trying to catch Penny's eyes and hoping I'm doing the right thing. She's standing where I left her, her ripe, cherry red lips in an "O," but I swear, there's something different in her eyes. Something I've never seen before when she looked at me.

Gramps leads me to his room. Penny's behind us. Things suddenly decide to go our way when I see there's a pair of sweatpants laid out on Gramps bed. Maybe he was changing when something switched in his brain. Is this normal? So many questions.

"Why don't you put those on?" I let go of him. "If you still feel like it, we can go work on the Corvette after you're dressed."

His eyelids flutter, and his shoulders slump, looking drained. Gramps sits on the bed and starts to put on the pants. "I'm not feeling very well, son. Think we could put off the car till tomorrow?"

My body stiffens at the word *son*. Not in a bad way, but in a way that actually makes me feel like more than the Bishop Riley I thought about earlier. More than any kind of Bishop I've ever been. A better Bishop. "Absolutely. I'll be here."

"I'll help him into bed." Penny steps up beside me and touches my arm. "There're some pills in his bathroom. They're color-coded. I need the ones in the purple container. Can you grab them for me?"

"Yeah…sure." I'm concentrating on the way it felt to hear him call me *son* and the feel of her hand against my skin that her words don't sink in until I'm standing in the bathroom, which I swear could double as a pharmacy. Sleeping pills, pain pills, I recognize them all. My mouth gets dry. My heart rate spikes. I want them. I can't believe how much. It's the stress. Has to be. Worrying about Maryanne getting in trouble, the band, Mom at home without me when Dad had called not long before. He's been leaving us alone now, but what if he doesn't? And Gramps…Jesus, Gramps. I could take one and no one would notice. I deserve that. After this crazy night, I could use something to take the edge off.

My whole arm shakes when I pick up the container.

One, one, one. I could take one. That wouldn't be so bad. The lid twists between my fingertips.

"Did you find it?" Penny calls from the other room. Her voice breaks through the daze taking me over.

Shit. "Umm…Yeah. Be right there." I peek out of the room. She's not coming. No one would know, especially if I do it right here. Drink some water from the sink or take it dry, and make this whole night disappear. I want it to be gone. Not to have to know Gramps goes through this.

Gramps.

The guy I work on the Corvette with every day. The one who treats me like an equal and talks to me. Penny jumps into my head next. She wouldn't be this damn weak. There's Gary, too. He just told me he's proud of me. And mom. It would kill her to think of me downing pills, especially at a time like this. It's still a fight. My fingers don't want to obey, but I manage to toss the bottle on the counter. I can't do it. Not from them. But damn, I want to…so bad.

I grab the purple container and get my ass out of the room as fast as I can. My hands are quivering so bad it almost slips out of them a million times before I get it to Penny. "Here. You good, now?" *Please be okay. I need to get out of here.*

She gives me a small smile before giving Gramps the pill. He seems to be better now, more like himself. He takes it before Penny tells him goodnight. We're to the door before he says, "Lucky? Bishop? I love you guys." And then he closes his eyes.

I love you guys… Maybe he wouldn't if he knew what I wanted to do with his pills.

"Follow me." Penny doesn't wait for my reply as she starts walking up the stairs. I feel like shit. I'm confused, ashamed, and on edge. My feet are begging to take me to Gary's again for my anxiety meds. Back in the house for Gramps…just to check on Gramps, but I follow her anyway up to a smaller set of stairs—almost like a ladder. She pushes open a door in the ceiling, and we crawl through into something the size of an apartment, but open with windows on all sides.

"What is this place?" I take in the open space, all the windows, and I bet if it wasn't black outside, we could see forever from up here. The walls are wood like everywhere else in the house, but there's actually carpet instead of worn plywood floors.

"Gramps built it for me after my dad died, but first I was too young and didn't want to be here alone, and now my room is close to where Gramps sleeps so I can listen for him."

There're a few blankets and stacks of massive pillows on the ground. She must come here often. Penny sits. Right as I'm about to ask her what just happened, she says, "Thanks... That was... Thanks."

I sit down next to her. "No problem. What's wrong with him?" I hate the words because I don't want anything to be wrong with him.

"Mild dementia. The beginnings of Alzheimer's. He's fine most of the time, but he loses it sometimes. I mean, he's okay a lot, but once in a while he isn't, and tonight... That's new."

"Damn. That sucks. I'm sorry. I didn't know."

She shrugs. There's a soft light in the corner giving me just enough lighting to see her. "He wouldn't want you to. It's hard. You know him. He's amazing. It kills me to see him lose himself like that." She blinks again before she pulls in this deep breath and tries to smile. Even now, she doesn't want me to think she's not tough.

"Yeah...me too." It also kills me to see her like this. To know that she's much more than the Snow Queen who has every guy in town wrapped around her finger. Which is bull because I've known that, but this takes it to a whole new level.

She pulls her knees up, resting her forehead in her hands for a moment before straightening. "How did the night get so screwed up?"

Damned if I don't wish I had the answer for her. All the answers to whatever she wants to know.

"The game was incredible and then the stupid party…and now Gramps. Ugh! Sometimes life sucks, ya know?"

Story of my life. "Yeah, I do know."

She turns to look at me. Her eyes are so blue, this wild shade that doesn't seem real, and it's like they can see through me, into me. And I want to see into her. To know what's inside her, but I don't. All I do know is I need to take away the pained look in them. To see them bright and happy like when we were on the snowmachines.

"Thanks." She glances down, almost embarrassed, and it does something to me because she's all strength and sure of herself, but *I'm* making her cheeks pink and making her tongue sneak out of her mouth to trace her bottom lip.

"You already said that."

And then she smiles, looking at me again. "You're such a jerk."

And damned if I know what comes over me, but I can't stop myself from leaning forward. From cupping her soft cheek and then pushing my hand through her white-blond hair. The light glimmers off and then I don't see, don't know anything else, but the feel of her lips as I cover them with mine.

She gives me a startled "Oh" and then opens up so I can slip my tongue inside. My lip ring presses against her mouth. She tastes sweet, but slightly salty like tears. Then her tongue is moving against mine, like she's trying to taste every part of me the way I want to taste every part of her.

I suck her lip into my mouth, before my tongue moves in to explore her again. Everything else is forgotten, only calm and need pushing me, making me lean forward to taste her deeper. One of my hands grabs her waist while the other slides behind her neck. Deeper, I want to get as deep as I can until suddenly her lips are gone.

"Bishop... I can't... Not... I just can't."

Penny gives me one last look and then she gets up and walks out.

Bishop Riley fucks up again. You'd think I'd be used to it by now.

Chapter Twelve

Penny

I sit in first period, wishing I could go home.

What's *wrong* with me? A guy I like kissed me. While sober. After helping with one of the worst nights of my life, and I said *I can't*?

My kisses so far include one with Mitch, which he didn't want, and a kiss that completely melted me from the inside out.

And *that* was the one I chose to reject?

I have some serious damage.

It was too much. Too soon. And Gramps—logically I know he's not going to get better, but his good days still make me hope. And then nights like last night crush any ideas I have of him going back to how he was before the dementia started.

But when I think about last night, Bishop sort of clouds over everything else. It's just that the kiss was *intense*. I didn't know how much he'd want. How far he'd want to go, and I panicked.

And without Bishop, where would I have been with Gramps? He wasn't listening to me at all, and Mitch never answered his text proving my theory that I've lost him in a way I didn't expect.

I pull in a deep breath, trying to clear my thoughts. I'll tell Bishop about why I backed away from his kiss after school, or at least hint that I'm all for doing it again. And try not to think about how I might have lost my best friend because he went from always being there to letting twelve hours go by without responding to my need for help.

The bell rings, and I jump. Crap. Good thing I don't need this class to graduate, because I have no idea what we talked about today.

"Penny?" Mitch's familiar voice crawls up my spine.

I don't stop moving. I was gearing up to talk to Bishop, not Mitch.

"Penny." He grabs my arm, spinning me around with this big, worried, sad face he does so well. "Is everything okay? I'm sorry, I—"

I pull my arm from him and start up the hall. "Check your texts, Mitch." If he gives me that sad face again, I'll give him a black eye. I hate it when he treats me like I'm fragile. It makes me feel breakable, which I despise. I'm not that girl. I'm the tough girl. The world needs both kinds, right? Only right now I feel like I could shatter.

"Penny." He touches my arm again from behind, but I jerk it away because facing Mitch right now might end in another wave of tears.

Three more steps to the stairs.

"Dammit! Penny!"

I start jogging down. Mitch is right on my tail. I spin before he grabs me and knock his arm away because I can't handle the kind of excuse he's about to give me.

"I just want to talk, okay?" His face is an even mix of the pity I hate and sadness.

"*Do* you?" This time it's me who steps toward him, and he backs up like I wanted him to, only I don't want to be arguing with him at all.

He shrugs with his armful of books. "I just got your text this morning. I'm so sorry, Pen."

I think about Gramps and the dancing and how for the first time Mitch didn't come when I called. "You left me," I whisper, only I didn't mean to. *The way Dad left me. The way Mom's leaving me now, and the way Gramps's memory is taking him away.*

"*I* left? Penny, you're the one who left the party." He pulls in a deep breath as he leans back. "Wait. We're talking about two different things. I think."

I try to shake my head, but I'm slowly going numb so I'm not sure if it works. "How long did it take you notice I was gone? I got home to a naked Gramps last night and you were the only person I knew to call. And you didn't answer."

He stares at me for a moment, absorbing everything. "Shit, sorry. I didn't check my phone until this morning. It's that I—"

"I don't want your excuses right now." I spin and walk

away.

"Penny," he pleads.

I grit my teeth. "Not. Right. Now."

I hear Mitch's books hit the ground about two seconds before his fist connects with the nearest locker.

Mitch's frustration or hurt or anger always ends in him bloodying his stupid knuckles. And he *should* feel bad. I feel hollowed out and horrible that he didn't answer when I needed him, but even as that thought goes through my head, I know it's more than missing one text. It's all the things that ran through my head at the party last night. How I'm losing him along with everyone else.

"I'm sorry, Penny," he calls. "Okay?"

I'm definitely not okay. Not yet.

· · ·

"Penny!" a girl yells from across the parking lot. It's hard to tell if it's an angry yell, or a get-my-attention yell. It's not like I have a lot, or really any girls that are friends, so I spin around.

Tiny little Rebecca's coming my way, her face flat. Not angry, not happy, just…confused. This is not what I need.

The snow's almost gone on the roadways now, and the slush is getting all over her shoes, but she doesn't seem to notice. This surprises me because she's someone who squeals at every tease, and the kind of person I'd expect to be worried about shoes.

But do I actually *want* to talk to Mitch's girlfriend knowing she probably knows about my freak-out in the stairway?

Not so much.

I jerk open my truck door, and she sprints to where I'm standing. "No! Wait!"

"I have nothing to say to you." I tighten my jaw but don't climb in. Why am I not climbing in?

"Yeah? Well have a whole lot to say to you." She sticks her chin out, but she's about six inches shorter than I am, so her action impresses me a bit because she's not backing down.

This whole situation is... It's just so cheesy teen movie ridiculous that I laugh.

She reaches out and pushes my truck door closed, stopping my laugh. *Whoa.*

Anger presses in where the hurt and fear and worry has been. "What do you want, Rebecca?" I'm tired and I'm thinking and feeling way too much for one person.

"I don't know where to start." But her manicured brows are pulled together in determination, and I'm not sure if I want to run away or wait this out.

"Why don't you start with why you're ruining your shoes just to talk to me?" I offer.

"Oh, shit." She stares at the ground for a moment.

And I know this is a jerk move, but I'm completely out of my comfort zone and I'm ready for it to be over. "Anytime today would be cool."

Rebecca bites her lip *again.* "I've lived under your shadow with him since we started dating. He talks about you all the time. I keep waiting for the day when he tells me he's in love with you. I've wanted to talk to you about it a million times, but I knew you'd probably laugh at me."

"Or give you a black eye." I keep my face straight, being kind of a bitch again, I know, but I don't know how to talk to her. I've always hung out with the boys—been the hockey girl. And to be honest with myself, I also want to see her reaction.

She takes a deep breath but holds her ground. I feel a random twinge of admiration when I really don't want to. "I really love him. A lot. And he was the one who asked if there was any chance I'd want to go to Michigan or Washington because he was leaving for hockey, and I never thought I'd get a shot at someone like him."

What? I lean against Bitty and take in Rebecca. Smooth curls today. Eyes huge with makeup. Dressed... Well, like she actually gives a crap. I figured a girl like her would *expect* to get a guy like him. I don't like that Rebecca's not fitting into the neat stereotype I put her in before now.

"And I keep waiting for it to all be some big joke, and he keeps coming back to me, and when he got detention over punching that locker during your fight, or whatever that was... Again. I thought he was about to walk away." She sniffs a few times before taking even breaths, and I almost tell her to hit something because it works better, but I hold it in.

Mitch walked away from me. *For her.* What does she want from me? She's got him already. "What do you want?"

"Please talk to him. It's making him crazy that he hurt your feelings. He said you needed help last night and he didn't know until it was too late. I know you don't care what things are like between Mitch and me, and I also know that me telling you to talk to a guy that I wish you weren't close to could seriously backfire…" Her words tumble over each other, and she actually looks serious. She cares if Mitch and I are getting along. Why is she being nice? Mitch's non-reply to my text stung, and now the niceness of Rebecca, and how I pushed away Bishop, and Gramps's episode all well up inside me. I can't cry in front of her. *Can't.*

I open the door of my truck. This is it. I have to get out of here. I should tell Rebecca she'll never have to worry about me and her guy, because last night was the final bit of proof that she definitely comes first in his world.

"Please, Penny." She grabs my door. "He's a grouchy ass right now, and it sucks knowing he's broken up over someone else."

"I gotta go," I say as I climb in my car.

"Yeah. Okay. Just… Please think about it, okay?" She looks down, and I shut the door between us, needing to be home. Away. On the ice. Anything.

Only now I start to get what Mitch sees in her. She's smart. Probably doesn't give him half as much shit as I would. And she wasn't afraid to come talk to me—that's something.

Plus, if I'm being honest with myself, my heart doesn't feel like it's cracking because I'm in love with Mitch—it's that we don't have the relationship I thought. He's leaving me behind, and like so many things in my life, I have no say in it. That's not Rebecca's fault, even though I want it to be.

I roll down my window. "I'll talk to him, okay?"

Her face snaps up, and relief fills her eyes. "Thank you,

Penny. Really. Thank you."

I open my mouth to say something else, but I don't how to do this girl talk stuff, so I mumble a "sure," roll up my window, and drive away.

The drive home takes forever, and I realize it's because I'm looking forward to seeing Bishop.

And then there's this wave of realization over how narrowing my sights on Mitch, who would never have me, has made me probably miss a lot of opportunities to be around kickass guys who maybe would.

I wonder if Bishop will be up for something today. Snowmachining or maybe he'd play drums for me, or we could go hang in the upstairs room or work on my car. As soon as I hit the driveway, I sprint to his cabin. Because I'm not the girl for most guys—not the kind of guys who would want to deal with me, at least—but *he* was the one who kissed *me*.

He pulls open the door with a smile and there's a girl behind him.

A girl.

I swear my gut hits the floor. She looks like… A girl's girl. A real girl. Like Rebecca but blond. And in every other way, the opposite of me. I can't breathe. No air. Chest still being pulled apart. Mitch saw me lose it today, and Rebecca nearly did. I don't need this.

"What's up, Penny?" He sounds like he's trying *way* too hard for his voice to be relaxed.

"You're busy. I'll go." Wow my voice sounds way more normal than I thought it would for someone who feels like she's drowning. Now I need to move, but I can't. It's like someone's put me on pause and slowed my world down—as if I really wanted *this* moment to last.

"I gotta take off for a bit." He shuffles his feet, looking nervous. "If um…Gary calls will you cover? Say I'm with you and that I fell asleep in front of the TV or something?"

I'm so stunned I'm not sure I'm breathing, and I'm still on pause. I need to not freak out for a minute longer because everything in me is splintering. I barely held on all day, and was excited to have the chance to see him, and now… Now I'm thinking I'll be the single girl who hangs with the guys, but doesn't actually date, for the rest of my life. I step back off his porch to go…I don't even know where.

"Penny?" he calls from behind me.

"Yeah. Fine. I have homework." My feet feel weird in the snow, like my body still isn't working right, and I begin to wonder if I'm totally overreacting.

Though, at this moment, I don't care because I have no idea how to shake this feeling.

I get that I walked away from him last night, but I expected he'd try again. That I'd at least have a chance to explain why I ran away. And now I'm offering to be his alibi so he can…*go somewhere* with a real girl. If we weren't making shitloads of money off these two—and if he hadn't helped me last night—there's no way I'd help him out right now. And I'm not totally decided that I will.

After what feels like an obscenely long walk across the yard, my insides chewing themselves up, I finally make it to the house and pull in a breath deep enough to force my chest to loosen. I'm such a raging idiot. Bishop. And me. The guy oozes something indefinably incredible—why on earth would he want me? Guys want "real" girls, even when they tell me that tough girls are hot. Because it's pretty obvious to me right now that I'm not what guys want.

Chapter Thirteen

Bishop

The urge to puke hits, and I actually have to fight it down. Last night I'd been all screwed up in the head. I couldn't believe I kissed her. Couldn't believe she told me no. Actually, what I can't believe is that it bothers me so much. She's just a girl, or should be anyway, so there's no reason I should have felt like someone kicked the crap out of me. No reason I should have sat behind my drums all night, beating out all my pent up energy, with nothing except Penny on the brain.

I should have just moved on.

So, I called Maryanne to make sure I did.

It felt right at the time, but now watching Penny walk away, I know it's wrong. Not because I think she wants me. She made it pretty obvious she didn't when she pushed me away, but because Alaska Bishop feels a little different than the other Bishop. Alaska Bishop kicks ass on the snowmachine, explores mines, fixes cars with Gramps, and watches Penny play hockey. Alaska Bishop may take something every few days, but it's only to keep him on track. He doesn't almost OD.

Maryanne knows the other me, not this one, and I don't think I can mix the two.

My head is so screwed up. There can't really be two me's.

"Who was that?" Maryanne snaps her gum, sounding bored. I'm sure she is. Even though she jumped on a plane to come here, this isn't Maryanne's kind of place. For her, it was an adventure, though. A way to hang out with me and party. Maryanne likes to party, and I like to party with her. Plus, it's one of the perks of money—of fame. The fact that all I had to do was buy a ticket and she was willing to come when I called her. That there's always someone willing to come.

"A friend," I tell her before closing the door.

"Bishop, are you hooking up with the locals?" she teases, trying to wrap her arms around me from behind, but I dodge her.

"Gary will be back soon. If this is going to work, we need to get out of here now." After walking over to the couch, I grab my bag. I can't believe I'm doing this while Gary's taking Troy to the airport. Can't believe I'm doing it at all.

"I'm still shocked they made you come here and sent you with a babysitter. That's such bullshit."

For a minute, I wonder if she remembers what happened to me. That she was there, laughing and dancing when I almost OD'd, but I don't because she's right. It is crap. Not that things aren't better here than I thought, but because they forced me. "It's not that bad. Like a vacation." We head out to her rental car.

On the way, I text Gary to tell him I'm with Penny. Tightness runs the length of me again, thinking about her. I feel like such a jerk, but I'm not even sure if I should or not. I guess the fact that I do should tell me something. Like I should stop and go back. Tell Maryanne to take the car back to the airport so she can go home. So I don't fuck up again.

I lean back in the seat and think about Gramps, wondering if he remembers what happened last night. If things will be weird the next time I see him. Maybe it'll be like tit for tat. He keeps my secrets, and I keep his. Not that his Alzheimer's is a secret, but I'm pretty sure it's not something he wants to talk about.

"You're awful quiet. You're not usually like this."

Maryanne reaches over and squeezes my leg. I try to smile at her but can't quite make it happen. I feel the beginnings of panic grip my insides, little scratches from nails threatening to slice me open. I don't know why, what I have to be freaked out about, but it's there, trying to claw to the surface. Maybe I *do* need a night of Maryanne to clear my head.

"You got anything to drink?"

Maryanne reaches into her huge purse and hands me a water bottle. I twist off the top and down the whole thing, which helps a little.

"Do you have any smokes?" She glances at me.

"Nah. I'm trying to quit." Just since last night, but whatever. That's what makes me suddenly realize what's different. Why I'm so freaked out. The Bishop Maryanne knows smokes. That doesn't feel like who I should be here. When I'm with Maryanne, we party. Partying is different than taking a pill every couple of days like I do in Alaska. The last time I partied, I almost died. Almost left Mom alone.

I don't want to go back to that night.

"Wow…that's new."

If she knew me, she would know it's not. I've always hated smoking. I just do it.

Finally, we pull into a tiny, hole-in-the-wall hotel. "Nice place," I say, trying to chill out.

"Whatever. You're the one who dragged me to this crappy town."

Her words make me frown, but Maryanne gets out of the car and leads me to her room.

It's about the same size as my cabin only not as nice. It's got a cheap picture on the wall and an old blanket on the bed. The TV looks like it's fifty years old. Dust flies up when I sit in the chair by the window.

Now what?

My leg starts bouncing and I start drumming my hands on my knees, wishing I was back at the cabin with my drums instead of here.

"Relax, Bishop. Damn, you're wound up tight." She tosses her bright pink bag on the bed and does the hair flip thing girls do. It's blond, but all I can think of is it's not the right blond. It looks fake. Maybe not fake, but not as…pure as Penny's, and then I feel like an idiot for thinking things like that about her. I shouldn't be thinking about her at all.

"You got anything?" Maryanne asks.

She doesn't even have to specify what she's talking about. Even though I just drank the water, I feel thirsty again. "Nope. Your stuff hasn't come. You?"

The memory of holding Gramps's pill bottles makes my palms itch. I squeeze my hands into fists, trying to forget. Trying to focus on my drums, working on the Corvette, and snowmachining with Penny.

The girl is exhausting. In a good way.

When I kissed her, it felt so fucking awesome I thought she had to be feeling it, too. But really it was just a screw up, since she obviously wasn't. And then I got back to my cabin, and the whole night came crashing back down around me. The hockey game. How it felt to hold Gramps's pills. The kiss. Back and forth between kissing and pills, kissing and pills. I hadn't been able to turn my brain off until I called Maryanne. She'd be able to help. She always had.

"Now, Bishop… What kind of question is that?" She winks at me before she opens her bag. "I have a bottle of vodka."

I want to tell her to stop.

I want to tell her to hurry up.

Not understanding either of the reactions, I try to ignore them and let her do what she wants to do.

Maryanne pulls a bottle out of her bag, shaking a couple pills out before she tosses them into her mouth and sucks down water from another bottle.

Both my legs are moving, and both my hands are drumming, and my heart is trying to find the same rhythm as my hands and my legs, and it all feels like too much.

And not enough at the same time.

"What'cha got?" I push to my feet, walk over, and sit on the bed. A little voice whispers that I should go—this nagging sense of wrongness overwhelms me. I'm so sick of feeling guilty for everything.

After grabbing the bottles, I fumble them in my hands. Then I read each one until I find what I want. My hands tremble as I shake three pills out.

Maryanne tries to hand me the vodka, but I grab the water. See? That's good. If I had a problem I'd drink the vodka. I look at the pills. Take another drink. Glance at the pills again.

Fuck it.

I toss all three in my mouth and swallow.

I expect the hyperactive limbs to slow, but they don't. Expect to feel better, but *I* don't. I'm still thinking about Gramps and Penny and that stupid guilt still spreading like a disease inside me.

Trying to relax, I lean against the headboard of the bed and grab the remote to the ancient TV. News blares through the speakers, and they're talking about hockey, which makes me think about Penny and how awesome and motivated she is. She wants to play on a men's team. That's pretty incredible. My guilt spreads even faster, so I turn the station.

"What's wrong with you, B.R.? Did they give you a lobotomy here or something?" She laughs, and I try to do the same, but it doesn't happen. This isn't me—this fucked-up, conflicted feeling cementing inside me. I pick up the vodka. Maybe I just need a drink to relax.

Before I get a chance, Maryanne takes matters into her own hands, crawling onto the bed and then straddling my lap. Her short skirt pulls high up her legs. "I know what will make you feel better."

She leans forward, but I again notice her hair is the wrong color, and she smells like cigarettes. Penny *hates* that smell, and now that I think about it, I do, too.

Maryanne's lips come toward me. I've kissed them before. I've done more than that with her and liked the way it felt, but this time, I turn my head, her mouth landing nowhere near its destination.

She isn't deterred, though, her lips just making a trail toward my mouth and this time, I don't stop her. Penny said she *can't* so there's no reason I shouldn't.

My mouth opens and Maryanne's tongue slides inside. Now I not only smell cigarettes but I taste them. Gramps would give me hell. So would Penny. And Gary.

This feels wrong. *I* feel wrong, so I turn away from her.

"Bishop?" She doesn't sound hurt, just confused.

"I can't." Penny's words from last night are now coming out of my mouth. It's almost like an out-of-body experience. Why am I being this way? It's just kissing Maryanne. It's not a big deal.

"Sorry, I'm just not in the mood." I lift Maryanne from my lap before getting off the bed myself. My gut is cramping up. I'm not sure if it's in my head or not. "I'm not feeling so well."

I close the bathroom door behind me before splashing water on my face. It helps a little, waking me up and shocking me into reality. My body has that light, floaty feeling it always gets when I'm high, but I can't tell if I like it or not.

Then I'm back in the main room again. "Listen... I think I better get back."

She just rolls her eyes. "Whatever, Bishop. You're losing it, you know that?"

Right now, I'm thinking she should be pissed, or at least care a little bit. Blake might be right. Would she be okay with anything just to be around me?

I'm not sure if I'm losing it or finding it, so I nod. When she tells me she wants to go back to L.A., I get on my phone and buy her a plane ticket. We drive back toward the cabins in silence. When we're almost there, I tell her to pull over so I can walk the rest of the way in. My body sort of relaxes at the thought, and I realize I'm not only walking so we don't get caught, but maybe because I need it. "I'm sorry about this. I just have a lot going on."

"It's okay. I've never been to Alaska. Got me out of town for a day." She shrugs. "Call me when you get back and we'll chill."

I nod. When I'm back home with her, things will be different. I'll be normal.

I actually feel pretty good about myself right now, like I did the right thing. Then, Maryanne pulls out a baggy, with about ten pills inside. "I brought these for you, since the package never came."

Don't do it. Don't do it.

Why shouldn't I do it? Why am I suddenly worried? I reach out and grab it before stuffing them in my boot. "Thanks."

Get out of the car. Close the door. Watch her drive away. One foot in front of the other. Walk. That's what each step feels like—a checklist of activities, and I'm not really doing them.

The baggy scratches my leg with each pace. There's a direct line from the spot it touches me to my brain, making it all I think about.

I stop, pull the bag out, and count them. Twelve. I was wrong. There are twelve pills. Now that I know how many are there, I push them back into my boot and walk again.

Sucking in a deep breath, I try to focus on the cold air, look at the trees, and remember the feel of grease on my hands. My mind flashes to Penny and her white-blond hair, and riding snowmachines, and working with Gramps.

I pass the driveway and keep going. Keep breathing and thinking. Soon, I don't feel the scratch of the baggy anymore, though I know it's there. The more I walk, the clearer my head becomes. On and on, I keep going, struggling to let it all go— to find that peace Gary tells me I have.

And then…there it is. I find it and wish like hell it will last.

Chapter Fourteen

Penny

So yesterday I was at school all bent over Mitch, and today I'm bent over Bishop. At least I'm headed to the rink. I left last period early for some time alone on the ice. Coach is going to bust our asses this week, but I'm looking forward to it. It's not like anything else awesome is happening right now. This is the last week of high school hockey, and the harder I work, the better the distraction is.

"Got a sec?" Mitch hollers across the ice.

After moping last night over…pretty much everything, I really just want to skate. But I slide to a stop in front of him anyway because I need one awkward part of my life to not be awkward anymore. "What's up?"

"Knowing you, I have about thirty seconds, so I'm going to spit it out."

Now that I've decided to let him talk, everything in me is still and waiting to hear what he has to say.

He shoves his hands in his pockets. Obviously nervous. "I love you, Penny. Like a sister. Like my best friend. Like if I'd seen your text, even though I haven't seen Becca outside of school in forever, I would have come to help. My phone was on the counter, and I hate that I didn't know you needed me."

I nod once because this is what we do as a team. Explain. Get over it. Move on. "Okay."

His head tilts to the side. "Okay?"

My chest loosens in a way it hasn't since Matt's party. It's not perfect, but it's better enough that I know we'll eventually be good. For real. "Get your gear on or you're going to be late. And yes. We're okay." I push away from the wall to keep warming up.

Mitch will never be mine like he is Rebecca's, and now that it's done, it doesn't hurt the way I thought it would. Like the idea of us together was my constant but not a reality I actually wanted. Crazy, but I think it took facing Rebecca and kissing Bishop to figure it out. An ache spreads from my chest at the thought of seeing Bishop with another girl. I suck in a breath and try to dispel the pain. I need to keep skating. Two laps and my brain is still spinning over the girl and Bishop, but when two laps turn into fifteen, into twenty, my head is finally starting to clear. At least a little.

Rebecca steps into the team box as I come around the corner and waves. She's biting her stupid lip again.

I slide to a stop, trying to be nice and forcing myself to recognize that she has more balls than I've given her credit for. "What's up?"

She shrugs her tiny shoulders. "Just came to watch you guys practice."

"Why?" I'm actually curious.

"'Cause it's really important to Mitch, and I want to understand that about him." She flicks a chunk of brown hair over her shoulder.

She wants to understand him, and she should. He deserves that anyway. "Then you need to be on the ice."

Her eyes widen. "Oh. No. No way. I don't skate. Like. At all."

I scan the area until I spot Rick, the rink owner, and then wave him over. "I'm serious. Coach doesn't get here for another fifteen minutes." I'm so full of good deeds. Seriously. "Rick! Get this girl some hockey skates!"

Her brows go up. "No. Penny. *Please.*"

I laugh. "I won't hurt ya."

Rick drops a few sizes on the bench next to us, and Rebecca just stares, uncertain.

Mitch practically sprints out of the locker room, only half geared-up and shirtless, looking between us with panic. Someone must have told him I was talking to his girlfriend.

I point my stick at Mitch. "I make *no* such promises to him."

He honestly looks scared as hell, which is ridiculous. It's not like I'm going to put her in skates just to knock her down. I shake my head like he's being stupid, and he nods because he knows me well enough to catch my meaning—*calm the hell down.*

He backs up a few steps without a word before turning and heading to the locker room. Just as I finish showing Rebecca how to tighten the stiff laces, Mitch reappears fully geared up, showing me that he's maybe not as chill as I want him to be. At least not yet.

His brows knit together as I skate away, leaving him with Rebecca, who's still staring uncertainly at the skates on her feet.

After a few minutes of Rebecca stumbling and slipping on her own, Mitch's arms are around her waist and he's skating backwards. Fast. She's just staring up at him with her girlie googlie eyes trusting that he'll keep her safe. I guess that's what Mitch wants. He couldn't handle a girl who isn't afraid to harass him. Mitch accepts who I am, but I feel like Bishop actually likes it. I didn't realize there was even a difference before now. It makes the whole blond girl situation that much worse. Maybe I just suck at reading people.

Mitch lifts Rebecca up on the side where the team benches are and stands between her legs for a kiss. She runs her hands through his hair, keeping their faces together, and I might be all charitable and nice about some things, but I'm not *that* nice. I hold in a smile as I flip Mitch's skate with my stick, almost sending him to the ice.

"What the hell, Penny!" he yells, grins wide, and scrambles to his feet. I push hard on the ice to get away, and we're back to status quo.

"I said I'd be nice to *her*, not you!"

And just as Mitch races my way to retaliate the way we all

do with each other, Coach hits the ice.

Time for what's probably going to be the best part of my day.

Rebecca's smile splits her face as she climbs off the wall and onto the team bench. And I hate admitting this, but I've got to give the girl props for getting out on the ice.

I guess Mitch could do worse.

· · ·

When I step upstairs into the kitchen, Mom and Gramps are watching some cheesy sitcom, and Gramps looks completely zoned. It makes me wonder how much of his meds he's on today. I hate it when she does that—it seems like cheating. Like she drugs him up so she doesn't have to worry, but it robs him of getting to be himself. I'd never do that unless I had to. I'd rather Gramps make ten steak and strawberry pies than watch reruns of Seinfeld all day while zombied in front of the TV.

"Hey, honey!" Mom smiles too wide and wanders to the table. "We got pizza. Is that okay?"

"Fine." I pause at the table and want to ask why she's home, but instead I just say, "Haven't seen you in a while. Must be busy."

"Yep. Been busy." This is her way of agreeing with me without opening up for anything further.

I wanted her to say something more personal than business or schools or hockey so I can, because part of me is dying to talk to someone. Irritation sets me on edge.

I pull open the box and grab two slices, not really wanting to see my mom if the conditions are a drugged up Gramps, a closed-off Mom, and bad comedy reruns. "I'm sore. Going to jump in the hot tub."

Her nod and smile feels forced, and I'm not sure when things got so weird. "Okay. Not too late."

I have to bite my tongue to ask why she cares how late I'm in the tub because she isn't here most nights. But I hold it in. Yep. Good deeds. I'm still on a roll. "Thanks for the pizza."

I stack my two slices and run downstairs before Mom starts in on more questions. Maybe I do like her new schedule.

After quickly slipping into my suit, grabbing a soda, and jerking off the hot tub cover, I slip into the nearly scalding water. Better. Feels like I'm practically living in the hot tub these days, which is fine. The cold air bites at my face, but the steam from the tub keeps me from freezing. The stars tonight are incredible—tiny dots of light in a black sky. I keep hoping for the Northern Lights, but it's probably not cold enough.

I close my eyes and try not to listen to the drumming coming from Bishop's cabin. Try not to picture how in the zone he is when he's playing. Try not to think about how cool it would be if he was playing for me. Or how the blonde feels about him playing for her. But then it stops. I try not to notice that either. My body floats, and I let it. Let my body hover in the center of the huge tub.

"Hey." Bishop's voice is close.

I don't jump. Don't move. Don't open my eyes. I don't want to do anything to show him how happy I am he's here because I should be more pissed than relieved. But I'm not. "What do you want?"

"What are you so pissed about?" he asks.

"You want a list, or do you just want to thank me for not ratting you out to your babysitter?"

"He's not my—" But then he stops.

"That's what I thought." I let the corner of my mouth pull up but still keep my eyes closed. I don't want to look at his brown eyes. I don't want to look at the guy whose lips were on mine, and who I turned away. I don't think I have the guts to tell him about Mitch when it doesn't matter anyway, because Bishop already has someone. "Where's your girlfriend?" I even keep the snotty out of my voice and try to sound bored.

"She's not at all my girlfriend."

I finally sit up and open my eyes, try not to notice the very nice shape of him in the dim light of the porch, and raise a brow.

"Okay. I mean…," He hangs his head for a second before his eyes find mine again. "Fuck, Penny. Why are you so hard on me?"

No way I'm letting him turn this back to me. "I'm not. I asked a very simple question."

His face falls as our eyes stay focused on one another.

"I screwed up. I was pissed and lonely and I called her."

Right. Now's when I should tell him to leave. Instead, I close my eyes and once again relax deep into the tub, resting my head on the edge. If he wants to take this as a fuck-off, he can. If not, he can keep digging himself in a hole.

"I didn't… We weren't gone long. Practically just turned around and came back."

Practically. I wonder what happened during that "practically." I hate that the thought of it hurts, and I hate how happy I am that he's out here talking to me because it's dangerous to like someone this way. Mitch proved it. And Bishop proved it last night. "Whatever. It's not like I have any claim on you or anything."

He takes a deep breath. "You can."

I can. I can have a claim on him? Does this mean that he wants me to? Is he trying to move forward again? I don't move, but open my eyes. Damn, he's not playing fair—looking vulnerable again. But I have too many questions to let it go. *It shouldn't matter. I shouldn't care.*

"So, did you just hang out with her long enough to get laid?" I close my eyes and slump again, trying to seem disinterested when in reality, I'm holding my breath waiting for his answer.

It's so silent he must be frozen. "I didn't sleep with her, but she kissed me."

"Did you want her to?" My heart's banging in my chest, making his drums seem like kid toys. I should not be reacting like this.

"No. And she's gone now. Back home. I mean, I only sort of kissed her back—"

"So, it doesn't count or something?" I swear guys have an excuse for every stupid-ass thing they do.

He slides his fingers across his lip ring again. "Damn, I

don't know. *Does* it count?"

I let the silence hang between us for a moment. "Depends on how you felt about it, I guess."

"I sent her home." His voice is quiet. "I'm here next to you. That's how I felt about it. *Feel* about it."

Something in not just his words but his tone makes me feel like I should share something. "The night—" *you kissed me,* is what I almost say. "The night Gramps had a hard time, and all that. I was at the party, and I realized Mitch doesn't and won't like me the way I thought I liked him. It's weird because things between us have been confusing for a long time, even though I thought I knew what I wanted from him. The other night with you... My head was a mess, and I ran."

"I've been known to ruin girls for all other guys." All it takes is one narrow-eyed look from me, and he laughs. "I'm kidding. Sorry, Penny."

There's a bit of silence between us, like he's processing, and maybe I am, too. Processing that some hot girl flew all the way up here to see him, didn't have sex with him, and then turned around and left. *Who is this guy?*

"I should also tell you that I was even nice and didn't kick Mitch's girlfriend's ass when she stalked me out."

"That was cool of you. I had no idea you knew how to exercise self-control."

Bishop's grin is immediate, and the moment our eyes connect, it softens, pooling warmth in my stomach.

He shifts his weight, but his eyes don't leave mine. "So... were you really into him?"

Despite the hot water, I shiver under his gaze. I've never responded to a guy just *looking* at me. Not this way.

"I don't know. I thought I was, but maybe I wasn't. We've been so close for so long that I think I just assumed we'd be together—and I thought I would like it. Then we weren't, and I was confused. I think…" I let my words trail off as my thoughts form in my head. Different puzzle pieces snap into place, and they make a truth I never realized was there.

"You think what?" Bishop scratches his neck like he's nervous.

"This is going to make me sound a little pathetic, but I think it's because I didn't want him to leave me. He was leaving me for her and…that freaks me out. Being left does." Not only can I not wrap my brain around this new piece of information, but also that I admitted it to Bishop. "God, I can't believe I'm telling you this."

He blinks a few times like he's absorbing what I just said. *I'm* absorbing what I just said. Before he even speaks, I know he's going to say something else that makes me know he understands.

"You can handle anything. It's crazy how strong you are. He wouldn't leave you, but if he did, you'd show the world you didn't need him. I've never known anyone like you." He rubs a hand over his face like he's also thinking he's revealed too much.

"Bishop…"

He shakes his head. "Can we not? I just wanted you to know that, okay?"

Honestly, I'm not sure what to say, so it's probably smart to let it drop.

Still part of me wants to ask a million questions about the girl, and part of me just has a million questions about him. "I know nothing about you except you're not half-bad on a snowmachine, you can beat the shit out of a set of drums, and you seem to see things in me people I've known my whole life don't. Want to fill me in on anything else?"

He runs a hand through his hair again and looks down, frowning. "I have a lot going on, but when we hang out, you kind of make me forget about the rest of it."

Am I flattered? Being used? More insecure than I should be? "You didn't really answer me."

"I know." He sighs. "I'm here because I have to be, but I wouldn't change it. Is that enough for now?"

"Maybe. I guess." I sit up on the edge, needing to cool off after being low in the water for so long. Steam rises from my body, and I watch him watch me as I move. There is no way he's not checking me out. Okay. I need to shake off whatever girl he had up here because I don't need another thing to over-think. I'm ready to just *be*. "If I'm so good for you, then strip down and get your ass in here."

"Yes, ma'am." His face loosens enough for a smile to hit the edges. It's the first time he's actually agreed to come in.

Guess we're okay. Or maybe just back to where we were before the kiss, and the California blonde pop-in.

I openly stare as he strips down. Drummers are hot. He's seriously toned in all the right places, and in about a minute he's down to his boxers.

Tight sides. Great arms. Impressive shoulders. Touchable abs, and he doesn't have chicken legs. The tattoo on his side is drumsticks, big and in an "X."

He must *really* like drums.

"Damn, it's cold." He half-jumps into the water, sitting across from me, and I'm still just watching, letting the steam float off my body. "What'cha looking at, Penny?"

"Oh, please. Like you didn't watch me slide out?" I lower myself back into the water. "I like your tat." *And might be thinking about touching you.*

"Thanks."

"Man of few words." I push his calf with my foot, needing to touch him.

"Girl of many smart-ass remarks." He leans back until his hair is wet.

I watch him and know that the only other guy I've had in here that I wanted my hands on was Mitch. If Bishop kissed me right now, I'd definitely kiss him back. There's no way to scoot closer without it being obvious. And maybe I should. Show him I'm okay with it. But maybe I just suck at being a girl, and I'm not someone he'd want to deal with anyway.

I can't sit here in silence with him, though. Not if we're not kissing. "I've wanted a tattoo since I turned eighteen. Just before Christmas." I want to touch his, but I'm not sure where we stand even though I'd like to be on his lap, so I keep my hands to myself.

"Do it… Let me take you to get one, Penny Jones."

Excitement rushes through me at the thought of it. "What, *now*?"

"I'm sure you know who runs a tattoo parlor around here. Maybe someone to do it for free or for a Penny discount or something," he teases.

In a few words, his whole face has changed. The way he holds himself, even though he's underwater, is different.

"You're lighter." The words just come out.

He nods, his face a shade more serious than it was a moment ago. "A little… I want to be."

"I don't know what I am yet." I wait for him to say something profound. Something that puts all this crap in perspective.

He winks, smiles and slides lower in the water. "You're a girl who's going to get inked with me."

I laugh and move as low in the tub as he did, letting my chin touch the surface. I pull my feet out to rest them on the sides of the tub next to Bishop. Part of me is curious to see if he'll touch me while I'm there.

His gaze travels up my calves like I hoped they would, and then his brow gets all wrinkled. "Damn, Penny."

"What?"

"That's a killer bruise on your knee."

I pull my leg out of the water, and his fingers rest on the edge of the purple mass, sending jolts through my body. Holy shit, touching a guy has never felt this good, and that's really saying something because I'm around them a lot. What else can I get away with?

"You should see the one on my side." I stand and turn for

him to see the blue/purplish and yellow-at-the-edges bruise on the top of my hip. The one I have to nudge my bottoms down a little for him to see. "That was courtesy of Chomps."

Bishop traces the edge of my bruise, letting his fingers linger.

My breathing stops.

The heat from my body is fogging up the air.

No one speaks.

He clears his throat twice before speaking. "Any more?"

I rest my foot on the seat next to him to show him the inside of my thigh where I got caught on the edge of the goal. My body's going weak on me again as his fingers slide up my thigh from my knee. His eyes follow the trail, and my leg is going wobbly at his touch.

"Penny!" Mom yells.

I jump, Bishop's hands splash back into the water, and we both exhale at the same time.

She's leaning from the second story window. Her voice has that forced brightness to it that says *I'm the friendly mom* to my friends, but it tells me she isn't happy about Bishop's hands on me.

"Yes?" I say with equally forced sweetness as I step back and sit down, much farther away from Bishop than I'd like to be.

"Not too late!"

I wave and grin to make her close the window and leave me alone. "She's never here, and now she's trying to be like super-mom or something."

Bishop swallows, watching me with the same want in his eyes that he had while touching my leg. "Guess that's our night then."

I'm hoping he doesn't want it to be the end of our night, because I definitely wish it wasn't. I stand and get out before the pull to him makes me do something else really stupid. Like kiss him. Or give myself another bruise for him to touch, which I'm seriously considering.

"Is it cool if I stay in for a few?" he asks. "I don't think I'm hot enough to keep my balls from freezing when I run back to my cabin."

I point to the cover without looking at him because it makes me want too much. "Just pull up the top."

"I can do that."

Once again, we stare at each other like there are a million things we both want to do and say, but neither of us makes the move.

I tighten my towel around me and stuff my feet in my boots. Best to get out of here before I make an ass out of myself, or we end up in a tangled mess in the hot tub in front of my oddly-present mother. "So, I'll see you tomorrow for my tattoo, unless you flake out on me."

"I'll be here." He turns but then stops and faces me again. "And Penny? I'm sorry…about everything."

Yeah. Me, too.

I had hoped to get inside and to bed without another confrontation. Unfortunately, Mom has different ideas.

She crosses her arms as she leans against the door to my

room.

"Yes?" I grip my towel tightly as I step around her to change out of my swimsuit.

"I'm not sure I'm comfortable with you being in the hot tub with a boy."

I snort. "Mom. I've never, ever been in a hot tub *without* a boy unless I was alone."

Mom sighs, and I pull out clean underwear and pajamas, wanting to rinse off in the shower so I can go to bed.

She's rubbing her forehead and frowning when she finally finds more words. "But I know your teammates, Penny. It's different."

"And you invited Bishop and Gary to stay here on our off-season and told me to be nice." I widen my eyes, daring her to contradict me.

Instead of fighting back, she pauses for a moment. "What do you know about Bishop?" And the way she says it makes me think she knows a lot more than she's told me. I'm dying to ask her, but I don't want to admit that I barely know anything about him, except how he makes me feel. I can't imagine that helping my case for hanging with him in the hot tub, so I turn to snark. "Bishop Ripe, from California. Spoiled, surly guy who thinks he can work on cars, and thinks he can ride snowmachines—"

"You took him *riding*?" Mom brows shoot up. "Penny. We don't have insurance for guests to do that!"

"Mom. Chill." I sit on the bed, feeling stupid for not even thinking about that. "He's a friend, that's all. I wasn't thinking, okay?" I sometimes hate the renting cabins business, but it does bring in some good cash. And she's right. One lawsuit over a broken arm would probably destroy us.

"Friends don't touch each other like he was touching you." Mom's jaw tightens. "I don't see the guys on your team doing that."

I can't answer her because it would involve thinking about things I don't want to think about right now. "You're never here, Mom. What's going on?"

She sighs and I swear looks guilty again somehow, staring at the floor but doesn't speak.

"Fine." I move past her for my shower. "You get to meddle in my life, but I can't ask about yours."

"Penny." Mom's voice has a pleading edge to it that I won't understand until she starts talking, which I can tell she won't. "You know that's not fair."

I'm still so amped up from everything I've been feeling over the past few days that I'm all out of patience. "You're right." Anger pours through me as I step closer. "It's not fair that I've missed the last two team parties because you were working and Gramps was having a hard night. It's not fair that I was told to be nice to the people staying here, and now you're upset about it. It's not fair that when I felt completely rejected by Mitch, my mom wasn't around to talk to."

Her jaw drops. "Honey... I'm so sorry, I—"

"I'm done." I take the three steps to my bathroom. "Night."

Closing the door isn't solving anything but my need to get away, and right now, that's enough. Why couldn't the last thing to happen to me before I tried to go to sleep was Bishop touching my bruise instead of this?

Chapter Fifteen

Bishop

"Do you know that I'm proud to be here with you?" Gary leans back against the couch while I fidget next to him.

"Why would you be proud of that?"

"I hate that we *need* to be here, but I'm honored to work through this with you. Like I was honored with Troy or when I got my degree."

Ah. I see where he's going with this. Opening my mouth, I almost tell him this is stupid. All these talks are lame, but that's not what comes out. "I'm proud of how I play the drums...of working with Gramps, being friends with Penny, and taking care of my mom." *Which I can't do if I'm dead...*

"That's good. You should be proud of all those things. You take good care of her. Don's talked to me about it a little bit."

The hairs on the back of my neck rise, but I drum my thumbs and try to settle down. It makes sense they would all know my dad's a prick. That there's a restraining order and secret money involved so he leaves us the fuck alone. "She's always taken care of me. It's the least I can do."

Gary nods and keeps talking. For the first time, we discuss my anxiety a little bit, how I feel and how often it happens. I'm sure he thinks it stems from my dad, but I don't. I don't think…

It's a struggle to make the answers come out, but I manage it. He was right. This talk is more than trees and cold air. But…my gut doesn't ache and I don't feel like I've downed a ton of uppers.

When the time is up, I stop at the door. "I'm going to be out with Penny for a bit."

He nods. "You know the rules."

"Yep."

Halfway out the door, Gary's voice stops me. "Hey, Troy's counselor tells him he should try to do one thing every day he's proud of. It can be something little, like opening the door for someone or doing someone a favor. And when you do, let yourself revel in that. Congratulate yourself. Think you can do that?"

My fist tightens on the doorknob. After what happened with Maryanne, I'm not sure I deserve it. "I don't know."

• • •

I watch Penny as she walks along the wall, looking at tattoo designs for the millionth time. I'm not feeling anxious. Don't want to push her into hurrying because I like watching her. She moves so smoothly, and I know that's not something I'm supposed to notice or not something I would have noticed before, but it reminds me of the way she skates, or rides the snowmachines, or hell, the way she does anything. All fluid movements, but with a practiced perfection that I know is all automatic with her.

The tattoo guy sees it, too.

I want to break his nose.

"You're slow as hell." I stop right behind her. When my hands start shaking this time, it's not because of anxiety, but because I want to touch her. We haven't talked anymore about the kiss, or Loverboy, whose nose I suddenly want to break, but that doesn't stop me from putting my hands on her shoulders, pretending I'm doing it to knead her muscles, when really I just want her skin beneath mine. She shivers.

Fuck, this girl is going to my head.

She said last night that I'm lighter, and though I still feel like weights are tying me down, I *do* feel more weightless when I'm with her. I want to hold onto that feeling even though I know everything else is still there, still threatening to pull me under. Shit, Maryanne came up, and I only took a couple pills *and* didn't drink. That has to count for something.

That's not the kind of thing I want to be proud of.

Maybe my talk with Penny last night could be, though. I think maybe I helped her. She trusted me to talk to me, and that means something.

"This is a serious decision, Ripe. You want to see me get inked, you're going to have to learn some patience." She turns around, which makes my hands fall off her.

"Don't call me that," tumbles out of my mouth. She looks at me like she's trying to figure me out, and I move my head, hoping she can't. It makes me feel like an asshole, but I'm not sure she'll like what she sees. Suddenly, I'm not sure I like what I see.

"It's your name." She nudges me.

"My name is Bishop." And then, because I want to kiss her, or because I need a little space because the way I'm acting is actually starting to freak me out, I step around her. "What about a flower? Girls are supposed to like flowers, right?" Like I knew she would, she gives me a dirty look.

"I'm going to pretend you didn't say that." She crosses her arms and clips me with her hip, and even though I thought I wanted space, I reach out and grab her waist. She sucks in a gasping breath before saying, "You're getting awfully touchy-feely there, Bishop. I don't remember saying you could put your hands on me."

Another weight drops free and sinks away. Leaning forward, my cheek touches hers. "If you don't want me to, tell me to stop." She still smells like vanilla and like her car, too. Who would have thought that could smell so hot? And I love how even though she's tall, even though she's a fucking *hockey* player, her body still feels fragile under my hands.

"You're cocky." She slips away from me and starts looking at the walls again. Looking at the same designs over and over again. "I don't see anything. I'm not marking my skin unless it's something really incredible."

"Wussing out?" This time, it's me who smirks at her.

"No, I have standards."

Ouch. I'm not sure if that's directed at me or not, so I ignore it. "I get it. That's why I only have one so far. I love ink, but I'm not putting something on my body that I'm not sure I'll want there forever. Like my drumsticks, no matter what happens, I know music will always be a part of me…so far, that's the only thing I'm sure of." I shrug. Maybe I'm being obvious and said too much, but it's true.

"You have trust issues, don't you?"

Laughing, I shake my head. "How did you get that out of what I just said?" But she's right. I don't have to answer her because both of us know it's true. "Now hurry up. If you don't decide, we're not going to have time to do this, and then I'm going to start thinking you did it on purpose because you're…" Again, I lean forward so my mouth is right next to her ear. "Scared."

She shoves me away and I almost trip over a chair, but I'm laughing too hard to care.

• • •

"Are you sure you want one there?" I ask. "It hurts like hell."

She's picked this feather design that breaks apart and will spread small birds across her ribs.

Penny climbs up onto the padded table and rolls her eyes at me. "I get my ass kicked on the ice every day. I think I can handle it." Then she looks at the tat guy. "I have a game coming up, so we can't let it be really big. I don't want it to screw me up on the ice."

"Cool. I'll shrink it down so it's only a few inches." He does and comes back to show her. She has to lift her shirt while they place in on her ribs. "Like this?" he asks her.

I think I'm going to like the view.

"If you sneak a touch, I break your finger."

Hell yeah. That's my girl. I look over at her tattoo guy and give him a cocky grin. He just rolls his eyes. She's lying down now on her left side and facing me. Her shirt tucked beneath her breasts. I've seen her stomach before—seen a lot of them, but I can't help myself from admiring the dip in her waist. The flatness of her stomach. And yeah... I want to touch. Want to touch so bad my fingers hurt. "You ready for this? For a needle to poke into your skin thousands of times, over each of your ribs?"

"Wow. You sound super traumatized over this. Did you cry when you got yours, Bishop?" The needle makes its first contact with her skin as she taunts me, but I'm pretty sure she's too busy talking crap to me to notice. It's what I wanted. There's only one little flinch before she adds, "I bet you did. Bet you cried like a baby."

"Always talking shit. You can't think a *girl* is tougher than I am, can you?" It's so fun pissing her off. And I wasn't kidding when I said tats on your side hurt. It's not that I don't think she can handle it, because I'm pretty sure she can handle anything, but I'm hoping the distraction helps.

I'm sitting in a chair, eye level with her as she lies on the table. Her skin is puffy and red as the needle stabs into her, but she's doing awesome. Keeping still and not flinching at all.

"So, tell me about this hockey stuff. How'd you get into it?"

"My dad played. Just local teams, pick-up games. 'Old-man hockey' is what they call it here. He's been on the ice since high school. It was the thing we did together. That, and all the guys said I'd never make it. So, you know. I *had* to then. And when I was out there proving them wrong, I fell in love with it." She pulls in a deep breath as the guy takes a short break, leaning back and stretching his shoulders and neck. "So, what about you? What started you with music?"

I check out tattoo guy. He's not paying attention to us. I'm almost 100 percent sure he doesn't recognize me, and if he does, he's not talking. I screw with my lip ring for a minute, trying to figure out how to reply. This is dangerous territory to navigate. Trying to decide what to say and it sucks because I actually want to talk to her about it. It means bringing up my asshole father, but I can deal with that.

"Touchy question?" There's a little accusation in her voice. Penny's not stupid. She knows something's up.

"We moved around a lot when I was a kid. My dad was a real prick. Abused my mom and shit."

Her brows pull together as she processes. "Oh my God. I'm sorry."

I shake my head, sort of surprised I'm even telling her this. "It was a long time ago. She was smart, though. She left him and didn't look back, but he was also a bastard and he'd follow her. We'd move somewhere. She'd get a job, and a few months later, he'd show up. Restraining orders don't do shit, by the way." The only thing that worked was money, but the piece of paper keeps it legal. "So yeah, we moved around a lot. Never had much…"

Guilt starts surging inside of me again—that weight that fell off trying to hook me. Mom always took care of me. No matter how hard it was, she took care of me, and I'm doing a shitty job of returning the favor.

"Did I lose you, Drummer Boy?"

Her words pull me back to the surface. "Drummer *Man*." I wink. "So yeah, one of the waitressing jobs she had was right next to this music store. I was like, ten. When she worked, I would go next door and hang out with the owner. He was cool to me. Played the drums, and he taught me stuff. I'd trade hours illegally working for him for lessons. We were there six months. I was fucking pissed when we moved, but like I said, dude was cool and he gave me an old kit. After that, I always played. I've learned guitar, too, but I'll always be a drummer." Shrugging, I attempt to play it off like this isn't the big deal it is. I don't do the whole baring-of-the-soul thing.

Her ink is coming along nicely. It's a contrast, the black ink and the red skin against what's usually such a pale white. I never knew how sexy it would be to see a girl get tatted. Or maybe it's just sexy to watch her. I'm not sure.

She's been quiet for a minute, so I watch her, wondering if the pain is getting to her or what, but it's not. She's looking at me, too. No, into me, and I'm actually scared of the answers she'll find. Nothing scares me. Not my asshole dad, not waking up in the hospital, but crazily this does.

"What?"

She bites her lip and then says, "So…I had a really bad night with my gramps once. Some hot, cocky guy who *thinks* he's better than me on a snowmachine confused me by showing me he's more than I thought when he helped. And then he kissed me…like the *best* damn kiss, but I pushed him away."

I'm trying to figure out what she's saying. Focusing on the fact that she thinks I'm *more* and hoping I really am. Suddenly, I don't want to be the guy who downs a pill every few days.

She breathes.

I breathe.

"I shouldn't have. Pushed him away, I mean. I wish I hadn't."

Heat runs the length of my body. Damn, I like this girl. Actually *like* her. And I'm totally wishing we weren't in this tattoo parlor right now. I brush my finger against her stomach, watching goosebumps spread across her skin. "Don't worry. You'll get a chance to redeem yourself. He *definitely* plans on doing it again."

• • •

I close the cabin door behind me. We just got home from the tattoo parlor, and I let her go inside while I ran over and gave Gary my check-in. She jumps a little and looks at me, her hand sliding over the bass drum. It usually pisses me off when people touch my drums, but this time, it doesn't.

"Play something for me." She gives me a smile. I normally kind of hate this—being on display when someone *asks* me to play. If it happens naturally, it's different, but I like the idea of her seeing me in the zone. She's incredible at everything she does, and drums are one of the only things I have. It's what *I'm* good at, and yeah, I want to show off for her.

"Are you sure you can handle it? I don't want you to be jealous because I'm so good. Plus, I know how hard it is for girls to resist a guy in a band." A sharp stab of fear hits me. I really just fucked up by saying band. *Please don't let her catch that.*

She pretends to gag. "Yeah, pot-smoking kids in a basement with a couple of their dad's old guitars is a serious turn-on. Oh, no. I don't know if I can restrain myself. Please, Bishop, take me now!"

"Don't say I didn't warn you." Shrugging out of my jacket, I toss it on a table before sitting at the drums. Penny sits down on the couch across from me. The room is so small, I know it will be loud for her. Only a few feet separate us.

I close my eyes as I slide the sticks through my fingers. *One, two, three, four,* and then my sticks slam down. I go up and down the line, finding the beat and the rhythm I want. Over and over, I pound down on it. My heart matches the rhythm. My arms feel the burn, but I welcome it—always welcome this kind of sting because it's what I crave. I don't think. Never do when I play outside of that stadium. Just feel. My body automatically knows what to do.

Sweat drips into my closed eyes, but I keep going, because this is the one thing I have to offer her. When I finally open my eyes, hers are closed like she's savoring the beat. *My* beat. It feels amazing. It makes me proud.

Playing right now feels better than it ever has, and part of me doesn't ever want it to stop, but I do. "Wanna try?"

She opens her eyes. "Do you have to ask?"

God, she's so fucking cool. I love that she's always up for anything.

I get up so she can sit in my spot behind the drums. "Okay, just—" My words are cut off by the worst sound I've ever heard. "What are you doing? You're abusing my shit." I grab her arm. "People don't realize this is an *art*. Let the expert show you how it's done."

We spend the next hour playing. Well, she tries to play, and I try to teach, but it's not coming off so well. I get to touch her a lot, so that's a plus. My gut hurts from laughing so hard, and I'm sure hers does, too. Finally, she throws the sticks on the floor. "I'm done. The drums suck, and you're a sucky teacher."

"Tell me you're kidding. I'm Bis—" *Bishop Riley. Drummer for Burn. Liar to the girl he likes*. "You hungry? I'd offer you pizza or something, but then I'd have to deal with one of your admirers, and I'm not in the mood for that right now." Hopefully, my wink shows her I'm kidding.

She gets up and falls to the couch, kicking her feet up on the table. "You don't ever let anything go, do you?"

"Nope." I sit down beside her, one of my drumsticks in hand.

We're quiet for a few minutes. I keep looking over at her, wondering what she's thinking.

"So… You told me about your dad earlier. I can tell you

about mine, if you want."

My insides turn to ice. I don't know why, but I know this is big. Know she doesn't like to talk about this, and I feel totally unworthy of knowing because I'm keeping so much shit from her.

But maybe this is a way to tell her. She'll tell me something, and then I'll tell her. She'll understand, I think. Get why I didn't tell her who I really am. "I want to know everything you want to tell me." And I put my arm around her, playing with the strands of her hair. It feels even better than the drumstick in my other one.

Penny looks over at me, all steel strength, somehow filled with softness. "It's not like a huge secret or anything. I just don't like to talk about it."

"You don't have to tell me if you don't want." But I want her to. Want to know she wants to tell me.

"You know my one-beer rule? The reason I watch the guys when they party? Some jerk who was stoned out of his mind hit him while he was on his motorcycle when I was ten."

Every. Single. Thing inside me explodes. Not the good kind, either. She tries to sound like it's not a big deal, but I know it is. My insides are shredded apart. I start to shake again. Panic simmering beneath the surface. *Don't let her notice. Please don't let her see I'm fucking cracking apart.* "Yeah?"

She nods. "I guess he downed a handful of his pain scrip, chased them down with a few beers, and left me without a dad. Sucks. It's why I don't drink and why I'd kill the guys if they ever did anything heavier than that. Why I make them give me their keys at parties, and why I hate leaving early because I can't be there to make sure they don't do anything stupid."

My mouth is so dry, it's hard to speak. "I'm sorry."

And I don't know where it comes from, but I feel like it was me. It could have been me. Not thought or cared about anything except getting messed up and then did something stupid. The Mitch conversation takes on a whole new meaning. Her fear of being left is because of someone like me.

I think about waking up in the hospital. About the pills I've taken since I've been here. About the pills *in my fucking bag* right now, and for the first time, I feel like a pill-head. I'm a loser. An addict. I'm sitting here with my hand in her hair, knowing what happened to her dad when she doesn't know about me. It makes me feel like a failure. Like I'm letting her down the way I let Mom down.

"You're quiet. Did I totally just ruin the mood or something?"

I try and shake it off, but I'm torn in half. Not one thing I've ever done makes me deserve to be here with this girl, but I've never wanted to be anywhere more. "We need to put the cream on your tat. I forgot about that." Getting up, I try to forget what she said. Try to take care of her so maybe I'll deserve to be here a little, because I can't stand the thought of not sharing this room with her right now.

I grab the tube and walk back over. Penny smiles, then leans back on the couch and lifts her shirt. When I sit on the coffee table in front of her, I don't know if my hands are shaking because I feel guilty, because I want something to take the edge off, or because I want her.

"You're shaking," she says when I pull off the bandage.

Yeah, it's definitely partly because of her.

"I know," is the only reply I can give her, and then I'm smearing the cream. My finger brushes her skin, higher and higher, just under her breast. So soft, so gentle because I don't want to hurt her. *You're already hurting her, she just doesn't know it yet.*

"It looks amazing on you. You did awesome today. You're not afraid of anything, are you?"

Instead of answering, she says, "I thought you were going to kiss me again, Bishop."

I know it's all kinds of wrong. I shouldn't do this, but I'm so broken up inside, I can't deny her. Not anything. I'm going to kiss her, and I'm going to start doing the right thing. I'm done with this pill thing. Done with it all. I kneel on the floor between her legs, pushing my hands through her hair and then I kiss her. Our tongues tangle together. Our lips mold to each other's. And I could swear that with each touch, she melts the ice in my veins.

I want to tell her everything.

I never want to stop kissing her.

"You don't even know who I am." My whispered words are probably the most honest thing I've said since we met. "I've screwed up...so fucking much." This is the first time it's hit me exactly *how* much. But she quiets me with her mouth, and I let her. She leans down and lies on the couch, and I follow her. I kiss her collarbone, behind her ear, before going up to taste her lips again, knowing the whole time I failed. Nothing I could ever do would make me proud.

Please, don't let me fuck this up.

Chapter Sixteen

Penny

I dream about lying in Bishop's arms. I dream about him playing drums with his shirt off. I dream about him kissing his way up my neck and how I can't get close enough to him. And how he whispers in my ear not to worry and then starts taking off my panties, and I'm kissing, and we're kissing, and I'm frantic, and some horrible ring won't stop…

I sit up and forget for a moment where I am. Bishop rolls over, catches my eyes, and smiles. "We fell asleep."

"Guess so." Holy. Shit. Only some of that was a dream. We did kiss. A lot. And there was definitely some under-clothing touching because the guy's sides are toned. And his back. And his abs. And his chest.

"Can you please get your phone?" He chuckles as he slides his hand down my arm.

My stomach hollows out. Crap. It's my school alarm. I was here all night. Mom is going to freak out.

"I gotta go before Mom figures out I didn't go home last night." I grab my phone, and it takes me four tries to shut the thing up.

Bishop half-leaps out of bed, but the grogginess all over his face tells me he's probably not much of a morning person. And he's not wearing a shirt, which stops me for a second so I can watch him. All the feelings from my dream send a rush of heat through me, and I reach out to touch his side.

Bishop smiles. His hand covers mine, and he steps close, pulling me into his arms. "I'm glad you stayed. I slept so hard last night." He says that like it's not something he usually does.

I rest my cheek on his bare chest, wishing with everything in me that I didn't have to go. But I totally do. "I gotta get out of here."

He plants a kiss on my temple before slowly releasing me. Like he wants me here as much as I want to be here.

"Right. Your stuff." He scans the small floor for anything that might be mine, but I'm sadly as dressed as I was when we climbed into bed together.

I pull up my shirt, remembering my tattoo. "How's it look?"

He kneels on the floor, looking more awake than he has yet. "Hot."

I laugh because it feels so good to have him say that. "I gotta run. State's coming up, and if I don't have a killer excuse, I have to be at school."

He stands and runs a hand over my hair, sending waves through me. "I can't wait to see you play again."

I love that he wants to see me play. For guys who don't

play hockey, it's usually a turn-off, or intimidation factor or something, and the guys *on* the team… Well, that obviously doesn't work out so well.

I grab my coat, let Bishop crush me into his arms again to say goodbye, and step quietly out the door into the darkness.

I'm outside, the door is closing, and my cheeks already hurt from smiling. Then there's movement at my house.

I freeze. I'm caught for sure. It's too late to hide, but then I stop and stare. The silhouette outlined by the small porch light isn't familiar. I tense, thinking some asshole's trying to break into my house as I step off Bishop's porch. Mom, in her bathrobe and slippers, appears, smiling up at some guy.

What the hell?

There's some quiet murmurs, then he leans forward, and she *kisses* him. And then again. And then his arms are around her, and he's kissing her like I was kissing Bishop last night.

I'm frozen and shaking. My stomach turns over.

His hand brushes back her hair.

With every gesture, my anger rises. Mom never even said she was *dating*! This is my *dad's* parents' house. And my *dad's* bed. And my *mom*!

The man turns toward an unfamiliar car.

Ben?

I try to suck in a breath, but I don't think it works, because I'm feeling dizzy, like I'm not getting enough air. Dad *knew* this guy! I know this guy! *And she lied. She lied to me.*

That's it. I need out of here. I head for my truck. And then I realize Mom and Ben are actually my perfect escape from

Bishop's porch. All I have to do is get to my car. I step down onto the snow.

"Penny?" Mom calls with a shaky voice. "What are you doing?"

Anger races through me so suddenly I don't think. "I'll answer that when you answer me what the *fuck* you did last night? Or did I answer myself with the question?" Okay. Probably not the smartest move when even I know that maybe crashing at Bishop's place wasn't the best idea. And maybe dropping the f-bomb was also stupid, and that maybe it was too early in the conversation for a counter-attack when I should be walking up to her to explain.

The door flies open behind me with a wide-eyed Bishop. Sadly, wearing a shirt.

"Penny. Please. This isn't…" Mom eyes Bishop, and her face turns from shock to anger.

We're way past explanations in this moment. And anyway, I'm a lot closer to my truck than she is. It's not like the cabins are parked directly under the house. And I'm parked next to Bishop's.

"Penny! Staying the night over there is completely unacceptable!" she yells and looks between Bishop and me.

I can't believe she thinks she's better than me in this situation. Can't believe she's been lying to me. "Are we *really* going to go there right now?"

Ben's gaze goes from me to Mom and back to me. He's about to be pulled into a mess because both Mom and I go too far when we're pissed. And we're definitely both pissed.

"I'm sorry, Ms. Jones." Bishop's voice is all apology. "We were watching a movie and crashed. I didn't mean—"

Mom holds up her hand. "I need to talk to my daughter."

Guess nice isn't going to work today. "Well I sure as hell don't need to talk to you." I run toward my truck.

"*Penny!*" Mom yells.

"Let her go," Ben says. Like he has a say in anything. Only, I'm sort of hoping she takes his advice, even though I know she won't.

"Mom. Seriously." I turn to face her. "I never hid that I spent time with Bishop, something you'd know if you were ever here. And for some crazy reason, you feel the need to sneak around with a guy when you're a grown-up! You didn't even know I was gone last night you were so distracted. I can't believe you would invite him here when you haven't even told me about him! You're sneaking around more than I am! You *know* how I hate being lied to."

Mom starts my way, the anger sliding off her face, but with how every cell in my body is tensed, now is not the time for us to talk.

I make it to the driver's side door and nearly *cry*. Emotions swirl around in my head. I blink a few times, like I'm not getting enough air and I'm about to pass out. Okay. Breathing. Right? Like Bishop did. I can try that. *In. Out. In. Out.* This time, my hands clutch the door handle. Why am I reacting this way?

Mom hasn't been here.

I've been here.

I've missed parties.

I've had nothing but craziness with Mitch and Rebecca, and Bishop, and now it feels like she chose Ben over *me*, over *Gramps*... She's left us alone for Ben. *Left me.* How could she think it wasn't something she could tell me?

I needed Bishop's help to get Gramps to bed, and Mom gets to be with a guy? And now she's pissed that I'm doing the same thing. Only probably not exactly the same thing because Bishop and I didn't have sex. I hold in a scream.

I try to pull in another breath when I remember this breathing shit doesn't work. I slam my fist into the door panel as hard as I can, sending a satisfying shot of pain across my knuckles, up my arm and the sound rings almost like a gunshot.

"Penny!" Mom yells, nothing but anger and disapproval on her voice, but she's in her slippers and stumbling through the uneven snow.

I can get out of here before she reaches me. Easy.

"Don't *Penny* me! A little warning would've been nice!" I jerk open the truck door and slam it behind me.

"Penny! Wait!" Bishop runs for the passenger door and jumps in with an armload of crap just as Mom reaches my truck, and just before I put Bitty in reverse and haul ass out of the driveway.

I can't breathe right, and I'm gripping the steering wheel with everything I have. Blood's running down my knuckles, but the damage wasn't enough. Not nearly enough to block out the mess in my head.

Bishop sits in silence as I fly toward the school. It's only about ten miles or so, but the road is windy up here. Bitty slides sideways on a steep curve, and Bishop doesn't even suck in a breath.

"What the hell are you doing in here?" I ask.

"Making sure you don't break your truck on the way to school."

I'm sure he wants me to react, but I don't. My chest feels different, though. Like I might be able to breathe.

"Watch the steering wheel. Your handprints might never come out." He chuckles, but his eyes are wide enough that I know he's also worried about me. Trying to distract me like he did when I got my tattoo yesterday.

My morning crashes in, and my chest feels emptied out. "She didn't... I mean, she never said anything. Ever. And now I don't know if I've been dealing with all the extra stuff at home because she needs to work or because of Ben. And I wouldn't have even minded her seeing him if she was *fucking telling me the truth*."

Bishop's silent for a moment. "I'm sorry."

I suck in a breath, trying to slow down my heart. "Please. You should be telling me that it's not a big deal. If I don't care that she's dating the guy, what does it matter?" Only it *does* matter because Mom and I used to talk, and I'm not sure what changed.

Bishop rests his hand on my leg. "I don't need to tell you stuff you already know. She kept something huge from you. That's not cool." His face falls for a moment before he recovers.

And hearing him say it that way cuts into me hard. I've been left at home alone night after night to deal with Gramps, and did not go out with my friends, because Mom would rather spend time with Ben than me. Now I'm blinking in a bad effort of trying not to cry in front of Bishop.

He gives my thigh a squeeze. "You're like me. You're hurt, but it's easier to be pissed."

Warmth spreads through me because I know he gets it. Just like he gets my need to stay in Alaska and play with the guys. Like he gets everything about me. "What are you?" I try to wipe my tears without it being obvious, but I'm sure I fail. "A shrink?" I'm still confused and a little angry and a lot hurt, but better.

"Nope. I just want you to know I understand. And that your mom is scary when she yells." He pauses. "But I want you guys to get along so I can see you and for selfish reasons like she brings me clean towels, and I don't want one that's used for a dog or something."

I love that he's trying to make me laugh right now.

"I feel like such…just wimpy." I slide low in my seat. "This isn't like me."

"Penny. How many people would bloody their knuckles before school on purpose, and still want to slam their fists into something else? You're not wimpy." He pauses. "I'm right, aren't I? That you'd like a good punching bag right now?"

"Yeah." I let myself smile a little. "I'm going to be late for school. How did you plan on getting back?"

He shrugs. "I don't know. I didn't really think about that, just wanted to make sure you were okay. I'll hitchhike or something."

He didn't think about how he'd get back because he was thinking about me.

I pull the keys from the ignition. Am I really going to do this? No one drives Bitty. *No one.*

"You can drive Bitty home, but if you scratch her, I kick your ass. And it means you'll have to pick me up from hockey practice at about four-thirty."

I set the keys in his hand, and his dark brown eyes rest on mine for a moment.

Bishop looks down then and starts tugging at the bundle of stuff in his arms, looking all busy like maybe being close to someone is as different for him as it is for me. "I grabbed a pair of my pants in case you didn't want to stay in sweats all day." A pair of jeans falls in my lap. "You're tall anyway, so I thought they should work. And I brought a hoodie, too." His black hoodie sits on the seat between us. "You know. Cover up so not *every single guy* at your school is drooling. And I think we're supposed to put cream on your tattoo again."

"Wow, *Mom*. Thanks." But I'm smiling wide because he did all this for me. I can't even remember the last time someone took care of me like this.

"Let's do the fun part first. Show me your tattoo." He waggles his brows, and I lift my shirt to scoot over. Well, and to feel his hands on me. And then I have a better idea.

"Let me change into your pants first." I pull my sweats

off, and it was worth it for the look on his face as I sit in my panties to pull on his jeans. Because, to him, I'm a real girl.

His pants are a little big, but I'll make them work.

When his hands touch my tattoo again, sending a rush of anticipation through me, I'm suddenly not sure if this morning is one of my worst, or one of my best.

When I finally flop into first period, Chomps gives me a raised brow and a smirk. "Whose ass did you kick for those clothes?".

I flip him off but smile because they smell like Bishop. And then I remember why I'm wearing his clothes, and that I'm still mad, and that he's home while I'm here, and if I didn't have to be at stupid school, we could be together, and all the sadness, anger and frustration from my morning starts flooding in.

No one bothers me for the rest of the day. I must look as furious as I feel. How could Mom not say anything about Ben? How many nights could she have been home and wasn't? And then, the other night when she did come home, she was all in my business, trying to get me to go to bed on time, and suddenly cares what's going on?

And then she makes it home too late to see if I'm home or not, but not too late to screw the guy she hasn't told me she's seeing?

Today is a timed mile for PE. I run four. It's still not enough to ease the tension.

Chapter Seventeen

Bishop

I slept with Penny.

Well, not *slept* with her, slept with her, but I actually fell asleep without lying around for hours first, and I actually slept through the night. And I'm not talking *passed out* either because those are entirely different things. All I know is, I was making out with her and it felt good, so good and *so different* and we were just lying there, and then her annoying phone had to go and wake us up.

I slow down before I hit the turn in front of me. I'd love to give her a little gas, see what it feels like to get Bitty's wheels spinning the way Penny does, but I also know I have enough marks against me that I don't want to add crashing her truck to the list.

That thought makes last night slam into me again. Not the good parts, either. The parts where she told me a loser who liked to party too much killed her dad. Someone just like me.

And I didn't tell her. I kissed her, touched her, but I couldn't make my weak-ass mouth open to tell her the truth. I'm not stupid enough not to realize this isn't huge. That I'm not doing the wrong thing by lying to her, but also because of everything else: the drinking, the pills, the hospital. Yeah, way too much to even count. All the ways I've thought I've been doing good since I've been here suddenly don't amount to much.

My fist itches to hit something the way she slammed her fist into the truck's side.

I remember her hands, and the way it felt like she punched me when I saw the blood dripping down them. It sucks to see your girl hurt, and all I wanted to do was make it better. All of it: me, the pain, and her mom. Damn, that was intense.

And then just now... I told her how huge it was her mom lied to her, but what about me? I'm doing the same thing.

I know I'm screwed when I get back to the cabins because her mom yelled at me to leave her alone this morning, but all I could think about was that Penny would freeze her ass off in that tank top. That she needed the cream for her tat so it heals right. That I didn't want her to be alone when she was hurt. It sucks to deal with that stuff alone, and I don't want that for her. Don't want any of the shit that clouds my life to rain down on her. She's too good for that. Too good for me. All this time, and I'm just now realizing how screwed up I am.

And when she finds out, she'll probably try and kick my ass.

I pull the truck into the driveway and park it right in front of their house, wishing like hell I didn't have to do this, but hoping it will fix the situation. If I tell her the truth, hopefully Penny won't get in trouble for it later. It's not enough to forgive my sins, but maybe it can be one thing to be proud of.

My hands shake as I jog up the stairs, but I ignore it and knock on the door. Half of me hopes Gramps opens up so we can work on the car and I can forget about her mom, but then that would make me a coward, and I'm done being afraid of everything.

Again, I knock, louder this time, so she knows I'm not going to let her ignore me. I saw her mom's car, so I know she's home. A couple seconds later, the door pulls open. She's wearing her scrubs for work and a scowl that's probably half the size of Seldon.

I'm so screwed.

"Umm, hey." My hands shove into my pockets. I've never had to do this kind of thing before. I joined the band so young, most of the girls I've dated have been groupies, so it's not like I had to do the whole meet-the-parent thing. "I'm Bishop… Well, obviously, you know I'm Bishop. I wanted to come by and apologize about this morning. It wasn't Penny's fault. We were playing the drums and then she fell asleep during the movie. I should have woken her up, but I didn't…so yeah, it's not her fault. It's mine."

If anything, the scowl is even deeper now. I wonder if Penny realizes her and her mom are alike in that they can both smell bullshit a mile away. Not that we didn't just fall asleep, but this woman knows there was more than movie and drums going on last night.

"It won't happen again." My words don't make her stop looking at me like I'm something she stepped in. "It was an accident, but my accident." *Shut the hell up, Riley!*

"Are you done?" she asks.

Yep, definitely screwed.

"I know who you are, Bishop."

My head drops back, and I let out a breath. This is it now. She's definitely not going to keep this secret. Not that it should be a secret anymore. Secrets mean lies, and Penny hates being lied to.

"I've seen your type before."

The weight on my chest lessens. She doesn't know. Not about the band and the other stuff.

"You came here with a chip on your shoulder, your family throwing money around and renting out the place. You buy your drums, which I know had to cost a fortune, and sit around banging on them all day without a care in the world, and I was okay with that. Okay that Gramps is fond of you, that you spend half your time here when you obviously think you're better than the rest of everyone—"

"I don't," I cut her off, knowing it's wrong, but at this point, I don't care. "I don't think I'm better than Gramps... Penny..."

She holds up her hand. "Like I said, I was okay with that as long as it didn't affect my daughter. Now it does. She's a good girl. She loves her family. She's smart. Incredible at hockey. She has a huge future ahead of her. She'll be leaving soon for college, and Penny's excited about that. I don't want anything to get in her way. Penny may be friends with boys, but that's the only way she's ever seen them. She's definitely not like that other girl I saw going into your cabin last week."

Ah, shit. She knows about Maryanne.

"Her attitude this morning was so unlike her. You're the only thing that's changed to make her act this way."

My first instinct is to tell her she doesn't know her own daughter. Yeah, Penny is all the things she said, and she's definitely not like Maryanne, but she also doesn't want to go. She doesn't want the future they're trying to shove down her throat, and second, she's much stronger than her mom gives her credit for.

Shaking my head, I know I'll regret this later. This woman can kick us out, make Penny stay away from me, but I can't keep my mouth shut. "I may be all the things you think I am, and in a lot of ways, Penny is as well, but you don't really know her. Not if you think she'd let someone like me stand in the way of her life. She's not afraid to step up and take whatever she wants. I don't know a lot of people who can say that, if anyone."

With that, I turn and walk away from her. I should probably go pack my stuff, but I don't. For the first time, I go to Gary's for something other than a pill or mandatory therapy session.

"Troy, I gotta let you go, baby," Gary says into the phone as I step inside. And for the first time, I don't even want to give him crap for talking to Troy so often. I actually kind of get it—

especially since this Alaska thing is something they usually do together. And if I wasn't here, I think I'd want to talk to Penny every day, too.

"Hey." He rubs a hand over his shaggy hair and sits down on the couch next to me, closing his laptop on the table. He's in a pair of flannel pajama bottoms, looks like he could use a shave, and I notice a new pair of earrings in his ears.

"Gift from Troy?" I nod at his ears.

"Yep. I doubt that's what you're here for, though. You doing okay?"

Yes and no. I'm not exactly sure why I came here. "Yeah, I'm good." Gary waits, and I realize he's good at this. He's probably sat with a lot of people like me who had the weight of the world on their shoulders but couldn't make themselves talk, to make some of it fall away.

"So…did you hear any yelling outside this morning or did you sleep through it?" This is kind of weird.

"Are you kidding? I sleep through your drumming half the night. I can sleep through anything."

I scratch my head, keeping my hand as a wall between us. "So, Penny was sneaking out of my cabin this morning, and her mom caught her. I just tried to—"

"No! No, no, no, no. I knew you guys were getting close, and it's actually kind of romantic, but no! Don's going to kill me. I can't believe you boinked the girl at her mom's house!"

"What?" My hand falls. "First of all, a guy should never say 'boinked.' Second, I haven't slept with her. I mean, I slept with her, but I didn't have sex with her."

Little heart thought bubbles start floating around Gary. "Aww, you slept with her! Why, Bishop Riley. I didn't think you had it in you. Are you in L-O-V-E?"

He's teasing me by trying to lighten the mood. I know that, but still don't like it. "Nice." I push to my feet. "I'm trying to be serious here, and you're giving me shit." When I start to walk away, Gary grabs my wrist.

"You're right. I'm sorry. You didn't have to come to me, and you did. That's important. Sit back down, please."

Rubbing my hands over my face, I fall back onto the couch. "Listen, I just got into it with her mom. I think it's safe to say she hates me and thinks I'm pretty much the spawn of the devil, so I'm not sure how much longer this gig is going to last. I know Don's going to be pissed, but I didn't mean for it to happen and…" *I'm not ready to go. I don't want to screw this up. I don't want to be like the loser who gets in his car after partying.* As soon as I think those words, I know what comes next. I am all those things everyone thinks I am, unless I can man up, at least about some of them.

"I'm sure Penny will agree with her mom pretty soon because I'm going to tell her." This is all eating a hole inside me, the lying. Her dad. I have to try to *do* something about it. "Don will probably be angry about that, too, but I don't care."

Gary is surprisingly quiet, so I keep talking. "She was so pissed at her mom this morning, man. So pissed because her mom lied to her, and I'm doing the same damn thing. She's going to freak out." I can't stop thinking about it. "You don't want to deal with a pissed off Penny, but I just…" Just can't lie to her anymore. She deserves better than that. *I* deserve better than that.

"So yeah, I just wanted to tell you. Be prepared or whatever." When I stand up this time, Gary is right behind me. He grabs me and pulls me into a hug.

"We all screw up. No one is perfect. You're a good kid, Bishop. Don't let anyone make you think anything different. No matter what, okay?" He's still holding onto me, and I let him. "If things don't work out here and you're not ready to go home, we won't. When you're not grumpy, you're not so bad to travel with." Gary laughs and lets me go.

"I... Thanks, man."

He gives me a nod. "I'm serious. Wherever you want, okay? And as far as Don is concerned, I'll take care of him. He's not so bad if you know how to deal with him."

I nod again.

"And Bishop, you haven't even needed much of your prescription. You're spending your time drumming and snow-whatevering instead of the things you would have done before. You're doing good. I'm proud of you, but I want *you* to be proud of yourself. You deserve it."

No, no I don't. "Like you said, something small every day."

"This wasn't small, Bishop."

His cell rings.

I shake my head, but not at him. At *me* because he thinks I'm much better than I am. Because the things he said I've done are pointless because they don't outweigh the bad—those bad things that I'm not even honest with him about. It makes my stomach ache. "Talk to your man." I move toward the door. "I'm going to go wait for Penny."

"It's not Troy and even if it was, we'd keep talking if you wanted."

"I know." And now I just need to do something to make myself deserve it.

I take a quick shower, wondering if it'll be the last one I get while I'm here. Before leaving, I push the baseball hat down low on my head. I'm so tired of wearing this stupid thing.

I head to the music store for a little while to hang out with Pat. "What's up, man?" he asks.

"Not much. Was just bored."

"Cool. Been a while since you came down."

Pat's good people. It's cool hanging out with him, and I wonder why I don't do it more often. Plus, he could have blown my cover a long time ago, but he hasn't. "Wanna play?"

His eyes light up. "Hell yeah."

We jam for a little while—okay, a couple hours, before a few kids come in.

"You like the drums?" I step up next to the one with the shaved head, eyeing the kit.

"Yeah! They're so cool!"

I look over at Pat and he nods. "Want me to play something?" I ask them and they look at me like I'm an idiot, so I sit down and show them what I can do. It's like it's coming from within me—this incredible feeling sprouting from my insides and coming out through the drumsticks.

"Holy cow!" The other boy says when I finish. "You're good! Can you teach us something?"

The next hour and a half is spent teaching them some rhythms and freestyle tricks. It's actually pretty cool. The bald kid reminds me of when I started playing. He's good. This—teaching him—feels even better than that.

Finally, it's close to time for Penny to get out of school, so I head out. She still has practice, but I go to the school anyway. I feel like watching her, since I probably won't get to see her game. I'm sure she'll be done with me after what I tell her today.

Standing in the doorway to the arena, I watch her on the ice. My mind flashes back to her in the truck this morning—how she just pulled off her sweats in front of me like I deserved to be there and see her. Like I belonged there with her.

Like I told her mom, nothing holds her back.

I realize I'm smiling when I head inside. She's skated to the back, but all the guys are out here, still in their big ass hockey gear. Mitch does a double take when he sees me and then skates over. "What's up, man?" Even though Penny used to be into him, he's all right. The least I can do is be cool.

"Hey." He has his helmet in his huge, glove-covered hand. "You here for our girl?"

"Whose girl? Nope, not here for *your* girl."

Mitch grins at me. Then Chomps skates up, doing the same.

"You guys got something to say?" This is the part where

they tell me not to screw up with Penny, and though I respect them for it, I don't need to hear it from them. I know exactly how lucky I am. And I know I've already fucked up, too.

Chomps's smile grows, but it's Mitch who speaks. "We're going sledding in a few days. You wanna come?"

Sledding? What are we, twelve? "Nah, I'm good. Thanks."

"It'll be fun." Chomps nods his head at me. "You can borrow gear from Pen, or we'll bring some for you."

"Gear? I'm pretty sure I can handle a sled without gear."

They both laugh, and Mitch leans over and puts an arm around me.

"This is going to be fun! Gotta make sure you're tough enough for our girl." He steps away.

My shoulders rise and fall in a shrug. "Believe me. I have what it takes."

They start laughing again, and I open my mouth to tell them to screw off, when Penny skates toward us, sliding to a stop next to the wall.

"What are you doing here so early? You're going to get bored." She leans toward me, her eyes bright. Yeah, she wanted to see me, too. She pushes her way through Mitch and Chomps who skate off, still laughing at something, but I couldn't care less. I didn't come here to deal with them.

For the first time, I want to take my hat off instead of pulling it lower. "I wanted to watch you, Pen."

She opens her mouth, closes it, and opens it again. For the first time, Penny Jones doesn't know what to say. "You can sit in the stands, but if I see you looking sideways at Rebecca, I might freak."

There's the girl I know. Reaching forward, I touch her face. "If she's not kicking ass on the ice, or challenging me at snowmachining, she's not my type." I wink at her before heading over to sit down on the bleachers. For the second time, I leave her speechless.

"So, you and Penny, huh?" I look over to see Mitch's girl a few rows up.

"Yep."

"Thank God." Rebecca laughs but then looks shy about it, looking away and kind of biting at her lip. "Seriously though… It's cool to see her happy and *not* just because she wants Mitch—"

"Used to want Mitch." My gut tightens. *And maybe will want him again after she knows the truth.*

"I didn't mean anything by it." Again she looks away. She's so different from Penny. Not that that's a bad thing. Just different.

"And?" I prompt her to see if she'll keep going.

"I know she wouldn't believe it, but I'm happy for her. Penny's cool, even if she hates me and insists on calling me Rebecca when she knows I like Becca better." Her voice is so quiet that I have to strain to hear her over the sound of skates on ice.

I chuckle. "That sounds like her, and yeah, she is cool. And I'm sure she doesn't really *hate* you."

I smile at Becca before leaning back in the seat to watch Penny practice.

I expect to see drills or something, but they're slamming into each other like they do in games, only they punch one another for fun when they get hit. This is some serious shit, and I like her even more for it. That she's not afraid to be out there giving as many hits as she takes.

Though, that could really backfire when I tell her what a prick I am.

Chapter Eighteen

Penny

Damn, the boy can give a compliment. He sits four rows lower, way off to the side of Rebecca, and watches until we finish.

"So, you and the renter, huh?" Mitch throws an arm over my shoulder as we head off the ice which feels nowhere near as good as it did before Bishop came along.

"It's Bishop, and he's just giving me a ride home." And hopefully more of last night when we get there.

He cocks an eyebrow. "He's been here for a long time for someone who's only giving you a ride."

I raise my hands in the air with a grin. "'Cause I'm awesome on the ice. Who wouldn't want to see this?"

Mitch leans in. "You're not fooling me, Pen. Just admit you like the guy."

"I might." I pull off my helmet to cool down.

"Feels good, doesn't it?" Mitch smiles. "That he came to watch."

"Screw off." I grin as I push him. But yeah, it feels good. Now I get it. Why Mitch likes Rebecca here.

I give Bishop a wave before heading to the locker room to shower and change. For the first time that I can remember, I know it'll feel good to get out of my hockey gear and back into something that makes me feel like a girl—even if it's wearing a guy's clothes.

• • •

We drive home in silence, but Bishop looks twitchy. He keeps readjusting his hat and rubbing his hands together. It's making me a little crazy.

"You were amazing out there," he says again.

It's obvious he has something he wants to say. "You said that already."

He shifts again.

"Bishop. Just spit it out. You're making me insane over here." I give my knuckles a little rub. After hitting Bitty, and then wearing my hockey gloves, they're all irritated again.

He pushes out a breath of air. "So you know how you asked me who I am?"

The edges of nerves are creeping in with how weird and tense his voice sounds. "Yeah…"

"Shit." He rubs his face. "Okay. My name's not Ripe. It's Bishop Riley. I'm the youngest member of Burn. I'm the drummer, and—"

I laugh. Hard. And then our eyes catch, and his are so wide and serious that it makes me laugh harder. "Shut up. I call bullshit." That band is hot. What is he trying to pull?

He fingers his lip ring and stares.

Is he *serious*?

"No." I shake my head, which is starting to feel light and floaty and strange with the possibility of who he is. "No way. I *know* that band." There's no way he's some rock star. No way. But even as I think that, it means that a lot of things about him make sense. How he's always hiding under that hat. The name. The drumming that's unreal. The babysitter. Freaking *Pat* who got all smiley when we came in, who should have *called me when he knew*. Maybe that whole anxiety crowd thing is a serious problem. I thought he was going lose it after my game.

"Your iPhone in here?" he asks.

I point to the front pocket of my pack, but I'm starting to tense up like he might not be bullshitting me. Was some *rock star* living next to me this whole time?

Bishop pulls it out and scrolls for a minute. "Here."

It's the label art for Burn. All five guys. It's black and white and a bit grainy, but holy. Shit.

"What the *hell*?" I mean, I knew he was keeping stuff to himself, but, "*What the hell*?" My heart feels like it's beating too high up in my chest, making it hard to breathe or swallow. How did I end up sharing a hot tub and kissing some guy who's part of a kick-ass band and *not know*?

"Part of me being up here is not letting on who I am. I want you to know, but I don't want you to know, because cool people turn into weird people when they learn who I am." He sounds so defeated. "They look at me different. Treat me different. I don't want—"

Usually, no one knows who the drummer of a band is, but when they're young—and *hot*—people notice. I can't believe I didn't see it before. I mean, maybe if I spent as much time in front of the TV or reading stupid magazines as some people I know, I would have recognized him. So, I'm freaking out. Honestly. But no way am I going to let him see that. "Wait. You think I'm not going to give you crap just because you're some drummer in a band?" I cock a brow. "Like I won't demand a rematch of your total fluke win on the snowmachine? Or double check all your work on my car to make sure you didn't screw anything up?"

I laugh, but it's a little forced because I'm sitting in the truck with a drummer from a band *that I know*.

"Are you actually pissed, freaking out, and trying to hide it?" He pulls off his hat and runs his hand over his hair.

"No." Yes. Totally yes.

He sighs. I look at him and he looks nervous. Upset. Like this is a really big deal to him.

"You answered too fast. I know you hate it when people lie to you… Fuck, this is such a screwed-up situation. I didn't expect to…" He shrugs, looking more somber than I've ever seen him look. "To fall for someone up here. Especially since—" He shakes his head.

Fall for someone. Something decidedly girly flutters in my chest. I clear my throat. "I *do* hate it when people lie to me. But I knew you weren't telling me everything. It's not like you kept that a secret. You even asked me not to dig, which is admitting something's up. I don't know. I guess that makes it feel different. Or at least, I want it to feel different." I stop Bitty in my driveway. I'm trying not to think about how *totally freaking out I am*, because a rock star drummer—*Bishop Riley*—is in my car. I'm wearing his clothes. And we *slept* together last night.

He sighs. "There's more, Penny."

Nothing could be bigger than what he's just told me, so it can wait. "Follow me." Mom's car is thankfully not here. "I need to hide for a while."

Bishop follows me in silence up to my top story room. I lock the hatch behind us, hoping Mom won't be back for a while.

I slide my arms around his waist, and enjoy feeling the warmth of him so close. I try not to do any kind of internal squealing at who he is.

His fingers slide across the back of his pants. The ones I'm wearing. "I like you in my clothes."

I gently bite his bottom lip. "You also might like me out of them…a little."

He moves his head when I try to kiss him. "Pen. I… Shit. I have a problem with—"

"Freaking out in large crowds." I chuckle, even though I'm still wound up tight. It all makes sense now: his reaction at my hockey game, why he didn't share, and why he's here alone. "I know. You picked a good spot if you don't like people but don't think that gets you out of watching me play. They have pills for that stuff, and I want you at my next game." I poke him in the chest and then stare for a moment at where my finger just was, because after last night, I want another shot at being that close to him. But now I'm wondering what happens when he leaves. When he goes back to his real life. Or maybe I need to be just thinking about now. What I want now. How I'm finally the girl a guy likes enough to *be* with and not just flirt with. Not just any guy, either. Bishop. The only guy who gets me.

He opens his mouth like he's got more to say, so I smile, hoping he'll smile. It's strange to see him like this—so uncertain. I want to ask him more about being famous, playing the drums, his band, but I don't want him to feel like I'm going to get weird on him over it, either. It's obvious this is embarrassing for him. Or awkward or something, which sort of makes him sweeter. Nicer. Like he could have come up here and been an asshole and demanded something different or special because of who he is, but instead he tried to blend. Or hide. "Come?"

"'Course I'll come." He sighs again and pulls in a deep breath. "That's not the only reason I—"

I cut him off. "Later." Or I'll lose my nerve.

"But—"

I grab the bottom of his hoodie and pull it over my head followed quickly by the tank I slept in last night. The move leaves me in my black bra and the pants he loaned me.

His fingers trace the top of my pants, and then slide up, fingering the bottom edge of my bra sending my whole body into a frenzy of wanting his weight on me again.

Instead of collapsing into the puddle of goo my body

wants me to, I hold out my hand. "So, can I have your shirt, or are you going to let me be the only one half-naked?" I ask.

"Um…" His fingers are still tracing, and his gaze hasn't left my stomach. "I'm sorry I didn't tell you about—"

"Stop. Bishop. I get it. You didn't want to be recognized. Can we talk later? I don't know my mom's schedule, only that she's not here *now*." I don't want being around him to be about apologizing for something that really is just a part of him. "This doesn't change who you are to me. Okay? So, do I get your shirt or not?"

He groans, but slides his shirt over his head. Our bodies come together at the same time as our mouths. The heat from his skin on mine tingles its way through my body, fueling my need to be closer, to have more. His hands dig into my back as he pulls us together, and I'm matching him pressure for pressure, touch for touch, kiss for kiss, as deep as we can go. I stumble backward as he slowly leads us toward my blanket and pillow pile. No matter how much of him I feel, it's not enough. In seconds I'm on the floor while he hovers over me, *almost* like I wanted.

He pauses and searches my face, and then his gaze floats over my body, looking at me so much the same as Mitch looks at Rebecca. My stomach tightens with anticipation and the feeling of being wanted. His eyes come back to mine, and something's different. Slower. Like he wants every touch to count. Every movement to count. He teases me with his lips a few times before I wrap my arms around him and pull him down.

So this is why people say they "melt together." I've always wondered. Like melting candle wax, and blending colors—the more we're together and kissing, the less I can tell where I stop and he starts. His weight's on me again. I want him. Seriously want him. And it has nothing to do with who he is in the world. It has to do with who he is *here*. The guy who dishes it out, but can take it, and doesn't just put up with me, but seems to like it.

My hands go up and down his sides, on his back, across his shoulders, in his hair, and I'm running out of places to touch that won't lead me *way* into new territory.

He rolls onto his side bringing me with him, and I sit up gasping for air. I'm afraid, but not afraid. Mostly, I don't feel in control of what my body wants, and that's a first for me.

"Your tattoo. I'm sorry," he says. "I didn't—"

"My tattoo's fine. I just want to look at you."

I sit on my knees and gently push on his chest. It takes him a while to relax enough lay down on his back the way I want him. "So weird. You don't act like a famous guy."

"I'm just me."

I keep staring at his bare chest and abs and arms, loving the newness of it all and amazed that I'm not more nervous or afraid. It's that I believe he wants to be here. Wants to see me, touch me, and have me do all those same things to him. My body warms up again, but it's not from the need to feel him closer like it was before. It's the closeness and the trust and the way I'm falling for a guy I'm still discovering.

He pulls in a long breath. "This takes a serious amount of

trust."

"Chicken?" I tease.

"Afraid of you," he teases back.

"Close your eyes." My heartbeat's flooding my ears, and my breathing still isn't normal.

I sit next to where he lies on the floor and wait. And wait. I don't blink, don't move, just stare into the dark eyes that pull me in, hoping he'll cave.

"Fuck," he whispers but does it. He closes his eyes, but his body's still tense.

I want to take in everything about him. I run my fingers across his forehead and down the sides of his face. I touch his cheekbones, and smooth my finger over his lips and lip ring. Instead of tensing up, he relaxes. The few pictures I've seen of him in magazines sort of float through my head, but they feel disconnected from the guy lying in front of me. Like that guy is one person, and this Bishop is someone else entirely. I start to think about the girl who came up here, and how many other girls there might have been, but I start to feel edgy and self-conscious, so I concentrate again on what's happening now. What *I* know about him. Who he is to *me*.

My thigh is pressed against his side, and I move my fingers down his neck and across his collarbone. And even though I don't want it to, it hits me again—this is Bishop Riley. I'm touching *Bishop Riley*. The guy who lets me be real, and likes me anyway. The guy who risked Mom's wrath this morning, and thought to get my cream and clothes for school today.

I run each hand down his muscular arms and trace all the

veins and contours—there are a lot. A very nice side effect of playing the drums. His palms are smooth, and he clasps my hand the moment our fingers touch. He opens his eyes and pulls his arms out to the side, which brings me close. We kiss once before I pull away.

"Not yet." I smile. "I'm not done."

"I might be insane by the time you finish." The need in his eyes should scare me, but it doesn't. It just makes me feel more like I made a really good decision in coming here.

"I'm okay with that." I sit back and run my hands over his chest, under the line where his pecs are cut and then down his toned stomach. My fingertips slide underneath the top of his boxers, and I run them back and forth at the edge of the waistband, which just shows above his jeans. I could sit here and touch him like this for hours.

"Yeah, definitely going insane." He sits up and pulls us together, while avoiding touching my tattoo. The heat from him almost gives my body what it needs to take over again, and he brushes his lips against mine. When I don't protest, his kiss is slow and deep, once again making me feel like he's exploring every part of me. "Time for *you* to relinquish control for a minute." His lips touch mine as he speaks.

My heart starts hammering at the thought. "I—" I was going to say I don't think so, but the way he's looking at me… I let him take my hands with his and guide me to lying down next to him. Close. Touching. I can't take in a deep breath with his bare chest against me, but I love it. Love that he does this to me, to my body. Love that he wants to be here. Wants to have this effect on me.

Our eyes lock in the dim light. "You're beautiful, Penny."

All I can do is smile because, for the first time, I *feel* beautiful.

Bishop hovers, holding my hands over my head, pinning me down. How far does he want to go? My muscles begin to tense as I wonder if I can do that. If I'm ready.

"I don't think I can go all the—"

"We're not going there." He kisses me softly. "I won't rush you."

I'm feeling too much at once, so teasing feels safer. "You know I could push you off, right?" I press up with my arms so he can feel how strong I am.

"I know." His face is still soft. "But don't."

Okay. Trust. Like he said. I can do this. I relax my arms, every nerve in my body aware that Bishop Riley is hovering over my half naked body, and I've just given up control.

I let my eyes close as his lips touch my collarbone.

This is a whole lot of firsts for Penny Jones.

Chapter Nineteen

Bishop

"This car is going to be the death of me!" Gramps wipes the sweat off his forehead, leaving a big trail of dirt behind. Quickly, I disregard the urge to tell him in case I need a joke later.

I slip my hand in and tighten one of the bolts he just screwed in. "Don't tell me you're giving up, old man. You can't take it? I thought you were better than that." I cock an eyebrow, waiting for whatever smart-aleck remark he has.

"And I thought you knew better than to try and play me, Rookie. I may be old, but all that means is I'm better. Had a whole hell-of-a lot more time to hone my skills than you. Here, let me get a tissue and wipe your nose for you."

He moves his hand toward my face, but I playfully push it away. A laugh rumbles from deep in my stomach and spills free. Gramps is so cool. He's unlike anyone I've ever known, but there's no way I'm telling him that. "Maybe you should sit down. I don't want you to get tired on me. Where's your walker?"

Gramps grabs for me, and I let him put me in a headlock. "You little punk! I don't have a walker!"

He's actually giving me a noogie (who can say they've been given a noogie from an old guy?), when a door slams. "Gramps, stop beating up Bishop." I look up to see Penny standing there with her arms crossed. "Seriously? You can't take him?"

I pull out of Gramps's grip. "I was letting him win. I thought you might get a little pissed if I injured your grandpa."

Gramps clears his throat. "No one was letting me do anything. Kids these days. No respect." He's trying to hide his smile as he backs up, but then his look gets serious. "Five minutes." He grumbles before walking inside.

"I thought he'd never leave." I back Penny up, my hands on her waist until I'm sandwiching her between me and her Corvette.

"I don't have five minutes. I have to go," she says as my lips trail up her neck. I love the way she tastes. The way she smells. The way she feels. I still can't believe I'm here with her.

"Four?" I nip her ear.

"Six, but that's my final offer."

I laugh against her skin. I'm not sure I've laughed this much in my whole life. Actually, that's a lie. Mom and I had problems, but we were happy when I was growing up. I was happy. Gary asked me once when the last time things were easy for me. It couldn't have been way back then. I mean, I've had hard times off and on like everyone, but I think I've been happy. I used to like riding my motorcycle and used to meet with my friend Ryan a lot, but those things are few and far between. When I'm high, I laugh a whole lot, but that's not the same. Not nearly the same.

Penny turns her head so our lips connect, and I kiss her.

Now totally isn't the time to think about those things.

My hand slides under her hoodie. Her hands thread through my hair, and I kiss her deeper. Needing more…always more when it comes to her. But I also don't want to push her too far, too quick.

"I like your hair. I hate that stupid hat you wear." She whispers the words against my lips.

"Me too."

"And your lip ring." She pretends to nip at it. "Totally hot."

I groan, wishing we had a whole lot more than six minutes. It's crazy how wild this girl makes me. How much different I feel when I'm with her—not just her, either, but at all lately. Working on the car, snowmachining. All of it.

Guilt tries to push its way back in, but I shove it away.

"You're really Bishop Riley?" It's different how she says it. I don't feel like she's a fan, trying to get a piece of me. It's just curiosity, surprise, and it makes that guilt squeeze in again. I give her a nod, and she shakes her head with a smile. "So weird."

"Not weird." I kiss her again. And it's not because when I'm with her I feel like only the good parts of me show.

"What are you doing today?" She squeezes me tighter.

"Your friends are picking me up in a few hours. I think they want to take me to the mountains and hide the body." Pulling away enough so we can see each other, I wink, my hands still on her waist. "Good thing I can take them."

"Ugh! Don't remind me. I'm pissed I can't go. My mom is seriously making me crazy. So damn hypocritical."

There's a way to bring the guilt back. Not only are Penny and her mom still fighting—partly because of me—but I'm still lying to her. "Maybe she hired Mitch and Chomps to try and take me out. I bet that's what this is about. Murder for hire. Drummer from Burn killed in the Alaskan mountains by his girlfriend's admirers, on order of her Mom."

Her grip tightens on me, and I can't help but lean forward and kiss her again.

"I thought you could take them."

"I can, but then you'd be pissed at me for beating up Lover Boy."

"Ugh!" She pushes me away. "Stop calling him that."

Gramps comes back into the garage at the same time. Five minutes are up already?

"Break it up, you two. I'm already public enemy number one with your mom, Penny."

I'm still in shock she hasn't kicked us out. That I'm even here right now.

Penny steps around me. "Don't get me started on her."

Isn't this awesome? I'm causing all sorts of family drama. I start breathing a little faster. My hands tremble. "Don't be mad at your mom about me, okay?"

She just rolls her eyes and kisses me quickly. "I gotta go."

I want to pull her closer. Let her kiss linger and touch her everywhere, but I don't. "Later," I tell her and try to walk away, but I feel her lips against my ear.

"I know it might not be huge to you, but the way you just talked about being in the band? Like it was natural and you didn't mind that I know? It means something to me. Thanks for being honest."

Sharp, stabbing pain pierces my chest. Not by her, though, because this one? This is all me. My hand holding the knife. Bishop Riley strikes again.

Gramps and I are quiet for the next hour while we keep working on the car. We can't figure out why she's giving us so much trouble, and it's adding to my already shitty mood. If I could just get the Corvette running, maybe I'd start to deserve Penny.

My heart's been beating way too fast since she left. I definitely could use one of my anxiety meds, but I can't make myself go to Gary. Not anymore. I'm going to stop all of it. I already feel like a sorry excuse for a man because—well, because I guess I am one, and that just makes it worse.

Without a word, Gramps tosses his tool down and goes to sit in a chair. We've been working together enough that he knows my moods. When I don't feel like talking, Gramps doesn't talk. When I need to laugh, he gives me shit. And I'm pretty sure he's the one who talked Penny's mom down the other day because so far, she hasn't kicked us out. The woman definitely wants me out of here. She gives me the evil eye every time I see her.

"I'm going sledding with Mitch, Matt, and Chomps in a bit. I think they want test me or something." I shrug. "Make sure I'm good enough for Penny or whatever." It doesn't even surprise me that I tell him. Gramps is cool like that. He has a way of getting stuff out of people and making it feel okay. Kind of like Gary lately.

Gramps chuckles, leaning back in the chair. He crosses his arms. "Eh, they're pretty good kids. Been around forever. They're good to Penny except Mitch has hurt her. Didn't mean to, but it still makes me want to slit his tires."

I hold out my fist and Gramps bumps it, just like one of the guys in my band would.

"I like Mitch, but he's not the one for Pen. She didn't love him. Just thought she did. He was there for her when we lost my son. And again when people gave her a hard time for playing on the boys' hockey team."

Jealousy creeps up inside me. "Yeah, but he also chose some other chick over her."

Gramps rolls his eyes. "Like I said, they're not a match, those two. Which is okay. Nothing wrong with that."

More silence. My leg is bouncing a little, but I'm actually feeling calmer than I was before.

"You really like her, don't you, son?"

His words make it hard to look at him. Because I do really like her, but I also know I shouldn't. I feel Gramps's eyes on me and know it's time to step up. "Yeah. She's awesome. I don't deserve her, though. She doesn't know everything. *No one* here knows everything about me."

Bounce, bounce, bounce. With my eyes, I case the place like I'm planning on robbing it or something.

"Then why don't you tell me?" Gramps's voice is softer than usual.

Can I do this? Can I open my mouth and say the words? It's so fucking hard to admit what's in my head. It's different, knowing something and admitting it. Knowing is personal. It's easy to lie to yourself. Or fool yourself. Admitting it? That's owning it. Making it real. It takes balls to own it. I'm not really an addict. I didn't almost die back home or get lost in Tokyo if I don't actually open my mouth and spit out the words.

I try the deep breathing thing I learned again. I feel like such a coward, and I'm tired of it. And I think if I could tell anyone, it would be Gramps. Looking at him, I realize he's probably the closest thing to a father I've ever had. That I ever will have.

"I kind of…have a problem with pills?"

"You—"

"No. I do. Not kind of." I scratch my head. My arm. Touch my lip ring. Bounce my leg. None of it makes me forget what I'm doing. The stalling makes it worse. "I started right after I got signed. The crowds, they kind of freak me out. It's like they're trying to get inside me, so I'd take something to chill me out. Then, I'd get tired and need to stay awake, so I'd take a pill for that. Then I'd need help sleeping, which would call for another one. It feels good, ya know? Like I'm flying or…I don't know… Light? It started to get fun. I started taking different kinds. Do you know how easy pills are to come by?"

For the first time since I started this confession, I look at Gramps. "I wanted to steal some from you."

His eyes are crinkled at the sides. He gives me a quick nod. "But you didn't, did you?"

"No. Not from you. I snuck some here with me, though. Took 'em all. Took more when my friend, Maryanne, came, and I have twelve sitting in the cabin, waiting for me."

It's almost like my words drift out but float back inside me. Whispering in my head to make sure it sinks in. I *am* an addict. Right now, my mouth feels dry. My heart is going wild again because I *do* have pills waiting for me. I could take them tonight. Or not all of them, but a few. Like for my last time, or whatever. Take some, dump the rest and then I'll be done.

No!

"You wanna know what happened for me to come here?" A part of me actually thinks I want to tell him. Maybe it's a warm-up because I know I have to tell Penny.

"I do." Gramps's voice is even softer.

More breaths. More bounces. More words. "My band had a show, and I was freaking out at it like I always do. The crowds…they get in my head. And then after, paparazzi were chasing me. When I got to Maryanne's, I just wanted to forget, you know? I just needed to forget, so Maryanne gave me a bunch of stuff…" *In, out, in, out.* "I don't even know what all I took. That's bad. Has to be bad, right?" Gramps doesn't answer, but then I don't need him too. "Alcohol, too. I'm not usually much of a drinker, but, yeah. I was feeling it that night."

I bite my thumbnail. "The room we were in was pretty quiet, but it all felt loud in my head. There was dancing, I think? Yeah, Maryanne was dancing and laughing." Flashes of that night pummel me. Drinking, spinning, dancing, laughing, falling… I haven't let myself think about it at all. "It's almost like I knew something was wrong. That I was way too messed up. My body felt it, like it was screaming and fighting against itself or something, but I couldn't do anything about it."

My cheeks are wet. Holy shit. I'm crying.

"It was like a fade to black, in and out. Part of me wanted to laugh with her, I think, because I stumbled and couldn't get up, and I knew that should be funny but not funny at the same time." I'm talking faster now, needing to get it out. It's like poison inside me, festering, and the only way to get rid of it is to hurry up and get the words out.

"Maryanne fell next to me. I think we were on the floor of her room. I can't even fucking remember, but I know my body needed to get it out. I wasn't conscious, but I was. Like my brain was on, but the rest of me wasn't. I knew Maryanne was rolling me over…hitting me on the back. And…that's all. Next thing I knew, I was at the hospital. I almost aspirated." I shake my head. "They had to pump my stomach. My mom… God, I think I broke her. She's been through so much with my dad, and then I broke her, too."

I wipe my eyes, wishing I could bring myself to look at Gramps.

My leg still bounces.

In. Out. In. Out. I try to focus on my breathing.

"Mom and my manager made me come here. I haven't done anything I'm not supposed to since Maryanne left. It's like I fucking hate it. Hate the pills in my bag, but I love them, too. I want to trash them, but I can't make myself do it." When I finally look at Gramps, his eyes are wet. "Does that count for anything? I mean, I know I'm still screwed-up, but the fact that I don't want to be that way anymore? Does that matter?"

Gramps's hand comes down on my shoulder, and he squeezes. "It matters, son. It matters."

I let his words sink in. Hear how he calls me *son.* That matters, too.

I let out a deep, shaky breath. "How do I tell her? I need to tell her." My voice actually cracks.

"The same way you told me. You can do it, son. I'm damn proud of you right now."

It feels good and bad at the same time. It feels so good for her to tell me he's proud, but I don't feel like I've done anything yet. This isn't enough to be my "one thing" Gary was talking about. "But they forced me to come here. I didn't do it on my own. And I haven't been completely clean."

"One step at a time. Can I have them? The pills in your bag?"

No!

In. Out. In. Out.

"Can you take them while I'm gone? My suitcase is in the closet. There's a slit cut in the back. They're in there."

Gramps nods. "One step at a time."

I can do that, I think. Some of the weight on me falls off my shoulders. "I'm going to tell her tomorrow after the game. I want to…" I clear my throat. "I don't know…maybe that's my first step to deserving her. And…rehab. I'm going to talk to Gary about rehab." They're my words, but I struggle to believe I said them. Two months ago, I never would have imagined this, but I need it. Need it for me, so I can take care of Mom and for everyone else who is important in my life. "I don't want to be a screw up anymore… It's time I was better. Try and be happy like Gary says."

Gramps puts his hand on my shoulder. "You're doing good, son. We'll get through this together. I'll be there every step of the way."

I pull Gramps to me and hug him, wishing I knew how to say thanks. That I need him. That he's been like a father to me, but more because he chose to be here. The way he squeezes me back shows me he already knows.

There's a loud rumble of a truck from outside. Gramps and I pull apart and I wipe my face again. Gramps gives my arm another squeeze before I walk away. I get to the garage door when he calls, "Just don't fuck it up, Rookie." There's laughter in his voice.

"You have some dirt on your forehead, old man. Maybe I'm the one who needs to clean you up."

Gramps laughs. "Like I said, no respect. You're lucky I love ya."

His words make me freeze. I *am* lucky. I try to tell him I love him, too, but I can't, so instead I say, "Thanks. And we'll work on the car again soon, yeah?"

"Yeah." He gives me a small wave before I run out to meet the guys.

We drive for, like, forty-five minutes. I'm seriously starting to wonder if these guys really do want to find a place to hide my body. It's going to suck to have to kick Penny's friends' asses, but I'll do it.

They're listening to Cyclops, who I hate. The urge to tell them what a bunch of assholes they are hits me, but then remember I'm not supposed to know famous people. My head's all out of whack after talking with Gramps—better—but still all messed up. If this sledding thing is as cool as they say, I'm anxious to get out there and do it. Hopefully, it will get my mind off of everything. Alaska's good for that, I'm noticing. When I'm feeling a little anxious, there's always some crazy way to burn it off.

Finally, Mitch parks the truck. We're so far up, if it wasn't a little too dark, I could probably see the whole valley from up here. This hill looks way bigger than anything I've imagined people sledding. It's more like a cliff. When I think about sledding, I imagine Christmas movies and eight-year-old kids.

"You're going to love this shit." Chomps rubs his hands together. We all get out and they start throwing gear at me. It takes me a minute to get on all the stuff I wear snowmachining. Even a helmet. This must be some hardcore sledding.

Mitch grabs the sleds, Matt right behind him. They're these thick, red plastic sleds with ridges on the bottom, and rubber pads to sit on.

It takes us another twenty minutes to hike up to the place we're going down from.

Mitch smirks at me. "Newbies first?"

This is definitely a test. Maybe I should respect them for it, and I guess I do, but I also can't wait to kick their asses. "Why? You scared?"

Chomps laughs and buttons up his coat. "Sounds like you're the one who's scared."

Not likely. I toss my sled on the ground and hold it with my foot. There are no trees this far up, but I can see some way below. If I sled too far down, I'm going to have some serious issues dodging them.

"First time, I go alone. Second time, we race." I don't hear if he replies because I sit down and take off. My first thought is *holy crap, they were right*. This is crazy. I grab on as I lean, hoping it helps me take the turn. It feels like I'm going a million miles an hour. Almost like I'm on the snowmachine, but it's even more intense because it just feels like it's me flying down the mountain.

I hit a bump and, no shit, I actually become airborne. "Woo hoo!" I shout. This is incredible. I'm so glad they had the goggles and stuff. Such a rush. When another turn comes up, I lean again. I'm getting close to the bottom now. My sled hits another bump and goes even higher than it did last time. When I hit the ground again, I lose control and catapult off, rolling away from the sled. My body comes to a stop a good twenty feet from where I fell off.

Lying in the snow, I look up at the sky. My chest is going up and down way harder than it should, and I can't catch my breath. Lying here in the cold-ass snow, all I can think about is how incredible this kind of natural high is. Way better than any kind of drugs. What I said to Gramps earlier is the right thing. This is the kind of thing I want to make me feel good, not pills.

I'm going to talk to Gary. I'm going to go to rehab.

Chapter Twenty

Penny

No one's saying the "grounded" word, but what else is it when it's the night before my big game, and I'm not allowed to go out with the guys? Mom and I have passed each other in stony silence dozens of times since I explained, again, that I fell asleep by accident at Bishop's house. Nothing I say seems to matter. She's struggling with what to say, too, but neither of us knows how to start.

I liked Mom better when she was spending too much time at work, or screwing Ben, or whatever else she's doing that she isn't telling me about.

"Loosen that frown, Lucky Girl." Gramps rubs a dirty hand across my forehead. "Bishop can handle himself with those boys."

I lean against the dusty garage wall and fold my arms. "Bishop's as crazy as the rest of them. He'll love it. It's Mom that's making me insane."

Gramps nods and starts opening drawers in the toolbox. He does this when he's not sure what to work on next. He'll pick a tool and then pick the job that goes with the tool. I've always loved this about him.

I push off the wall and slump into one of the greasy camp chairs resting in the garage.

"No, no." Gramps shakes his head. "You don't need to talk to me, you need to go talk to that mom of yours."

"*Pfft*." Not likely.

He chuckles. "I just had this talk with the boy. You like him, don't you?"

I nod and am only a little successful in hiding my smile. "A lot."

Gramps's eyes light up. "He's got history, you know? But those people are the best kind because they already know what's out there and are ready to figure out what they really want. Do you know what you really want?"

I'm not ready to answer that question. "You going to give me the *great opportunities are in front of you* speech? *The sky is the limit?*" If he brings Bishop around to college and leaving, I might freak out.

"No." He shakes his head. "Go talk to your mom. I think she has a lot of guilt stored up over this and over starting to fall for someone new. Try to see this from her point of view. I'm sure she's been afraid to say anything. Just give her a chance to explain before you come at her with your attitude."

I stand. "Fine, fine. I'll go."

"I'm not trying to scare you off. I want you to have some

of the pie I made this morning and tell me that I'm a regular renaissance man because I'm so multi-talented." Gramps winks.

I stop in the doorway. "Anything else?"

He pauses for a moment, his brows pulling together. "Bishop asked me to do something, and I can't for the life of me remember what it was. You got any ideas?"

"None."

Confusion fills his features before his face relaxes. "It'll come to me. Good luck with your mom."

Right.

He's engrossed the moment he leans over the engine. Apparently, he found the tool he wanted to work with.

As I hit the top of the stairs to grab some dinner, or Gramps's pie, I figure I should see if Mom wants to talk. Her voice carries from her room into the kitchen. Good. She's awake. She's here. We can talk. Maybe it was just guilt that kept her from telling me. I mean, it's weird, but I knew she'd find someone eventually. When I get to her door, I pause.

"I'll need to get the story on that kid. He's obviously a bad influence. I've never had to worry about her before. I'm so sorry about the outburst... No, of course it's not your fault. She's just a kid... Yeah, I know... She has a temper, that's all."

Mom sighs. I ball my hands into fists. *Kid*? Playing off how pissed I am because of my *temper*? What the hell? Who is she talking to? It can't be—

"I know, Ben. I want to see you, too."

My whole body tenses. She's talking about me to her

boyfriend?

"Once we work past how she's dealing with this, it'll all be fine, and she's heading off to college soon."

What, does she want me out of here so she can hang with her man anytime she wants? It hurts to breathe. My fingernails press into my palms.

"Okay. Thanks." Her voice has that same ridiculously over-dramatic tone that Rebecca has with Mitch. "I know. Kid hormones. I'm just not used to it, that's all... Well, he can't stick around forever, but it makes me extra determined to get her out of here... That whole situation is strange... I know. Okay, goodnight."

Now is when I should sulk in my room, but I don't. I'm not the smartest girl when I'm this worked up.

Mom opens the door and freezes when she sees me.

"Don't talk about me to your boyfriend!" I yell.

Mom slides her phone into her pocket with shaky hands. It's as if she's about to tiptoe through a room with a glass floor. I want her to yell. Tell me I'm being petty. Instead, she goes weirdly stoic. "Penny. We need to talk. I—"

"I'm not a *kid*. It isn't a *hormone* thing. It's that my mom's left me here to take care of things while she runs around with some guy she didn't see the need to tell me about!"

She blinks a few times, still seeming unsure of what to say. "The night you called, I was at work. I couldn't leave, and—"

I put my hands on my hips. "And what about every other night?"

"Penny," Mom warns. "I need you to lower your voice."

"No!" I yell knowing I'm about to unleash and that it won't be pretty, but I'm past caring right now because it's been building for way too long. "What about when you weren't at my games, or when I had to come home instead of going to the party after? What about then? God! The least you could have done was to tell me you were seeing someone!"

"It's not that simple, Penny."

"Of course it's that fucking simple!" And I just shattered any chance we had of making this civilized.

Her nostrils flare, and her mouth pulls into a thin line. We might be about to step into the fight that's been simmering since I pulled away from her in my truck. "And what have you been doing with Bishop?" Her voice is teetering on the edge of serious anger. "Because it's not like you to be…to be… sleeping over, or…"

"Don't. Even." I point. "This isn't about me. This is about *you*!"

"Not when you're screaming at me like this it isn't!" Mom yells before pulling in a deep breath, like she's actually trying to control her frustration. "We need to talk about you now. Not me."

"Oh. Really? Because you don't know anything about what's been happening in my life. Bishop's the first guy I liked who actually *likes me back*!" But he's so much more than that. I just have no idea how to explain, or why I'd want to bother trying with her right now. It's all in a red haze of frustration and anger anyway.

Mom steps toward me, her face stony, still not pushing

back the way I want her to. "Did you know he had a girl up here?"

I suck in a breath, ready for anything she has to say to me. "Of course I know!" I yell. "Why are you so determined to make my decisions for me! Or to *ruin* this for me?"

Her careful façade breaks, and her face reddens. "Because you're a kid and don't know what you want!"

I laugh a harsh laugh, anything to hide how I'm starting to shake apart inside. "I'm a kid?" I know exactly how to send her over the edge, and I can feel the words making their way to the surface even though I'm sure it's the stupidest thing I could do in this moment. "The tattoo parlor doesn't think I'm a kid."

Anger blazes in her eyes, and the silence is weighted enough for me to know it's time to retreat.

I spin and head for the stairs, my vision and my brain still clouded with frustration. This was supposed to be about her, not me.

"Penny Jones!" Mom's voice has turned into a low growl. "Get. Back. Up. Here. Now."

Not going back up will be stepping way into new territory that I'm not sure I'm ready for, but then I hear a quick knock at the door.

"I'll get the door," I say as I jump down the last couple steps.

I swing open the front door and come face to face with Rebecca.

My jaw goes slack. What the…? I cannot conceive of

any reason for Rebecca to be at my house, but her timing is definitely perfect.

Mom starts stomping down the stairs. "You are not to see him—" She stops as soon as Rebecca comes into view, with a delightfully stunned look on her face—one that makes me know I might be off the hook for just a little bit longer. "Oh. Hello." Mom's voice is suddenly bright and happy.

"Mom. This is Becca." I even try to use the name I know she likes. "She came to help me study since you won't let me go anywhere." I try to lay my nicest voice on thick. Thick enough that she knows I'm doing it, but it hopefully won't make her more angry.

Rebecca's mouth opens, but she's quick. "Yeah. I knew Penny would want to get ahead in Government before the big game, so I came by to help her out." Her sweet voice and the timid way she stands are the perfect counter to Mom's ferocity.

"Okay. Well. Penny." Her lips purse together. She's not happy, but I can tell she's going to take it. "Don't stay up too late."

I give Mom a salute that I hope says *fuck you* as much as it says *yes ma'am*.

I slide my arm through Rebecca's—something I *never* thought I'd do—and we head for my room.

"What's going on?" she whispers as we step through the door.

"Long story." I sigh and flop on my bed.

It's silent for a few moments, which is fine with me. I have no idea what to talk to Mitch's girlfriend about.

"Your room looks like a guy's room, Penny. It's all blue and black and hockey." She shakes her head but still stands just inside my doorway, as if she's not sure if she wants to be in here.

"You've been over here before." I grab a puck off my nightstand and spin it in my hands.

"Actually, you make me change for the hot tub in the tiny unfinished bathroom downstairs."

I cringe because it now seems pretty harsh. "Yeah. Sorry about that."

Her smile is wry. "Sure you are."

I fiddle with the edge of my blanket and try to figure out what I'm supposed to say next. "So... What are you doing here?"

"Waiting for Mitch. I knew you couldn't go with them, but I thought I'd come in and wait for the guys to come back if it was okay. Ever since they caught us together, my parents think Mitch is the devil's spawn or something, so I'm still on lockdown. I had to lie and tell them I was helping you with Government to get to the party the other night."

"Yeah. Okay." This should not be so uncomfortable. Being friends with a girl should be easier than this. "Have a seat." There. That seems friendly. I scoot up on my bed to make room. If she's trying, which she obviously is, I should try, too.

"So, you okay?" she asks.

I'm not sure where to start, but I am sure I don't know Rebecca well enough to be baring my soul here. "What?"

Rebecca cringes. "I could hear you and your mom."

I roll my head around trying to get rid of some of the tension. "She's pissed over Bishop, and I'm pissed for other things, and I get my temper from her, so…"

She smiles. "So when you two argue, it's like world war three?"

I grin back. "Pretty much, yeah."

She rests back on her arms. "My parents are, like, insane about everything."

"Which is why they freaked out over Mitch." And the cool thing is that Mitch doesn't come close to Bishop in a million ways, so having her here… I don't know, but it feels okay.

"And why is your mom freaked out over Bishop?"

I could tell her my mom probably thinks Bishop and I had sex like her and Mitch, but that's way into personal territory. "I don't think my mom knows what to do with the idea that a guy could like me." *I* barely know what to do with it.

"Don't worry, Penny." Rebecca smiles a bit. "I have a feeling Bishop has a way with people. I'm sure he'll turn your mom around."

I hope so. And then I realize that a girl and I just talked about boys, and I didn't sprout pink fingernails, hell hasn't frozen over (that I know of), and it might even be okay.

Chapter Twenty-one

Bishop

Another sleepless night. I thought this shit was over. Telling Gramps, deciding to go to rehab, and talking to Penny should have taken all the stress away, but it didn't. My brain was still going, my eyes still open as I tossed and turned. I would have done anything for an anxiety pill, but I'm determined to be clean now. It makes sense to start now, to make myself proud *now*. Which I am sort of proud, so why couldn't I sleep?

I got my ass kicked sledding down the hill. My body was exhausted, but it also hurt. But again, no pills, so I tried to deal with it. Alaska sledding is no joke. I will seriously never look at it the same way again.

Actually, I wonder if I'm going to see anything the same after Alaska. Which is crazy. I never expected to come here and have an epiphany or whatever, but I can't stop myself from thinking that's exactly what happened.

Maybe it has something to do with all the internal musing

I've been doing… Definitely didn't spend as much time contemplating life's mysteries when I was back home. The walking helped with that—giving me time to just be in my own head. Who knows if that's a good or a bad thing. Sometimes I like what I discover, and other times I feel like a whack-job.

When my cell starts beeping, I roll over in bed and grab it off the nightstand. Maryanne flashes up on the screen. Part of me feels like it's shitty to ignore her, but the other part doesn't want that life to bleed into mine anymore. Plus, it feels wrong to talk to her because of Penny.

After hitting ignore, I toss the phone back onto the nightstand.

I wish it was always that easy—to hit ignore when a thought or craving slips into my mind. When L.A. Bishop tries to resurface and all I want to do is wipe him away and become Alaska Bishop for good. Even though the thought of rehab makes my skin crawl, that is why I have to do it.

I push out of bed and go take a piss before my memoir starts writing itself in my head: "If life was a cell phone—blending two versions of yourself" by Bishop Riley.

Yeah, Alaska is making me crazy.

But I like it.

After a quick shower, I get dressed, knowing my morning is going to be boring. Today's the game and Penny's out to breakfast with her team. Her mom's home so I can't risk her wrath by going over to see Gramps. Which helps, I guess. Not being able to see Gramps takes away my excuse not to go talk to Gary. After everything he's done for me, he needs to know about rehab. He helped me get here.

I'm feeling a little antsy. Nothing bad, but a little bit of jitters. Reasons to go into my room, into my closet so I can find my suitcase, keep tugging at me. I'm proud to say looking at my case is all I've done. Before talking with Gramps yesterday, I checked for my pills every day. Recounted the twelve at least once to make sure they were still there.

Now, I haven't touched it. Haven't stuck my fingers in that tiny slit in the fabric to make sure Gramps didn't accidentally leave one, to make sure there aren't any old ones from before. Gramps wanted to take them, and I'm glad he did.

And honestly…it makes me a little proud.

I head over to my drums and grab the sticks. They're about to slam down when I remember what Penny's mom said—about how loud I am—and I toss them to the ground. My hands are itching to play, but I don't want to give her another reason to hate me. The list is already too long.

I use my hands to drum on my knees instead, and it's totally not the same thing. I think about going over and borrowing one of the snowmachines, but then remember Mama Bear is home and I can't even do that.

I'm not sure any of it would chill me out today, though, because I know what's coming. I'm telling Penny everything. Part of me wants to do it right now. I should have done it last night, but it wouldn't be fair before the game. I'm already in douche-bag territory, and that would tip things toward unforgivable—if they're not already there.

That's when it hits me, and just thinking about it the

tension starts to slip out of me. Walking. I need the cold and fresh air. To see how open that big world is and realize my problems aren't the end of it. There's something freeing about it, and right now, I just want to be free.

Not giving a crap that it's early, I slip on my boots and coat before trudging my way over to Gary's place. He can go with me and tell me stories and ask questions that I might feel okay about answering now. I'm finally doing something I can be proud of—telling Penny and going to rehab.

As soon as I hit the steps, I realize the door is partway open. Time to have some fun. Sneaking up on Gary and scaring him to death will definitely distract me for a few minutes.

I'm quiet as I finish walking toward the door. I'm about to sneak inside when I hear Penny's mom inside.

"I need to know what you guys are doing here." Her voice is as fierce as I've ever heard it. Right then, I know I'm fucked.

"With all due respect, ma'am, I'm not sure that's your business. We haven't caused any trouble. We're paying guests, but I don't think that entitles you information on our private affairs."

I want to yell "Go Gary!" and "Shut the hell up! She already hates me!" at the same time.

"It's my business when it involves my daughter. When I catch her slinking out of his cabin in the morning, with all due respect, *that* makes it my business."

It hits me like a punch to the gut, because she's right. Or maybe not her business, but Penny's. Penny's my girl, and she should know the big shit about me.

Gary speaks up again. "I understand your concern, but I trust him."

Now it's a knife, not just a punch. Gary trusts me when he doesn't know half the truth. When he doesn't know about Maryanne or the pills or any of it.

He keeps talking. "I'm not saying Bishop, or *anyone* for that matter, is perfect, but he cares about your daughter. He won't hurt her."

Her mom sighs. "I've seen it before—girls who throw their lives away for a boy. Penny is so much bigger than Seldon. She needs to get out of here. Go to college. Do you realize she's getting scholarships from schools that have some of the best women's hockey teams in America? I don't want Bishop in her way. I can see it in his eyes. Something's not right, and I'll be damned before I let him drag her down."

Drag her down... It's not that I have anything to offer Penny. She's right. Money doesn't matter to a girl like Penny. She wants Alaska and hockey. Even when I do get clean, I'm one of the youngest drummers to ever win a Grammy. I've had way more success in two years than I ever imagined, but Penny is bigger than any of that will ever be. It's not like I can expect her to give up hockey for me. I wouldn't if I were her, but could I give up Burn? We couldn't have a relationship if I'm traveling all the time.

Her mom is right. The thought of holding Penny back makes my gut churn.

Gary is quiet for a few seconds. "You know, people like

you piss me off. He's a fucking *kid*. He hasn't had a lot in his life, but he tries. Tries a whole hell of a lot harder than a lot of people I know. I hate this judgmental bullshit. I don't care what anyone says, I'm damn proud of that kid. He's a *good* boy, who I know will grow up into a *great* man. Is he perfect? Nope, but at least he knows it. He doesn't sit up on a pedestal and condemn everyone else."

Twist, twist, twist. The knife just keeps getting pushed in deeper and deeper. I clutch my stomach so I don't puke. Gary's wrong about me. I'm none of the things he said. It doesn't matter that I've booked a flight home, and that I'm planning to call my Mom to help me get into rehab. I'm a liar. He's defending me without knowing about the pills and Maryanne.

"Is that why he snuck a blond girl in here? I can't help but wonder if he started seeing my daughter before or after her."

Ready. Aim. Fire.

I'm dead.

I should have been the one to tell Gary about Maryanne. He deserves that and a whole lot more for the faith he puts in me. After kissing Penny, I snuck Maryanne here. She has goals and a future. She needs someone a lot better than me.

Gary's quiet.

"Did you know about the girl?"

More quiet.

Finally, he replies. "We'll be out by tomorrow."

There's never been a time I hated myself more than I do right now.

As soon as Penny's mom goes back to her house, I come out from my hiding spot. Everything inside me is yelling… screaming at me to run away, but I'm so fucking tired of being weak, so I climb the stairs to Gary's cabin again and knock.

There's no typical Gary smile on his face when he opens the door. No joking. No nothing. That's not true. There's disappointment, my legs buckle, threatening to collapse. Everything inside me aches. I want to run away. I'm scared as hell to do this, but I have to. I can't keep running anymore. I head straight over to the couch and sit down. "I'm sorry."

"Was it Maryanne?" His voice is tense.

"Yeah."

"Did you get high with her, Bishop?"

"Yeah."

"Shit," he mumbles, and then, "I should have known this. It was my job to fucking *know*." His guilt over my screw-up jams that knife in me again. "How many times?"

I hate this. I'm so tired of disappointing everyone. Of disappointing myself. "Only once with her. That's the only time she's been here. I snuck some pills with me here, though. Took them off and on. I've also had one beer. And Maryanne mailed me some pills, but they never came. She also left some when she bailed, but I didn't take them. Wanted to a million times, but I didn't. I started to realize—not that it matters."

"Where are they?" he grits out, pacing the living room.

"Gone. Gramps took them—I told him about everything yesterday and he said he'd take care of them for me." It's so crazy spilling it out for him like this. It hurts. It sucks. I hate this person that I am, but it also makes the tightness in my chest loosen just a little.

Those words soften his stance a little bit. Gary sighs again before sitting on the coffee table in front of me. "How did I let this happen? I've done this before with Troy. I've been *trained* to do this. I should have known… I had faith in you, Bishop."

His guilt makes me feel worse. "Fuck, I *know*." Here comes the shaking. I run my hands through my hair hoping it will stop. "I know, and I hate that. Hate it all. It's so screwed-up, but I swear, I'm done, Gary. I don't want to touch anything anymore, and I'm sorry. I know that doesn't matter, but I am. I'm coming clean to Penny after the game and then…I was going to talk to you. I want to go home and, you know." I shrug. "And go to rehab."

Gary looks me over. "Funny how you've decided to go to rehab all of a sudden. It doesn't work that way. You can't just throw words out there because you got caught. It has to come from in here." He touches his chest.

Fear climbs up my spine. "It does. I'm not lying. I'm so fucking tired of *lying*. You can talk to Gramps. I told him everything yesterday. I made the decision about rehab and telling everyone the truth before you found out. I just hadn't told you yet."

He just stares at me, and I never realized how much I need Gary. How weak I was before he started helping me. He dropped his life for me, and he trusted me. He's walked with me and talked with me and, hell, he's my *friend*. I could have pushed him too far to go back, and that thought makes the words start rushing out of my mouth again. "It's not your fault. I swear I'll do better. Don't turn your back on me…" *Please, don't turn your back on me.*

He sighs. "You've really been thinking about his before now, Bishop? You talked to Gramps and this isn't you grasping at straws here?"

"I swear." I stare at the ground. "I know my word doesn't mean much right now, but I'm telling you the truth. I…I need you."

"And I'll be here. You can't get rid of me that easy. I'm not going anywhere."

My head jerks up, and I look at him. He's staying? "Really? You really won't bail?"

"But I won't be as easy on you. You've lost my trust. You're going to have to earn it back, and I'm not letting this rehab thing go by the wayside. You want my help, then it's happening."

The urge to hug him hits me. "Thank you. I will. I'll do whatever it takes. I just need to see Penny's game and tell her where I'm going, then we can go."

Gary reaches over and grabs my shoulder. "I told you, we'd take care of this together, and we will. I'm not bailing on you. Never."

It's like each of Gary's words start to pull the knife free. He's not bailing. I can still do this. "Thank you. You won't regret it."

Chapter Twenty-two

Penny

"Your mom's going to be pissed," Bishop says as I turn off Bitty in the parking lot of the ice arena.

"Aww... Does my mom scare you?" I tease.

He shakes his head. "No, but I don't want to cause problems, either."

"Mom's the one causing problems. And did you or did you not have to *ask* Gary if you could ride with me?" I scoot over and slide a leg across his lap until I'm straddling him in the front of my truck. This is what I need before my game—a little distraction to help me focus.

Bishop's thumbs trace my cheekbones, and the warmth in his eyes turns my body to mush. I love everything about the way I feel with him. It's a rush, like being on the ice, only softer, and warmer... His hands rest low on my waist, the way I'm learning he likes. And the way I'm learning I like.

I lean in for a kiss, which Bishop dodges by kissing my

cheek.

"We need to talk about a few things, okay?" he says. "There's stuff I need to tell you—"

I slide my tongue across his lower lip until I hit his lip ring, hoping to distract him. "Are you turning into a girl, Bishop *Ripe*? Talking about my mom and feelings and—"

He kneads my shoulders, staring at his hands. "I'm serious, Penny."

The warmth in his eyes has turned sad, and that's not what I need right now.

"And *I'm* serious when I say we can talk *after* the game. I need to kiss you." I tease him with my tongue again, upper lip this time. "And then I need to focus."

He narrows his eyes while trying to hold in a smile. "You're impossible."

"You love it." I part my lips and barely touch them to his, pulling away when he opens his mouth for a kiss.

"I *do* love it. Now come here before you put all that gear on, and I can't feel you anymore." Bishop wraps his arms around my waist, making me forget everything but him and how I need to be closer. Need my body closer. Need more of his hands on me.

But the kiss is over way too soon, and Bishop's pulling away.

He brushes a few stray hairs off my face. "You should probably go in. Hockey's your thing. State Championship. This is a huge deal. I don't want to distract you."

"It *is* my thing." I kiss the corner of his mouth. "I love

hockey. I couldn't function without it."

He gets a far off look in his eyes like there are a million things buzzing around in his head.

"Hey, what's wrong?" I slide my hands down over his chest. Because Bishop and I touch each other that way. And we kiss. And after kissing him, I really want to know what it's like to do more. I also know in a few minutes, I'm going to have to shake off this amazing feeling so I can get ready for the game. Just not yet.

Bishop takes a deep breath before smiling at me. "Nothing. Can't wait to see you kick ass out there."

Grinning, I lean forward to kiss him again.

"Jones!" Someone's hockey stick clanks on my window. "Get off the guy and get your ass in the locker room!"

Mitch laughs, and Becca gives me a wave. Chomps and Matt are behind him and make kissy faces at me as they walk by.

I flip them off. Jerks.

I close my eyes for a moment, trying to clear my thoughts as I slide my fingers through his hair. "I love the way you mess with my head."

"I love the way you mess with mine." He stares into me. Deep. Like he always has. "Know that, okay?"

"I have to go." I lean forward and press our lips together again. And then just touch his tongue with mine. He's becoming a very nice addiction.

"I know. Go kick ass." He leans forward and kisses me back. "We'll talk after."

"Bishop!" Gary pounds on the window as he laughs, but

he's also shaking his head.

"Okay." I slide off Bishop, not thrilled with our interruptions, but ready to get into the game.

I even let him carry my bag.

. . .

Lucky bra. Lucky socks. Lucky leggings. Lucky shirt. I shake out my quivering hands. I slide on my pads and my jersey. My heart's thrumming. Hammering. Thrumming. State. Senior year. I'm the only girl playing. I'm in the locker room alone. It's quiet. Perfect.

My whole high school hockey career has come down to this. I'm not going home on the losing team.

Skates. I pull each step of laces tight before moving to the next. They have to be just right. Just so that I don't have to touch them again. Tight. Ready. Helmet. Check. Mouthguard. Check. I shove Bishop out of my mind. Shove Mom out of my mind. Push away the picture of her and Ben. Thank Dad for making me love this game, which twists in my gut, but just for a moment. Reluctantly push away the picture of Bishop drumming without his shirt. Push away Gramps, after I imagine him giving me a thumbs-up.

For big games like this, I can't even look for them in the crowd. I need to be in the zone. On the ice and nowhere else. I'm good. My head is clear. I've got lucky everything on, and I'm ready. I can kick ass. I can do this. My team can do this.

I stand up and head out to the ice knowing once I'm there, it'll all fall into place. Like always.

• • •

I haven't had a clear thought in the four minutes since the game started. There's no time. The puck's mine. Now Mitch's. Now stolen. I fly toward number ten and ram him into the wall. Chomps flicks the puck back to Mitch, and ten is on my tail as I try to position myself in front of the goal.

I know Mitch. I know what's he's doing. He goes around the backside of their goal, and I fake like I'm moving back, but come forward just as the puck goes from Mitch's stick to mine. I smash the thing with everything I have and hit net.

Holy. Shit. *Goal one in State is mine.*

I scream and throw my hands in the air. The crowd screams. Mitch slaps my back as I spin around.

"Way to go, Penny!" Matt yells from the goal.

Wow, this feels good. Better than good.

The puck's on the ice. Back to game.

Number ten's after me now. I can't shake this guy, and he's almost as big as Chomps.

At the end of first period, the score is still 1-0. Just me. Just mine. I'm gasping for air as we hit the bench.

Coach yells some words of encouragement. My whole body already hurts from being slammed. This is brutal.

"You okay, Penny?" Coach says more quietly as we head back out.

He never singles me out. "Good, why?"

"'Cause ten has it out for you. He's a big guy."

I just nod. This would piss me off coming from most

people, but Coach has never treated me like I can't handle myself. I hit the ice and look at the hulk of number ten again. Not a good idea. I can't be afraid to get hit. Can't. That's the number one killer in a game.

I'm Penny.

No fear.

I'm fast.

I'm good.

I can play.

The puck hits the ice, and I'm back to instinct. I've never skated so hard, worked so fast, let instinct take over more. I can't wait to watch this game because I know I'm playing good. UAF's men's coach will take me for sure after this. Still no goals from the opposing team. We can do this. I'm weak, like I've run ten miles, but only one more period's gone by, which means one left and we win. *One.*

The whistle blows to start the final period, and number ten clips my shoulder, slamming me against the wall. A searing shot of pain goes through my arm, stealing my breath, but I can handle it. I can deal. I'm okay. My skates slice across the ice, and both teams race and weave to gain control of the puck and the game. I get slammed again. I fall. Exhaustion is taking over almost as much as the pain. Mitch flies behind the goal again, puck at the ready. I need to get in there to make sure we stay ahead.

My legs are starting to weaken, my shoulder's a throbbing mess, but there're less than ten minutes left. I can take Advil later. Right now, I need to play with everything I have.

Chapter Twenty-three

Bishop

Something's not right. I don't know what it is, but Penny doesn't seem as fast as she was. She's not letting anyone close to her. Yeah, I know she's supposed to be dodging guys, but she's doing it differently. It takes everything I have inside me not to jump out on the ice and take down number ten. He's been on her ass all night, and it's pissing me off. Hockey or not, he hits her again, and I'm out there.

Chill out, Riley, I tell myself. Penny doesn't need me. She doesn't need anyone. She can take care of herself. She'll go off and play hockey, which is what she should do. Leave my ass behind.

I look around, starting to feel freaked out.

It doesn't make it easier that the crowd is double what it was at her last game. People pushing, screaming, cheering, grabbing. It's every fear that taunts me alive. If this wasn't her game, I would have been gone a long time ago, but what kind of man am I if I can't deal with a crowd for her? I need to find a way to calm my shakes before I spiral out of control.

Penny makes a turn, ice shooting up from her skate, and it calms me a little bit. She's incredible out there. Everywhere, actually, but it's so cool to see her skate like that.

And they're going to win because of her. I know it.

I look a few rows behind me and see Penny's mom with Ben. If you ask me, it's pretty janky that she brought him here. She gives me a look of death, so I turn away. I'm not dealing with her tonight. It bothers me that Gramps isn't here, though. Gramps and our talk and the pills are playing on a continuous loop in my mind. The more I think about them, the more it feels like everyone is gravitating toward me, squeezing around me tighter and tighter until I want to scream for a whole different reason.

Bishop! Bishop! Bishop!

I flinch, try to take some deep breaths, pretend I'm walking with Gary. *They're not here for me. No one's yelling my name.*

I hate that it's like this. It shouldn't be this way. It sucks that I'm teetering on the edge at a hockey game. Trying to shake it off, I look for Penny. Just as I do, she starts skating our way. Number ten is right behind her. He slams her into the wall so hard, I swear I feel the rumble. And then she hits the ice. My chest is getting tighter, like someone is squeezing the air out of me.

The crowd gasps. Pauses. I stare, waiting for her to get up. She doesn't.

Everyone starts racing toward her. Coaches, an EMT, her team, I don't know who else, but I know I have to get to her. To be there for her the way she's unknowingly been there for me. I start shoving my way through the crowd.

"Bishop!" Gary yells from behind me, but I ignore him.

Deep breaths. Calm the fuck down, B. You can't lose it right now. The crowd is tight. No one wants to let me through, and I'm struggling to breathe. It's like they're a wall, fighting to keep me from her, so I start pushing bodies with everything I have in me.

My chest cinches tighter.

Deep breaths.

In. Out. In. Out.

I feel like I've downed a bunch of uppers. My insides are twitchy, like they want to bust out of my body. I can't control any of it. Nothing. Me. The crowd. No control.

"Bishop!" Gary yells again.

I just need Penny. Need to get to Penny. There are too many people around me, in front of me, to see her.

Hands clawing at my skin. People grabbing me. Bishop! Burn! Bishop, burn! Don't crack up! It's not real.

Deep breaths, deep breaths, deep breaths.

She's not getting up. Why isn't she getting up?

Finally, I push my way onto the ice. If I took the time, I might be able to breathe right now, but it's not important. I'm slipping like crazy, but again, it doesn't matter. A million years later, I get to the people blocking her.

They're crowding around her. *Give her room to breathe!*

"Pen," rushes out of my mouth when I get to her. Her mom is by her side, and she gives me another one of those evil looks. Right now? Fuck her. I don't care. This is about Penny. Ben steps in front of me when I reach for her.

"Her mom doesn't want you around her. Maybe you should back up."

"And I'm pretty sure Penny wouldn't want *you* around her." I shove him aside and he falls to the ice. Someone yells, "Hey!" and a ton of hard stares come down on me. *Burn, Bishop, Burn!* Hands grabbing me.

They're loading her onto a gurney.

"Penny." I reach out and touch her hand. They took her gloves off so it's just her skin, all soft. Her bones, all fragile. So fragile. Her eyelids flutter a few times, but her body's still slack.

Ben grabs my shoulder. "Back up!"

I just want to make sure she's okay. They should understand that. I need her to be okay. I shake him off. My finger is latched onto Penny's. Her Mom is there again, breaking our contact, leaning over Penny. "What's wrong? How bad is she hurt? Is she awake?" She can hate me later. Right now, I just need to know about Penny.

"Get out of the way," she replies. Ben grabs for me, and I shove him again. People gasp all around me.

A coach grabs me this time. "We need you to get off the ice!"

Everyone is staring.

Mitch skates up and tries to grab my arm, but I jerk away.

I can't handle being touched right now.

"She'll be okay, Bishop."

I ignore him.

Breathe, breathe, breathe.

Sweat makes my eyes sting.

They're wheeling Penny away.

Dizzy. I can't believe I'm fucking dizzy right now. I feel like I could puke. Pass out. Fall down. Something. Everything is blurry. The crowd is both loud and muted at the same time. People are looking at me. Somehow, they're transformed into a crowd at one of my shows. Waiting for me. Penny's gone, and all I can think about is her. Gramps. Gramps isn't here. He would be down on the ice if he was. Gramps has to know she's hurt.

They're not going to let me see her, but Gramps will make sure she's okay for me. Get me in to see if she's okay.

Breathe, breathe, breathe.

I start to run. The ice is slippery as hell. My heart feels like it might burst, but I keep going.

I'm out of the building and don't even take the time to suck in a deep breath. I run for Bitty, pulling the keys out of my pocket as I go.

I slam the truck into first, the tires spinning as I peel out of the parking lot.

I almost run off the road three times, the tires slipping and sliding, but I just need to get home. *Tell Gramps. Check on Penny. She'll be okay. Everything will be okay.*

The only reason I know I turned off the truck when I get home is I use the keys to unlock her house. "Gramps!"

Breathe, breathe, breathe. Don't lose it right now. Not when it counts. She can do anything. She's way better than me. I need to do this for her. "Gramps! She's hurt. She needs you. We need you!"

Music is playing, but I can't find him anywhere. My legs are shaking so bad I can hardly stand, but I push myself. Keep going. Have to keep going. "Gramps!"

I make it to the kitchen. I'm not breathing anymore. My heart isn't beating, but somehow I make myself run to Gramps who's lying on the floor, a pie teetering on the edge of the table.

"No! No, no, no! Fuck no!" I fall to the floor next to him. Grab him. Pull his head to my lap. My hands are shaking so hard I can't even tell if there's a pulse. Get it together. I need to get it together. Don't fuck this up.

My chest is cracked open, everything inside me spilling out. Gramps. Penny. How can this be happening? "Wake up. Wake up, old man. Penny needs you." *I need you.*

I shake him. Please wake up. I need him to wake up. *I love you, too.* Rocking. With his head in my lap, I rock. Look down at his beard. There's grease on his face again. Crazy old man, always has grease on his face.

And then it's wet, my tears hitting him the same way Mom's hit me in the hospital.

"You're doing good, son. We'll get through this together. I'll be there every step of the way."

"You said we'd do it together. You said you'd *be* there. You have to be there." More rocking. My head is blurry. The room is blurry. I just want it all to go away. Everything. It's too much. *Please be there. I need you. I can't do it, Old Man.*

Fighting, I try to stop shaking, to stop rocking, but I can't. It's taking me over, possessing me. *Penny, Gramps…*

"Bishop! What are you—oh shit." Gary falls to the floor next to me. He's on his phone. Yelling into it. Yelling at me. Pushing me out of the way so Gramps is flat on the floor. My brain tells my body to do something, but I'm frozen.

"Snap out of it, Bishop! I need your help!" Leaning over, he breathes into Gramps's mouth. CPR. Gramps is gone. *He loved me. He knew all about me and still loved me.*

"Push on his chest. Snap the fuck out of it and help me!" he yells.

I'm screwing it up. Like always. *Get it together!* For once, I need to not mess something up. Fighting down everything else inside me, I find the spot in the center of his chest and start compressions.

Gary gives him more air. Gramps has no air. Gary's breathing for him. I'm trying to start his heart when he's always been able to do everything.

Over and over, we try to bring Gramps back to us. I'm on autopilot, no idea what I'm doing, but managing to do it. EMTs show up. Shove me out of the way. Give Gramps air. Push on his chest.

Gary's pacing. Talking to an EMT. My legs are so weak I reach out so the table can hold me up, but I miss and almost crash to the floor.

I'm numb. More numb than I've ever been. I can't feel

anything. Don't know if I'm breathing, but I know I need out. Out of the house. Out of my own skin. Out of everything.

Staggering, I stumble to my cabin. I have no idea how I get inside. With all the strength and anger inside me, I kick my drums until they topple down, smash my foot over and over into them. Pain shoots up my leg, but I don't care. Penny is hurt. Gramps is *gone*. I know it. Know he's not coming back. How can he leave me? Doesn't he know I need him? How much Penny needs him? He was fine yesterday. Fine. We worked on the car, and laughed, and talked, and he told me we'd do this together. He made me believe. He made me feel strong.

More stumbling and then I make it to my room. I don't know why I go there, what I want. Actually I know what I want, but I can't have it. My foot catches on the chair, and I fall forward and let loose. Cries climb up my throat. My gut cramps. I wanted to save him. Couldn't save him. He's gone. *Gone*. Penny's hurt, and I couldn't save Gramps for her—for me. I'm losing it.

It's not like I did anything to deserve being happy anyway.

I roll on the ground, my eyes blur with tears. My suitcase sits in front of me, taunting me. I can hardly make it out through the blur of my vision. My shaking increases. My heart slam-dances in my chest.

He could have missed one.

I actually *crawl* to my suitcase, rip it open. *Please let him have left one.* It takes me three times to push my fingers inside. Finally they're there and...harder, my heart pounds harder. There's a baggy inside.

He didn't take them. Why didn't he take them? Maybe he didn't get a chance. Maybe he forgot. What matters is they're here when I need them. I rip it out. Open. Twelve pills.

I want to throw them across the room.

I want to take them all.

Gary giving Gramps air. Pushing on his chest.

Penny getting slammed into the wall. Falling, falling. Her mom's words. She'll never let me be a part of Penny's life. I don't deserve to be, never have.

It'll be my last one. No more.

Why didn't I tell Gramps I loved him, too?

I dump them into my shaking hand and toss I don't even know how many into my mouth. The rest fall to the floor and scatter. Stumbling, I go to the bathroom, then turn on the tap.

What am I doing? I don't want to do this.

I need this.

I cup my hands, fill them with water, and drink down the pills and liquid before sliding down the wall and hitting the floor.

I'm floating away…further and further the longer I sit here. The pain is masked, hiding behind the clouds of high. I can breathe. I'm free. It feels so good. I shouldn't have fought this. Why did I fight this?

Soaking in this light, fluffy feeling, I kick my legs out in front of me. This is the freedom Gary talked about. The pain keeps getting further away, and it feels incredible.

Alaska Bishop is gone.

Gramps pushes his way through the haze. He worked with

me. Believed in me. Loved me. I'm letting him down.

Gary shoves his way in next. He stood up for me. Protected me. Took time from Troy to help me. Walked with me. Talked with me. I'm letting him down.

Mom's hand is in my hair. She always loved me. Took care of me. Let me have my dreams. She did everything to keep Dad away from us. I want to take care of her. There's no way to do it like this. I don't want to let her down anymore.

Penny. *Penny*. Her hands on my sides. Her lips against mine. Vanilla and gasoline. I feel the adrenaline when we race. How good I felt just carrying her hockey bag. She trusts me. Talks to me. Likes me. Bishop Ripe, not Bishop Riley. I don't have to be a rock star for her. And I lied to her. I don't want to lie to her anymore. I want to deserve her trust.

This is my biggest fuck up of all. All my plans, what I told Gramps, Gary, rehab. I'm blowing it to hell. It makes me sick. I make myself sick. Gramps just died, and I don't know what's wrong with Penny, and I'm high. Hatred burns through me.

Lurching forward, I stick my finger down my throat trying to get rid of the poison inside me. Trying to be the Bishop I want to be. It tastes like crap. My throat burns. My stomach feels like it's shriveling I puke so hard, but I don't want to leave anything else in there. I don't want it inside me ever again.

When nothing else will come out, I pull out my cell and type two words.

I'm sorry

After hitting send, I push to my feet and run outside.

Chapter Twenty-four

Penny

I blink and try to open my eyes, but it's like they're filled with mud. Everything's heavy. Someone's holding my hand. Bishop. Bishop has my hand. I remember at the rink. I turn, and Mom's blurry face is looking through the railings of a hospital bed.

"You're fine, sweetie." Mom's voice carries to my ears from someplace far away. Or maybe I just think it's far away. "You got a nasty concussion, and—"

"Where's Bishop?" I jerk my hand away, but I can't find the thoughts to form the words. Wait. Game. "The game. How did we do?"

"Mitch stopped by. You won."

I let myself relax. How much did I miss? *What* did I miss?

"Yours was the only goal scored. I'm proud of you." Mom's voice hitches.

"Why am I here?"

Wait. Her face is seriously red and blotchy, and tears are streaming down her cheeks so fast she can't keep up with them.

"Did I lose an arm or something?" I ask. The foggy, floaty feeling is still keeping me from putting any pieces together. I'm just here.

Wait. I'm mad at Mom. I think.

"No, honey, but—"

"Bishop?" That's what I was after. He had my hand. Not Mom. Bishop. This isn't right.

"He's not here," Mom says, but her voice is sorry, tired, not frustrated like I'd expect. "Penny. Listen to me."

She's being too quiet. Why is her voice so quiet and hesitant? Why isn't Bishop here? I turn toward Mom. "Did you tell Bishop not to come?"

"Yes, but we need to talk about something else right now."

I never know what to do when things get this intense, so I try to tease. "Am I dying or something?"

She shakes her head and squeezes her eyes tight before looking at me. "You'll be fine honey, but we lost Gramps."

"Gramps?" The room spins, turning my stomach over. "What are you talking about?"

"He passed away." The words come out on top of one another in this weird, whispering voice.

They linger, hover, and then start digging their way in, but I won't let them. Won't let them sink in. Won't let them be replayed.

I choke. "No. He's fine." I can't lose Gramps. *Can't.* My

head is so clogged up and heavy that I'm not processing right. No way can this be happening.

"I'm sorry, Penny. He had a heart attack. He was gone before the ambulance got there." Mom's hand squeezes mine again, but she feels like a stranger right now who is saying things I can't understand. Gramps isn't gone. I'll figure this out. I just need out of here so I can find him.

I try to sit up, but a shot of pain rushes through my shoulder, and the room spins like I'm on a roller coaster.

"Whoa." A nurse pushes me back down. Where did *she* come from?

"She's going to give you something for the pain," Mom says as she continues to hold my hand in her two.

I don't want anything for the pain. My chest hurts way worse than my shoulder, and I don't think whatever she's putting in my IV is going to help with that. I don't want Mom to hold my hand. I want to be out on the rink with Gramps screaming my name from the bleachers and grinning every time I get stuck in the penalty box. He's the only thing that takes the sting out of Dad being gone. My eyes are too heavy. I open my mouth to say *stop with the drugs*, but nothing comes out.

Gramps dying is all too real. I scream and yell, only I think it's mumbles because my lips are so numb I can't feel them. Mom told Bishop to leave me alone, and now Gramps is gone, and if I can't have Gramps I need Bishop. I try to tell her how I hate that she lied to me and that she hasn't been home and that she never gave Bishop a chance. I exhaust myself talking in slurred words. I'm still fuzzy with drugs, and none of it makes sense. Finally, the doctor insists my mother leave the room. "You're not mad at me, Penny. You're just mad," she keeps saying over and over. Right now, it's all the same.

I lie through a CT scan to check for permanent damage to my brain and wonder why Bishop hasn't fought his way through to see me yet. I've been here all night. A doctor explains that my clavicle is broken in several places, which is not his biggest concern. His concern is the huge bundle of torn ligaments, which was probably the hit I took and ignored. Because I kept playing, I shredded the torn ends. He's scheduled surgery on my clavicle and isn't sure yet how best to treat the rest of the damage. That's a different kind of specialist. I've also got some serious bruising on my hip and thigh, which will make walking tricky for the next couple weeks. The damage sounds bad, and I wonder how long it'll be before I can get back out on the ice because I can't even *think* about the possibility of losing hockey right now.

The doctor keeps Mom from my room for my recovery. I'm angry and she's here and I want all of this to be over. I want to be home with Gramps working on my car and giving Bishop shit for not keeping up—even though he does.

I hear long recovery. Physical therapy. Pain medication. Rest. Calm. Nothing I want to hear.

Bishop still hasn't made his way to me. I think that hurts almost as much as losing Gramps.

. . .

Mom and I drive home together, and she's sort of understanding I need her to be quiet because she's said nothing. I feel empty. I should be worried I'll never play hockey again or that my arm won't work right or wonder how far behind in homework I'm going to be, but I don't have it in me to care about any of that. Gramps and Bishop are the only things swirling in my head. As soon as we stop in the driveway I push open my door, determined to do this on my own.

"I'm going to see Bishop. I'll be inside in a minute." Though, I haven't totally figured out how to walk by myself yet.

She sucks in a breath like she's bracing herself.

"What?" But before she can answer, Mitch slides into my driveway in his truck. Driving like an ass, as usual.

Before Mitch opens his door, Mom says, "He's gone, Pen. He and Gary left. I have a number for you."

"He *left*? Why didn't you *tell* me?" The hollowness grips at my insides in a feeling that's a million times worse than my shoulder. "Give me the number."

Mom slides out her phone and scrolls to Gary, handing it to me.

I hit send with shaky hands. It hasn't even sunk in that he's not here. Bishop would *never* just leave. Not with me hurt. Not with Gramps's death. How crazy is it that I never even got Bishop's number? He was just *here*.

"Hello?" Gary answers.

"What's going on?" My voice has nowhere near the strength I need for it to. My *body* has no strength.

"Penny…" He sighs. "I'm sorry. He was really trying hard."

"What are you talking about?" I'm blinking back tears again. Even my lips are trembling, I'm feeling so much. How could he… "Was he sick or something?"

Mitch stops next to me, his brows pulled down, and he's leaning forward, trying to see my face.

"You know who he is, right?" Gary asks. "The drummer for—"

"I know who he is!" I yell, pain spreading through my side so sharp I gasp, and Mitch wraps an arm around me. "Where *is* he?"

He sighs. "He has a drug problem, Penny. Pills. Drinking. That's why he was here. To get clean, but he couldn't control it on his own anymore."

It's like someone's just stuffed my head with cotton—something that makes it hard to think. To see. To breathe. Drug problem? He's on drugs, and he never told me? My world tilts. I don't get how Bishop could be on drugs. He never seemed like a junky to me. Never once acted high. And he knew, *knew* how I felt because of my dad. *And*. And he knew how I hate being lied to. In a strange way, that's not the worst thing he did. How could he have all the faith in me—tell me I can go to school where I want and play on the men's team—when he wasn't even staying *clean*? In a way, he was another person making choices for me. Or allowing me to make choices based on a *lie*.

And he left. Left me the way Dad did. I know it wasn't his choice, but I feel left all the same. Mom chose Ben over me. Mitch left me for Becca. Gramma and now Gramps... Why am I so easy to leave behind?

"Do you know my dad died?" I ask. It's all I can think of—easier to focus on this instead of the fact that two people I care about are gone in one swoop.

Mom's hand goes to her mouth, and she blinks as a few tears fall. I'm not sure if this makes me feel bad for her or more angry. Probably, I should feel bad.

"You mean Gramps?" Gary asks.

"No!" I snap. "My *dad*!"

"No," he whispers.

"Some stupid asshole who liked to get wasted killed him. When you see Bishop—*if* you see Bishop—tell him to leave me the fuck alone." I hang up the phone, hand it to Mom, and the first sob hits me, sending shocks of pain from my shoulder through my body. It's not taped tight enough. No one could tape me tight enough.

My hip aches as I move back to my house a half step at a time. I know I should be leaning against someone, but Mitch doesn't feel right anymore.

Bishop's gone. Walked out on me when I needed him most.

I lost my *Gramps*. His happy face, his freaking pies, and his horrible country music.

I don't have enough people to lose two at once.

There's too much hurt. Too much cracking apart. Too much everything. Every kind of pain. Bishop's gone. The bastard left. God. And the reason he was here. I can't breathe. Don't want to move. I'm stopped in my driveway wishing I could pass out again. Wishing to not feel. To escape. Anything. I'd do anything. My body shakes, spreading the shoulder pain, which is nothing compared to how my chest burns.

Mom tries to touch me, but I push her away because I'm just not ready to deal with our mess right now. Mitch tries to support me as my thoughts continue to spin.

Shit. Bishop did want to talk. Was this it? What he wanted to tell me before the game? The thing I made fun of him for? It's just that the other thing was so big, I didn't see this coming, and I feel stupid. I'm still pissed. Him being some kind of rock star was an okay thing to share because it didn't make him look bad. But him being some drugged-out drummer wasn't important enough to share. Fine. Whatever.

"Penny?" Mitch's voice sounds panicked, but close. Too close. "Can I help you up?"

Am I down? Mom's wiping away her tears and kneeling in front of me. I'm sitting in the snow, and Mitch's arms are around me, pulling me to my feet.

"Penny," Mitch whispers. "Come on."

I let him half carry me to the door. I've never let anyone see me this weak. I've never been this weak. It just fuels my anger.

"Can I—" Mom starts.

"I got it for now," Mitch whispers as we pass her on our way into the house.

"He left, Mitch." More searing pain. "He just left."

• • •

I'm not sure how long Mitch stays. I sob when he brings me a piece of Gramps's apple pie. And part of me smiles because Gramps was right. He said it was a good one—renaissance man and all that. I sleep. I wake up. I sleep. My surgery is one long day of more haziness and drugs. Mitch is still around. It's crazy how I thought he was more than a friend. This feels nothing like being next to Bishop, which sends another hit of searing pain through me.

Right now, Mitch is the best friend I have. Maybe the only real one. I'm snuggled against his warmth, with days worth of paper plates and cups strewn about my room, scrolling through everything I can find on my phone about Bishop Riley. None of it meshes with the guy I knew. Drugs. Girls. Hotness… Okay. That one came with him. There's such a disconnect from the famous guy to the guy I know. Or…*knew*, I guess, since he's not here anymore, and it would appear I didn't know him all that well anyway. He sent me one short, pathetic message on the day he left.

I'm sorry

Anyone and everyone is *sorry*. It changes nothing.

When my bedroom door opens, I quickly disconnect from the Internet, and Rebecca steps in.

What? I slowly scoot to sitting in bed and double over the pain is so intense. "You just walked into my house?" How long has it been since I took something for pain? It's like there still isn't enough tape to keep my bones from feeling like they're scraping around inside me, and my surgery scar itches like crazy.

Rebecca glances between Mitch and I a few times, and then crosses her arms. "I lent you my boyfriend for nearly a week. Where he slept, with you, after finally admitting to me that he loves you." Her whisper is harsh. "Though he claims its just friendship, I think I'm allowed to walk in."

Just then Mitch lets out a snore, his mouth still hanging open in sleep. And we both laugh—it's sort of a nervous, need-to-break-tension laugh, but it works.

But then the weight of losing everything at once crashes into me again.

Rebecca's face changes. "Have you eaten?" she whispers.

I shake my head and clutch my stomach. "Not for a while." I've *never* not been able to eat. And then I gesture to the mess in my room. "Mitch hasn't had a problem with his appetite."

Becca smiles as she watches him drool on my pillow. Only someone crazy in love could see anything endearing about Mitch's drool. "Of course he hasn't had a problem with eating. He's Mitch. At least he's friend enough to stick around." She gestures with her head to my door. "Come on."

Humiliation burns its way to the surface, and I open my mouth twice before getting it out. "I need help to stand up."

Becca says nothing, just comes to my side of the bed and puts her arm softly around me to help me to my feet. My head pounds, my shoulder throbs, and my hip feels like it's not only frozen stiff but aching.

"We'll get you some medicine as soon as you get food,"

she whispers.

I'm about to ask where my mom is, because I'm still not in the mood to run into her, but Becca keeps talking.

"Your mom's at work. She'd already taken some time off and is trying to give you space, so—"

"You guys are talking about me?" I frown as I baby-step out of my room. Hurts to stand, hurts to move.

As soon as I'm in the open area downstairs, I see Gramps's freezers and then his trailer, and the panic and loss seize my chest again, wiping my brain clear of whatever we were just talking about. Becca's hand rubs my back a few times.

"Breathe, Penny. Come on," she whispers.

I follow her up the stairs, one pathetic step at a time, and into the kitchen.

"This is so weird." She shakes her head. "Never in a million years did I think I'd find myself wanting to help Penny Jones. Or that you'd even take help from anyone."

I'm sort of amazed I'm taking help from her, too. So much has changed. "Not like I have a choice. I can barely walk." I lean on the counter, afraid that if I sit I won't be able to get back up again. The pain of my hip and my shoulder and my ribs is making it hard to breathe, but not like the ache in my chest.

Becca stands in front of the windows, suddenly looking a little small and lost. "I know Mitch had the same clothes on, and I feel horrible for even asking, but…"

I don't move my head but hold up my hand. "After kissing Bishop, I totally see I don't feel that way about Mitch.

Lying next to him was nothing like lying next to Bishop. And the stupid ass thinks I should be playing on a girls' team for college anyway."

A corner of her mouth pulls up. "Only you, Penny, could find the drummer of a rock band in freaking Seldon, Alaska and make him fall in love with you."

I snort. "He did not fall in love with me, or he'd be here." The last few words come out all shaky, and tears threaten my eyes again, but there's *no way in hell* I'm crying again. Flashes of pictures I've found of him while stalking the Internet roll through my brain even though I wish I could erase them. Way too much of his cocky smirk and way too many girls who look like Victoria's Secret models.

Becca pushes two pieces of bread in the toaster before folding her arms. "I sat sort of near Bishop when you practiced and watched that boy when you got hurt. Whether he fully knows it or not, he's kicked-ass, insane-crazy in love with you. Trust me."

Her words press into the anger I'm holding on to—it's so much easier than hurt. "And that's how Mitch is with you, so why are you worried about him?"

She fingers the clip in her hair for a moment. "Because I know he loves you, and he swears it's not the way I'm thinking, but it can turn so easy. That's why. Honestly, Penny, I think if you wanted him you could have him. You're like… You're like the girl who can do anything. It's a pretty big shadow to be living under."

I shake my head, feeling both empty and weighted at the

same time. "Trust me. I can't… I don't know what I want right now."

"When you figure it out? Do it. You have to see that you have a knack for getting what you want because you work your butt off for it."

So much of what she said echoes Bishop's words. It's too much to think about him right now, but maybe, *maybe*, Becca's right on one count. Maybe I can just decide for me. Whatever I want. And make it happen. "Why did you come help me?"

She laughs as she moves to the fridge. "Two reasons. One, your mom asked, and before you get upset about that, it's because she's trying to be nice. Two, so I could watch you with Mitch." She sets the OJ back in the fridge and doesn't make eye contact. "If I'm being perfectly honest."

I grin, feeling a little lighter since it looks like Becca and I can be straight with each other. "Fair enough. And…I think you're good for him." Crazy thing is that I mean it.

Becca slides the toast onto a plate, taking one for herself. "I'm scared because he wants me to follow him to Washington, but I'm staying up here. I just… I don't want to spend the money, and I don't want to be so far away from home. I think it's got him nervous."

I take a few nibbles of the toast Becca sets in front of me. "Mitch is crazy about you. You two will be fine."

"And so will you, Penny Jones." She gives me a knowing smile as she sits. "Mitch thinks you're crazy for wanting to stick to Alaska, but I happen to know that the coach from Fairbanks has called like three times to ask how you are."

I stop chewing as I think about the amazing things this could mean. "Which team?"

She pauses and takes a huge bite of her toast with a smile. "The men's coach. He's pulling strings right now to take you, if you want to go."

I'm stunned and thrilled and hoping Mom won't put up too much of a fight because, in this moment, I know I want it enough that I'm going to find a way to make it happen, injury or not. I rub a hand through my greasy hair and know I have to say it. Know it. Some words are just a lot harder to find than others. "Thanks, Becca."

. . .

We climb in the car after Gramps's funeral. It was nothing of what he would've wanted and everything that every single funeral is—crying people who didn't know the deceased nearly as well as they thought they did. As soon as I figure out what I really need to do for him, I'll do it. Until then, I'm going to do everything I can to erase this day from my memory.

Mom hits a bump in the road, and I flinch. My stupid brace isn't much of a brace, and the pain meds just aren't keeping up, especially on a day like today when I'm moving around so much.

Mom clears her throat and shifts in her seat. "I have things to say."

Nervousness builds as the silence stretches, and mom regrips the steering wheel like fifty more times. "Things to say?" I prompt.

She pulls in a long, slow breath. "I judged Bishop harshly, and I'm sorry. He tried to be next to you when you got hurt and were on the stretcher, and I lost it. I was angry because I felt like he was intruding and I was pushing you away when I didn't mean to. I wasn't fair to him when you got hurt, and I'm sorry."

How would things be different if she hadn't told him to stay away? Would they be? I'm so tired of being angry that I'm not sure what to do or say. If she didn't sound so...sorry, it would be different.

"I know that I give you a lot of freedom, but the morning you walked out of his cabin... I could see you throwing away everything for him. Did you know a nurse I work with was two semesters away from being a doctor?"

"No." I'm afraid to look at Mom, so I stare at the snow-filled trees flying by as she drives.

"Two semesters left, and she gave it up for a guy from Seldon."

I chew on my lip, a little annoyed that she thinks I'm weak enough to push aside what I want for anyone, but I'm starting to understand that she's paranoid because I'm her daughter.

Mom tightens her hands on the steering wheel, feeling things she wants to force me to understand. "And now, ten years later, she's the single parent of three kids and working as a nurse instead of what she could have been."

"Mom." I raise my brows and finally look at her. "I'm not going to lose myself in a guy. Ever. And if you really want me to follow what I know I want, what I've given a *lot* of thought to, you'll be okay with me going to UAF. I really want it, Mom. Really." The words I don't say are the ones we both know I'm thinking. *I'll go there with or without your help.* Mom and I are enough alike that she'll know.

She nods, her hands finally resting more loosely on the steering wheel—a sign that we might be moving forward. "I'll keep thinking on it, Penny. It's hard for me to see so many big opportunities and to reconcile myself with that not being what you want."

"I'm decided, Mom." And feeling lighter the more I think about my decision.

"And if I'd been a better mother, we would have talked and I wouldn't have made a mess and underestimated you. I'm sorry."

"And Ben?" I ask because she opened the door to talk about guys, so I'm keeping it open.

"And Ben…" Mom lets out a sigh. "I haven't dated since your father died. I loved your dad so much, and it felt too wrong to even look at anyone else—especially living with Gramps. I ran into Ben on my way home from work and, for the first time in years, I felt good. Pretty. Like a woman again. And then the guilt kept me up all night. It felt like I was cheating on your father, even though he's been gone for years. I wanted to tell you, Pen. But I couldn't. I felt guilty, and I knew if you didn't approve that I'd walk away. After taking care of you and Gramps, there was finally someone who wanted to take care of me. Who wanted to see me. To talk to me. To spend time with me. I was terrified of losing that."

We should have talked because Mom and I share a lot more than either of us realized. "That's what Bishop did for me."

She takes a long, slow breath, and I know her well enough to know she's considering what I've said but hasn't totally converted yet. "I hate what I've done to us. Hindsight is twenty-twenty, though. I was scared, but the longer I kept quiet about Ben, the harder it was. I swear to you, I'd do it differently, but it was something that I wanted to be just mine for a while. Does that make any sense?"

"A little." I slide a bit lower down. "I miss him."

"Who?" she asks. "Bishop?"

"Both of them."

We drive in silence for a few more minutes. "You know Gramps would have rather died like this than as a crazy man strapped to a bed somewhere."

"I don't think they do that anymore, Mom." I almost laugh, even though I'm too heavy for laughing.

"Probably not." Something like a smile plays on the edges of her mouth.

Since the mood is finally lightened in the car, and I'm smart enough to want to keep it that way, I have the perfect thing for our drive home. "Jeremy is working McDonald's this afternoon."

"Sounds good." Mom chuckles. "I do want you to meet Ben."

"Mom. Small town. I know Ben. He's nice. I like him. I just—"

"You don't like that I didn't tell you." She steals a glance my way to gauge my reaction.

"Yes."

She reaches over and squeezes my arm. "I won't do that again. I promise."

More than it ever has, it feels like we'll be good. "Okay."

Again, we drive in silence. Mom and I have never been great at the emotional stuff. "If you need to talk about Bishop or anything else, you know you can come to me, right?"

"Not at all ready for that." I stare out the window. "And I'm trying not to wonder if things would be different if you hadn't pushed him away."

A few moments pass before Mom answers. "Fair enough."

And we're not perfect, but we're better. Mom and I need to learn how to be without Gramps around as our buffer. I just have no idea what's next for me. If I'll be able to play hockey, if I'm going to college, if I'm ever going to talk to Bishop again.

Chapter Twenty-five

Bishop

Dear Penny,

I feel like an ass for writing this. It's such an easy way out. I'm pretty sure if I would've written you before... everything, I never would've heard the end of it. You would have talked shit, and then I would have kicked your ass on the snowmachines to show you how cool I am.

This isn't a few months ago, though, is it? I'd be surprised if you're even still reading this. You've been known to have a bit of a temper, ya know?

I'm sorry it took so long for me to write. Sorry I screwed up so badly. Sorry I lied. But most of all, I'm sorry about Gramps. Sorry he's gone and I couldn't save him. That I couldn't hold you while you cried. Wiped your tears in a way you never would have wanted someone to do, except after something that huge. It kills me that I walked out on you—just left without a word, but that's because of me, okay? Not you. And I didn't want to leave you, but I needed to get well. Remember that.

God, I miss him. I can't imagine how you feel without him.

He was so cool . . . I loved him. He knew everything about me, and he still loved me and thought I was something special. Gramps was special.

You're a lot like him. Not sure if I ever told you that.

I seriously hate doing this through e-mail. I deserve having to face you in person, to admit what I did. To actually see how much I disappointed you.

That's not going to happen, though, so I'll say it now. I started taking pills because I couldn't handle the crowds. Couldn't deal with being on the road. After that, it escalated until I couldn't stop.

My mom and manager sent me to Alaska when I almost OD'd. I didn't get it. It took you, Gramps, and even Gary to start to make me see. It wasn't enough, though. What did it was hearing about your dad. Someone like me took your father away from you. Then I realized I was an addict and a coward.

It doesn't excuse shit, but I want you to know I planned to tell you. After the game, I was going to come clean and then leave for rehab. It didn't go down like that, though.

The night we lost Gramps . . . the night YOU lost Gramps, I lost it. All I could think about was you being hurt and Gramps being gone, and I downed a bunch of pills.

Fuck, it's embarrassing to even admit that. While you were in the hospital and Gramps was dying, I had to get high. I've never hated myself as much as I did then.

I don't know what you know, or what you want to know, but I've been in rehab ever since. I went straight to the airport. Got off the plane and went straight to rehab. Not like that makes anything better, but it's true.

So yeah, that's all. Today's my last day, and I wanted you to know that I'm sorry. For the lies, drugs, not being what you needed, Gramps, everything.

Hopefully, one day, I'll deserve everything you guys gave me.

Kick ass out there on the ice. Show those guys Lucky

Penny can take them all. I know whatever your injury was, it won't hold you back.

Love,

Bishop

PS... When Gary and I used to walk, we used that time to talk. He told me about making schedules, so I now I have one. Every day, I'm going to work on my Ranchero—to fix her up. I've wanted to do that for so long but never took the time. I will now. And don't laugh at this next one, but I'm also getting a snowmachine. I already picked it out online. She's all white like the snow—gorgeous. Mom thinks I'm crazy, but I know you'll understand.

I hit send on the email as there's a knock on the door. "Come in," I call, knowing its Mom. She's the only one who's come to see me since I've been here. The only one I've wanted to see.

"Hey, sweetie. Are you excited to go home today?" She's smiling as she sits next to me, but I can tell she's nervous. Makes sense. I'm not sure if I would trust me, either. I feel good, though. Better than I remember feeling in a long-ass time. It's kind of like Gary said, I'm going back to when things were simple, going to hold on to the things that matter—the things that ground me. I know there's a lot to deal with. A long road ahead of me, but I actually think I might be looking forward to it.

"I don't know if excited is the right word, but I think I'm ready."

Mom's wearing her hair in a loose ponytail like always and a pair of jeans. She smiles at me before leaning forward to put a hand on my knee. Instead, I pull her into a hug.

Struggling, I try to remember the last time *I* hugged my own mom. God, I was so screwed up.

Mom's shoulders start to shake, and I know she's crying. The sniffles start, and I hold her tighter. "I'm sorry, Ma... I can't believe everything I put you through. I'm so sorry."

"It's okay," she tries to tell me, but I shake my head.

"It's not okay. None of it. You protected me. Gave me everything. Let me follow my dream, and I wasn't man enough to handle it. And I took it out on you... Not letting you go with me to Alaska? God, I can't believe that."

"It was me." She holds my hand. "Who insisted you go... Or do something. I wanted rehab, but I knew you'd never go for it. I'm the one who pushed Don to give you the ultimatum."

Wow... I didn't see that coming. "Thanks. For doing that. I probably wouldn't have...yeah, I might not be here if you hadn't."

She cries harder. We sit like that for a long time. Finally she pulls away. Her nails are still the same shade of pink as always. She wipes her eyes. Smiles at me. "I love you, Bishop. I'll always love you. And I'm looking forward to your future. I *know* who you are, and that other guy? He wasn't you. I can't wait to watch you shine."

I hug her again. Tell her thank you and that I refuse to screw up this time. I want to be the person she thinks I am. The person I want to be.

She tells me she loves me again, and I know we're okay. It's only the start, though. I'm going to keep proving myself. For mom, Penny, Gramps...for me.

"You ready to get out of here?" I'm going home with her instead of my old house. I don't want anything to do with the guy who lived there.

• • •

The last thing I ever would have thought I would say is that I actually kind of enjoy going to my meetings. Maybe *enjoy* isn't the right word, but I don't dread them, either. There hasn't been one I've missed. It's crazy what realizing you aren't alone can do. I was a druggie and screwed-up. Screwed-up a lot, but it doesn't define me, and I'm not the only one.

Talking with people, I see that my dad could have been responsible for some of my anxiety, too.

My car gets a lot of my attention. It's my own form of Troy's trees.

When I need to be alone, I walk. Sometimes with Gary, sometimes not. Troy and I have even started working out together. Even though I shouldn't, I can't help but wonder what Penny would say if she saw how ripped I am now.

I send her emails, but they're usually just little things here and there. It took her a while to answer my first one—not that I blame her, she did because she's strong like that. And like I knew she would, she's going to school in Alaska. She'll kick those guys' asses.

There's a cab waiting for me outside my meeting. After waving bye to my sponsor, I get in the car and give him the address to my old house. Mom is there when I arrive, waiting on the porch. It's the first time I've been here since I came back to L.A.

"She's running late. She said she'll be here in about ten minutes. It won't take long to sign the papers, though." Mom stands from where she'd been sitting on the steps.

"Okay." Staring at the house, something hits me. It wasn't this place I should be scared of, it's the old me. Maybe this house, saying goodbye to it, is another way to say goodbye to the old Bishop.

My hands don't even shake as I unlock the door. It's empty. Mom took care of that for me.

And...it's only a house. Yeah, it's the place I've done a lot of drugs and other things I shouldn't have, but that's all it is.

"You okay?" Mom's arm slides through mine.

"Better than okay."

She gives me a small squeeze. "Yeah, I think you are. This is a big step, though, Bishop. Not just the house, but everything. Are you sure it's what you want? You're really sure about this?"

Turning toward her, I smile. "More than sure." And it's true. So incredibly true.

Chapter Twenty-six

Penny

Mom and Ben drop me off at the motocross track on my way home from physical therapy. If I'm careful, I'll be playing hockey for UAF in just a few months, practicing with the team in a few weeks.

"Penny!" Chomps jumps off his bike. "You know the rules."

My body tenses, preparing to fight them off. "Oh. No." I hold my finger up in warning. "Don't you *dare*. I wore a skirt as a show that I'm not going to try to ride."

"Help me with the cripple!" he yells, and in seconds four guys have me in a lock as they duct tape my right arm to my side, wrapping the stuff around me at least four times.

I'm laughing so hard my sides hurt as I try to kick them away. "You assholes!" I yell.

Mitch smirks as he throws his arm over Becca's shoulder. "Can't have that arm getting hurt."

"Seriously?" I widen my eyes and stare down at the tape

crisscrossing around my middle. "The stuff hurts my arm hairs, and this shit is getting old."

Only I'm snorting as I try to keep a straight face, and the guys are still laughing and putting their helmets on for a few more laps.

"Come sit." Becca moves toward the stands, and I follow her with my stupid arm taped to my side. I wonder what my physical therapist would say about this.

I itch to get on my bike as they tear up the track. Chomps is being sloppy today, and I know I'd kick his ass. "I hate being on the sidelines." I growl as I sit while wearing one of the many outfits Becca made me get before she agreed we should be roommates. Actually, I think she said we were going to be roommates, but not until I started dressing like a girl instead of a jock.

"You look hot, Penny Jones. I'm impressed." She giggles as she takes another sip of her Diet Coke.

"Yeah, well…" And it's not as weird as I would have thought. I get glances no matter what—being as tall as I am with white-blond hair does that. And anyway, I like the skirts. Fuel for my ego at the very least.

"Go University of Alaska! The school I can afford!" she fake cheers.

"And Mitch is cool with you not following him to Washington?" I ask.

She shrugs, keeping her gaze on him as he runs the track. "He's not paying my tuition."

"Right." But they're solid. I know they are. I've seen the

way they stare at each other, and just thinking about it makes me miss Bishop in a way I wish I didn't.

Becca sits back, and then nerves settle into my stomach as I try to pick out the end of the duct tape to unroll myself and know I'm about to tell her about him. I'm seriously trembling all over, which is crazy because it's just a few emails. Everything still feels so raw and fresh, even though it's been more than three months. "Bishop wrote me." I cough a few times trying to push out the words. "Well, a few times…" This is so strange, having another girl to talk to about this stuff. Kind of cool, too. "Actually, one long email and then every few days he sends something else."

"Holy shit." She sits up so fast her feet slap on the old wood. "Why didn't you *say* anything? Have you written back?"

I slide my foot across the bleachers, staring down. "Wasn't sure how to talk about it yet." His words have been rattling around in my head for weeks.

"Have you written back? Like…are you two *conversing*?" She leans in, eyes filled with excitement.

All his words hit me again like punches to the chest. "He went to rehab. Told me everything. Hated how he left things… It took me a while to answer. Like two weeks. But we've been writing. A little."

Becca sips her Diet Coke, still staring, waiting for more story.

"I don't know what we are." I set my feet on the bench in front of me just for something to do. Mostly his letters make me hate him and miss him all at once. I don't know what to do with so much emotion.

She pokes my side. "Look at you. You're all affected."

I finally find the end of the tape and start to tug. Anything to keep my hands busy while we're talking about things I don't know how to talk about. "Shut up and help me with the duct tape, would you?"

Becca's grin is completely giddy. "He's *writing* you. You're writing *back*. You're so sunk."

I stand up and turn as she continues to pull on the tape, wincing every time we go over my bare arm. *Assholes*. Seriously. "Nope. Not sunk. I'm actually not going to complain about you dressing me because I need a normal boyfriend at college, not someone who makes me crazy."

She scoffs. "Whatever, Penny. We leave in a week, and you're obviously still in love with him."

I freeze. Am I?

Chapter Twenty-seven

Bishop

"Thanks for meeting with me, you guys." I look at Don sitting behind his desk. The rest of my bandmates are in chairs, but I'm standing by the door. I think they've known this was coming. I knew it was coming, and I thought it would be harder. Being in a band was always my dream, and I'm not stupid enough to think I won't miss it, but leaving is what I need. It's what's best for me.

"No problem, B.R." Blake says. He's the only one besides Don who might get my decision. The only one who comes over to jam with me for no reason. That's cool. There've been enough fake people in my life. I'm ready for real.

Twirling my drumsticks between my fingers, I start to talk. "I'm out, you guys. I know it's shitty timing, but I also know Don's smart enough to have a backup plan." When I look at him again, I get a nod. "I can't do it anymore."

"Seriously?" Chase, our guitarist, spits out. "When you

checked into rehab and weren't getting out 'til after our first few shows, we pushed back the whole fucking tour for you."

"I know. I'm sorry about that, but I don't think it's smart for me to go out there. I don't *want* to go out there… It's… I can't do it anymore." Ever since I got out, I've been all over the headlines. Exactly like Don said, rehab is hard to keep quiet. Paparazzi follow me. Old pictures of me are splattered all over magazines. "The media will be a distraction for you guys, too. It's better for us all."

Chase looks at me like he's really confused. "Don't pretend you're doing this for us. We've had your back this whole time for nothing."

Regardless of what he says, I know this is the right choice.

Blake stands up. "No matter what you want to do, I'll support you, but you love to play, B.R. You're the best I've seen. Are you sure you want to throw that away?"

I think about the nights on the road. The girls, the parties, the drugs. The pressure, the fights. And then I think how my heart feels alive when I'm sitting behind my drums, keeping rhythm for the guys. How it feels when we nail a new song. "I can still love to play. I can *still* do it, but…I don't know. It's different now. There are other ways to keep music in my life."

Blake nods. "Yeah… I know. You ever want to come back, we're cool. You got that?" He gives me a hug, slapping me on the back. The rest of the guys tell me good luck, shake my hand. All surface stuff. There are a lot of people like that in the world, and I'm done surrounding myself with them.

When it's only me and Don in the office, he speaks for the

first time. "You're under contract."

"I know."

He huffs. "We'll get it worked out. Have to take care of yourself and all that shit." He doesn't look any more sincere than he sounds, but I know he is.

I nod and walk away. Almost to the door, I turn to him. "Thanks, Don. For having the balls to send me away. I never would have gone if you didn't make me."

For the first time ever, I get a smile out of him. "You have problems with your dad, still come to me, okay? I'll help you work it out."

His words settle into me, build me up. There are more people here for me than I used to think. "If I can do anything for you, too, you know I'm here."

"I know and…you did good, kid. You did good."

The *kid* doesn't even bother me this time.

Gary texts me as I'm about to leave the building.

PAPS ARE OUTSIDE.

Fucking paparazzi. They're always sniffing around for something.

Without much choice, I push through the door.

"What are you doing here, Bishop?"

"The whole band was here?"

"How do you think you'll handle your addiction while on the road?"

"Are you still in Burn?"

A few camera flashes go off. Doing my best to ignore them, I jog to Gary's SUV and get in. "Asshole."

He chuckles and pulls away from the curb. "Hello to you, too."

"You know I wasn't talking to you." I watch the paparazzi while we drive away. "Thanks for the ride. I can't believe you're on time. Troy must not have been home."

"Don't be a hater, Ripe. I'm not always with him."

I'm quiet because we both know he's full of it.

"Okay, *fine*. So I'm always with him—when he's not with *you* that is. He's going to be bummed to lose his workout buddy."

"Me too. He's cool." We even know how to talk to each other now. When I need to talk to someone who's been where I am, Troy is there.

"He had to go out of town. I won't have you to keep me busy, either."

I can't help it, I laugh. I knew something had to be up. But I also remember that as much as Gary never wants to be away from Troy, he left him for months for me. Would have stayed longer. Would probably go back if I asked him, too. He's probably the best friend I have. I'm okay with that. "Bad timing, huh?"

Gary shakes his head. "Absolutely not. This is your life, Ripe, and I'm stoked for you." He pauses for a second. "Have you talked to her?"

I know exactly who "her" is. I also knew this was coming. "Same as it has been. We email back and forth a little. It took her a while to answer my first one, but I didn't give up."

Gary chuckles. "Push your way back into her life? You've

always been such a cocky jerk." There's teasing in his voice.

"I'm cocky for good reason. But no…not pushing my way anywhere. I like talking to her. Maybe one day, I can really apologize to her."

He tries to weave through traffic on the 405 Freeway. "Look at you. You're all sentimental now."

"I can still kick your ass, though. Keep talking shit, and I will."

"So violent." He teases. "She still doesn't know, though, right?"

Traffic piles up around us. "Nope." Let's hope that doesn't backfire. "You shouldn't have gone this way. I hate this freeway." Not like all freeways around here aren't bad, though.

"You wanna drive?"

"Sure."

"Shut up." He gives the line of cars ahead of us the evil eye. "Ugh! Traffic sucks."

We're at a dead stop. It's always like this. And it's hot, too. I put my feet on the dashboard. "Wake me up when we get there."

I fucking hate Los Angeles.

Chapter Twenty-eight

Penny

I'm glad I decided not to tell Mom I'm home from college early. Halloween weekend and freaking Chomps is getting married. Crazy. It took them more than the two months I predicted, but it's still weird. Becca gives me one last wave as I step out of her car, then peels out. Mitch just got home, and I know that's her next stop.

A pang hits my chest when I step in as I see Gramps's trailer in the corner, and some random old rock music is playing instead of his country, but it's better than it was. I'm okay. Or will be.

I hit the top of the stairs, and Ben freezes over the stove. "Penny!"

"Hey." I glance around. No Mom. Weird. Oh, wait. She said he moved in. Still weird, just not bad weird. "Where's Mom?"

"You're a day early." He keeps smiling. I don't *think* he's faking.

"Yeah." I shrug. "I wanted home."

"Your mom went to get something from one of the cabins. Should be back any minute. I was just finishing dinner." He shakes his head. "You're more grown up all the time."

I glance down at my skirt, boots, and tight sweater. "Becca." I shrug.

He chuckles. "Well. I was going to set up a good time, but it looks like it's just been given to me." He leans back and glances out the window.

"Good time for what?" I'm a little on edge, because he's rubbing his palms on his legs. Definitely suddenly nervous.

"I know you weren't thrilled about your mom and I..." His smile is gone, and some bizarre expression has taken over. He's totally freaked out.

I laugh at how nervous he seems to be. "I was pissed that she didn't tell me what was going on. I didn't object to *you*."

He pulls in a big breath. "Okay. I'm just going to ask." But the pause is long enough for me wonder if he ever will ask. "I want to marry your mom."

A bubble of happiness for them swells in my chest, but I try not to show it. He should sweat at least a little. "How does this involve me?"

"You're her family. I thought you were the one I should ask." He runs a hand through his hair. "I don't even know if she'll say yes—"

I can't hold in my smile any more. "She'll say yes."

"And you?"

"Scared?" I smirk and narrow my eyes.

His shoulders relax a little as something like a smile starts to play on the edges of his mouth. "You're a force, Penny."

"I learned from the best—you sure you want to tangle yourself with her?"

"Very sure." There's nothing but sincerity in his voice. It'll take me a while to get used to the idea, but it's okay.

"Well, I'm going to go check on my 'Vette and maybe take Bitty into town to catch up with friends. Tell Mom I'll be back later, and good luck." I wink.

As I jog down the stairs, an engine in the garage roars to life, and my heart leaps into my throat.

Who has their hands on my car?

I sprint down the stairs and throw open the door.

Bishop.

Riley.

With his hands on my car. Well, not on her now because he's grinning from ear to ear in the driver's seat, and my mom is on the other side of the car, watching him and looking just as happy.

I'm so stunned I'm frozen in the doorway.

Bishop smiles even wider as his hands run over the steering wheel.

I'm choking on words, and my heart's hammering because he's *here*. And Mom hasn't killed him.

I have no idea where we stand after three months of giving each other crap through email, and now…

He glances to the side and our eyes catch. Mom gives me

a quick half squeeze before stepping around me and into the house. I can't register any of it. Just Bishop.

God, he's the same. But…better. There's shock on his features that is also probably on mine. And then it's like he finally snaps into the present. He reaches over slowly and turns the key, letting my Corvette shudder 'til she stops.

I've forgotten how to move or breathe or…

"What are you—"

"I can explain—" We say at the same time as he steps out of the car with his hands up in surrender.

I want to throw my arms around him and bury my face in his smell. Feel his hands holding me. Glancing away, I see a box of pizza on the counter. It's easier to look there than at him right now. "So…you got Ditch to deliver and Mom not to kill you?" It's a stupid distraction.

"What can I say? I'm good."

At that, I turn to him and shake my head.

"I wanted to surprise you…" He looks back at the Corvette and then toward me. "Surprise." He gives me his cocky half-smile that makes my insides melt. And he looks good. Healthy in a way he didn't look before, only I hadn't noticed then.

"I'm just…" And after only talking through email, I want to feel him again. I can't handle weird or awkward with him. "I've missed you so much."

"You have no idea." He gives me a real smile, and it's like I'm seeing all the best parts of him at once. His eyes. The way he really takes me in when he looks at me…

He glances lower and tenses up a little. He gets this sort of faraway look.

I snap my fingers a few times as I let out a nervous little laugh. "Are you seriously checking me out?"

"You look… There is no way you wore that thinking no one was going to check you out."

We take a few steps closer, and I really look at him again. His hair is back to rocker band blond, and he's in a snug grease-stained T-shirt with even a little more muscle under it than before. And he still has his lip ring. I love that lip ring. He looks every inch of the rock star he is. Or was. Or…

"What are you doing here?"

"Wanted to show Mom Alaska. Wanted to see you. I've been working on your car and helping Pat at the music store. I had to figure out who I am when I'm not trying to be someone else. Just taking it a day at a time. I have the time and money, you know, so…"

Uncertainty creeps in as him being here feels more real. "Why didn't you come see me? Tell me you were here? I'm, like, four hours up the highway."

He fingers his lip ring and blinks a few times. "I didn't want to come too early. Didn't want you to turn me away. The second I got your first email, I was itching to throw my arms around you, but I felt like… I felt like I wanted to earn you—to make sure I was okay. Like I told you in the emails, I'm doing my meetings, working on cars, working out, and it's great, but I wanted to fix her for you, too." He nods at the car. Then he smirks. "Plus, if I waited long enough, I thought you might miss me enough to forgive me."

Warmth spreads through my chest because he's completely right. He knows me well. "You look happy," I say as he reaches forward to slide his fingers through mine. I stare at where they come together for a moment before daring to see what's in his eyes.

"I am happy." His lips press together. "So…it's okay that I'm here?"

I swallow hard as nerves settle in again. "Yes."

"And that I've had my hands on your car?" His voice is quiet. More quiet than I've ever heard him. Every breath from him, every word, every movement is something that I feel, something I want to be a part of. How did I stay away from him for so long?

"Yes. All okay." And feeling so much I step closer, like all this newness is something we can share. He's holding both my hands in his two, and I realize I might actually get him. Emotion pours through me as I stare at his rough hands holding mine.

This moment is more intense than anything we've shared so far. Like everything we've gone through together and apart is starting to lead to something really amazing. Something I'm finally ready for. Maybe it's good that we had so much time apart. Maybe I'm ready to appreciate all the good things that come from his experiences. Gramps was right. People who have been a lot of places make decisions about what they want, and those decisions really mean something. Bishop choosing to be here with me *means* something.

He lets go of my hands, and his thumbs wipe my tears away. "God, I wanted to be there, Penny. I did. You have no idea how much. It killed me that I left you…still kills me. But even when everything was good with us, perfect, I was still barely hanging on. I had to get help…had to get better so I would be what you deserve. What both of us deserve. I know how I did it sucks, but in the end, and for the long term, it was the right thing to do."

I step into his arms and let Bishop hold me. "I don't hate that I love you anymore."

He squeezes me tighter. "Only you would admit to loving someone that way." He's quiet for a moment, and then I feel his hand slide through my hair. "I missed this…your hair…the way you smell…the way you feel. I'm so fucking in love with you, Penny Jones."

I can't lift my head from his shoulder, can't stand the idea of his arms not being around me. I pull on him even tighter.

"I'm going to regret not having recorded this conversation," he says. "You totally said you loved me first."

"Guess that means I win." I lean back to see him. His eyes are full of love and friendship and *everything*.

He laughs. "I'm pretty sure I'm the winner."

Whatever. We can argue that one later. I'm determined to best him in *some* way.

"So, Ben's going to propose to Mom, I'm guessing tonight. I say that since my car's running, we should test it out. Maybe go check out your place." I'm not scared. I'm not embarrassed. It's him. Us. Everything. I've never wanted something the way I want him. Ever. It's scary, but being next to him makes me feel like not even skating can, and I can't wait to see what happens when we're even closer.

Bishop grins. "I was fully prepared to get my ass kicked for fixing your car, and you're asking me out?"

I lean in and whisper, "I'm here for a long weekend, and I really want some firsts with you." I hold him tighter, afraid to see his face but afraid to look away, afraid for him to tell me no. "And I sort of need a date to Chomps's wedding."

He chuckles. "You know, I was going to try to be all nice and tell you I wanted to start over, and if all you could do was be friends that I'd be okay with it."

"I don't work like that." I shake my head and let my smile take over. This is actually going to work. I don't doubt him. It's not just in his eyes, it's in everything—the way he looks at me, the way he touches me, the way he can tell me he loves me one minute and tease me the next.

"I know."

I blink, still amazed that he's holding me, but it's more easy and perfect than I thought possible. "I know what I want."

His nose touches my cheek, and he closes his eyes. "I think you always know what you want, Penny Jones."

"And I want you." I slide my lips against his, and his reaction is immediate. I don't melt into his kiss—I *dissolve* into it. Into him. And as screwed up as everything got, it's pretty perfect right now. And there's no way in hell I'm going to let that change.

Acknowledgments

Nyrae would like to thank:

My husband and my girls. You guys put up with so much from me when I'm in the zone. I appreciate it, and I love you for all the support. To Jolene Perry for writing with me. Thanks for creating Bishop's perfect match and for being a great friend. Wendy Higgins because you are a rock star of a bestie and a great beta reader. Kelley York, Cassie Mae, Morgan Shamy and any other early readers. I couldn't do this without you. I would also like to thank everyone who reads my books. Your trust in me means the world to me. To Heather Howland for all your knowledge and for seeing something in Bishop and Penny's story. Thanks for giving us a chance. And to all the folks at Entangled. Thank you for believing in this story.

Jolene would like to thank:

My family, whose endless patience enables me to do what I love. Definitely to Nyrae for writing with me. She writes the *best* boys—I fall in love with them all. I can't imagine not having her as a friend. Thank you to all the people who gave us feedback on this book: Lauren Hammond (the agent who sold this book), Wendy Higgins, Kelley York, Cassie Mae, Morgan Shamy, and my husband, who listened to *Out of Play* not once, but twice, as we wrote and edited.

I'm grateful that I grew up in Alaska and have known so

many girls who are like my Penny Jones. I'm also *so* thankful to Heather Howland for her enthusiasm and insights on Bishop and Penny's story. Also to Entangled for their hard work in getting *Out of Play* into the world.

There is no way I could thank the people who read my books enough. Ever. *You. Are. Awesome.*

If you loved OUT OF PLAY, *check out*

SIDELINED

by Kendra C. Highley

After being pushed to excel her entire life, high school basketball star Genna Pierce is finally where she wants to be. University scouts are taking notice, her team is on its way to the state tourney, and Jake Butler, the hot boy she's daydreamed about since ninth grade, is showing some *definite* interest. When he asks her out and their relationship takes off, Genna believes things can't get better.

Then, it's over.

A freak accident ends her career before it's even begun. Her parents are fighting more than ever, her friends don't understand what she's going through, and she's not sure who she is without basketball. And while he tries to be there for her, Genna doesn't understand how Jake could ever want the broken version of the girl he fell for.

Her life in a tailspin, Genna turns to the only solace that eases her pain: Vicodin.

AVAILABLE SUMMER 2013

Fall in love with Cash, the troubled bad boy in

BLURRED

*the highly anticipated second book in
Tara Fuller's Kissed by Death series*

Cash is haunted by *things*. Hungry, hollow things. They only leave him alone when Anaya, Heaven's beautiful reaper, is around. Cash has always been good with girls, but Anaya isn't like the others. She's dead. And with his deteriorating health, Cash might soon be as well.

Anaya never breaks the rules, but the night of the fire she recognized part of Cash's soul—and doomed him to something worse than death. Cash's soul now resides in an expired body, making him a shadow walker—a rare, coveted being that can walk between worlds. A being creatures of the underworld would do *anything* to get their hands on.

The lines between life and death are blurring, and Anaya and Cash find themselves falling helplessly over the edge. Trapped in a world where the living don't belong, can Cash make it out alive?

AVAILABLE SUMMER 2013

Grab the adorkably cute summer read

THE SUMMER I BECAME A NERD

by Leah Rae Miller

On the outside, seventeen-year-old Madelyne Summers looks like your typical blond cheerleader—perky, popular, and dating the star quarterback. But inside, Maddie spends more time agonizing over what will happen in the next issue of her favorite comic book than planning pep rallies with her squad. That she's a nerd hiding in a popular girl's body isn't just unknown, it's *anti*-known. And she needs to keep it that way.

Summer is the only time Maddie lets her real self out to play, but when she slips up and the adorable guy behind the local comic shop's counter uncovers her secret, she's busted. Before she can shake a pom-pom, Maddie's whisked into Logan's world of comic conventions, live-action role-playing, and first-person-shooter video games. And she loves it. But the more shedenies who she really is, the deeper her lies become…and the more she risks losing Logan forever.

AVAILABLE SUMMER 2013